MURDER AT THE LIBRARY

Murder at the Library

North Dakota Library Mysteries
Number 1

ELLEN JACOBSON

Murder at the Library

Digital ISBN: 978-1-951495-49-7
Print ISBN: 978-1-951495-51-0
Large Print ISBN: 978-1-951495-52-7

Editor: UnderWraps Editing

Cover: Cozy Cover Designs

Published by: Ellen Jacobson
www.ellenjacobsonauthor.com

For everyone who thinks tater tots are one of humanity's best inventions.

CONTENTS

1	Flip-flops in the Snow	1
2	The Disappearance of Paul Bunyan	20
3	Fluorescent Bananas	40
4	So Much Twine	58
5	Sibling Squabbles	69
6	Clown Shoes	88
7	Keeping Score	109
8	Game Night	125
9	Tater Tot Hotdish	144
10	Plastic Wrap	166
11	Did She or Didn't She?	183
12	Cats Just Gotta Have Fun	204
13	So Many Books	220
14	Gleeps!	233
15	Chameleons versus Geckos	256
16	One-Word Answers	282
	The Card Catalog	297
	Grandma Olson's Recipes	300
	Author's Note	304
	About the Author	305

CHAPTER 1
FLIP-FLOPS IN THE SNOW

"Oh, for Pete's sake," I muttered to myself as I circled the airport parking lot for what felt like the millionth time. The flight from Minneapolis landed twenty minutes ago, and the VIP I was picking up was probably wondering why no one was there to greet him.

I pleaded with the universe, "Please don't let him call my grandmother to ask where his ride is."

Grandma was a stickler for a number of things. Never dog-ear book pages, don't even think about tracking dirt on newly mopped floors, and keep your elbows off the table. But the worst sin of all? Well, that was being late. Not being on time was practically tantamount to committing murder.

Okay, perhaps I'm being a bit extreme. I don't

really think my grandmother would compare being tardy to killing someone, but it was still a pretty serious crime in her eyes.

No wonder my stomach was churning. If Grandma found out that I hadn't been at the arrivals gate *well* before the plane landed, she'd be quietly disappointed in me.

The problem with quiet disappointment is that it can linger. Guilt smolders inside, threatening to overwhelm you. But my grandmother doesn't do loud, showy displays of emotion. No one in my overly reserved Norwegian-American family really does. To be honest, there are times when I think a heated exchange might be preferable to keeping it all inside. You have a blow up, clear the air, and then you move on.

A couple walking across the parking lot distracted me from thinking about how people deal with their emotions differently.

"Here we go," I said, doing a fist pump. "The parking gods have heard my plea."

I drummed my fingers on the steering wheel. It was taking these two forever to clear the snow off their sedan. When the last snowflake was finally banished from their windshield, I inched forward, ready to slip into their spot once they pulled out. But just as I was about to claim victory, a blue pickup truck cut in front of me and swooped into the parking space.

I'd recognize that battered, rusted-out piece of junk anywhere. It belonged to Bobby Jorgenson, a guy I'd gone to school with. He had a reputation for causing trouble, and was certainly causing me some now. I laid on the horn.

"I was waiting for that spot," I yelled when he got out of his truck.

"Sorry, Thea." Bobby's cocky grin indicated that he didn't feel any remorse whatsoever. He jammed a gray beanie on top of his shaggy mullet, then said, "Gotta go. Don't want to be late."

Bobby ran toward the terminal, darting between cars and jumping over barricades like someone who was trying to elude the police. My parking nemesis was no stranger to evading law enforcement. Whenever there was a report of petty theft, vandalism, or disorderly behavior in our small town of Why, Bobby was usually the suspect. Unfortunately, this afternoon the police were nowhere to be found, and I was stuck circling the parking lot yet again.

Unlike Bobby, I didn't usually flaunt the rules. But this was an emergency. So, I pulled into the loading zone and said a silent prayer that the airport security guards wouldn't tow my car.

I had to elbow my way inside the small terminal, which was insane. This was a small, regional airport in western North Dakota with three or maybe four flights a day. Why did it look like half the county was here?

Someone bumped into me and I inadvertently jostled the older woman in front of me. The petite lady had been standing on her tiptoes, trying to see over the people in front of her. She twisted her head to look back at me.

"Sorry, ma'am," I said.

She smiled good-naturedly. "Can't be helped. We're packed in here tighter than the bras in my underwear drawer."

Okay, that was an interesting tidbit about this woman's unmentionables that I didn't need to know. "Why are there so many people here, anyway?" I asked.

"Don't you read the newspaper?" Her eyes were bright with excitement. "We have a celebrity arriving *here*, right in our very own county."

I scanned the area. Folks of all ages were humming with excitement, a high school band was tuning up in the corner, and a reporter from the local television station was testing his microphone. I snorted when I saw Bobby Jorgenson poised by the arrivals door, clutching a bouquet of red roses. He'd probably swiped the flowers from the gift shop. He certainly hadn't been carrying them earlier.

Although my grandmother thought the guy I was picking up was a VIP, I was stunned that anyone else shared her view.

"Wow, I can't believe everyone is here to see Why's new library director," I said.

The older woman gave me a funny look. “Library? What are you talking about?”

“The board of trustees hired a new director for the library,” I said. “His name is Hudson Carter. He’s flying in today. Well actually, he should already be here.”

I scanned the airport terminal. My grandmother had only given me a vague description of what Hudson looked like—in his 30s, dark hair, and above average height. Normally that would have been enough to go on, given how few people flew in and out of the tiny airport on a daily basis. But with this crowd, I wasn’t sure how I was going to spot him.

“We have a library in Why?” The woman shook her head. “I didn’t realize libraries were a thing anymore.”

I bit back a smile. Thank goodness I was here instead of my grandmother. As Why’s former library director, Grandma would not have been amused by the woman’s comment. There would have been a lot of that quiet disapproval going on.

“Yep, we have a library,” I said. “It’s next to the bowling alley.”

“But there’s so much to watch on streaming channels. Why would anyone need to read a book?”

She appeared genuinely perplexed. Unfortunately, it wasn’t an uncommon reaction these days. People liked to unwind with their favorite shows rather than immerse themselves in a book. Personally, I did both, but with the caveat that I never watch a movie or TV series based on something I've read. No matter how hard they try, the Hollywood versions always disappoint.

Rather than try to convince her that books are worthwhile, I changed the subject. "If you're not here for the library director, why are you here?"

A huge grin spread across the woman's face. "The minute I saw on my Instagram feed that Seatrina was going to be here, I made this." She unfolded a sign and held it up for me to see. Large turquoise letters spelled out, 'Seatrina.' Silver glitter flew off the poster board as she waved it enthusiastically in my face.

"Who's Seatrina?" I asked.

Her jaw dropped. She started to reply when the crowd erupted. Whoops of excitement competed with the high school band's out-of-tune rendition of 'Celebration.'

"She's here," the woman shrieked repeatedly as she jumped up and down.

I put my hands over my ears to muffle the noise, then looked in the direction of the arrivals gate. The first thing that drew my attention was the enormous fluorescent green beehive on top of the twenty-something woman's head. Her eyes were the exact same unnatural color—clearly the work of contacts. It looked like Seatrina was struggling to hold her head up due to the immense size and heft of her hairdo. Or maybe it was the dinner plate-size earrings that were weighing her down.

My eye was drawn next to her sequined halter top, cut-off shorts, and high heels. Apparently, she hadn't gotten the message that this was February in North Dakota. The minute she got outside, the woman was going to freeze her tush off if she didn't slip and fall on it first.

Seatrina held up her hands for silence. I was mesmerized by the way the iridescent makeup covering her exposed skin sparkled in the harsh overhead fluorescent lighting.

A hush fell over the room, everyone waiting with bated breath to hear what their idol was going to say. But before she could speak, Bobby pushed his way through the crowd screaming, "I love you, Seatrina. I want to have your babies."

Everyone roared with laughter. Bobby's face reddened. "I mean, I want *you* to have my babies," he spluttered.

Someone in the back shouted, "No one wants to have your babies, Bobby."

"Leave the girl alone," someone else said.

As other people chimed in with rude comments about Bobby's suitability as a baby daddy, I started to feel sorry for him. But then I remembered how he had stolen my parking spot.

Seatrina took pity on Bobby, squeezing his hand and bestowing a quick kiss on his cheek.

Bobby looked like he was going to faint. "Does that

mean you'll have my babies?" he asked in a squeaky voice.

She looked horrified. "Uh, no. That's a hard pass."

A member of Seatrina's entourage grabbed Bobby's arm and steered him away. Bobby looked dazed. I guess it's not every day you offer to impregnate your celebrity idol, only to be turned down in front of a large crowd.

The news reporter called out, "Can you tell us why you've decided to take a break from filming and visit the area?"

Filming, huh? So, this Seatrina was some sort of television or movie star. I peered at her more closely, trying to place her, but I came up with zilch.

When Seatrina didn't answer his initial question, the reporter added, "Do you have connections to the county?"

She cocked her head to one side, as though considering how to answer this. Her beehive was tilted at an odd angle, giving off a leaning tower of Pisa vibe. Not that I've ever been to Italy, mind you. While I've traveled extensively around the States for work, I've never been to Europe. Hopefully, one of these days, I'd take a vacation there.

Seatrina straightened her head before replying to the reporter, her beehive snapping back into place. "No comment," she said firmly. Gesturing for her entourage to follow, she sashayed out of the terminal.

The party-like atmosphere ramped up as people

excitedly compared pictures they had snapped of Seatrina and shared theories about her mysterious appearance in our county. Eventually, folks decided it was time to head home, and the terminal cleared out.

A lone man stood next to the arrivals and departures screen. He was dressed in a t-shirt, shorts, and flip-flops. Clearly another person clueless about winter weather in North Dakota.

Assuming he was a lost member of Seatrina's entourage, I pointed at the exit. "She went that way."

He frowned. "She already left?"

"Uh-huh, about fifteen minutes ago."

"Really? I thought she would have waited for me." He ran his fingers through his dark brown hair, causing some of the curls to stand up at odd angles. "Okay, I guess I'll have to take a taxi then. Do you know where the baggage claim is?"

"Um, right behind you." I pointed at the lone carousel. The conveyor belt was slowly whirring around, but it was devoid of any luggage except for one small cardboard box.

"I don't see my bags." He looked around. "There must be another carousel around here."

"No, that's the only one," I said. "Maybe your friends took your luggage with them?"

"My friends?"

I bit back a smile. I guess being part of someone's entourage didn't necessarily mean everyone was buddy-buddy. Well, at least he was honest about it.

"Your colleagues then."

"Colleagues?" He chuckled. "No, it's just me and Dr. McCoy."

"Wait a minute, aren't you here with Seatrina?"

"Who's Seatrina?" he asked.

"Honestly, I had never heard of her before today," I said. "But apparently, she's famous. But if you're not with her, then . . ." My voice trailed off as I put two and two together. "Oh, wait a minute, are you the new library director?"

"I am." He held out his hand. "Hudson Carter."

"It's nice to meet you," I said as we shook hands. "I'm Thea Olson. Rose Olson's granddaughter. She sent me to pick you up. But she didn't say anything about a Dr. McCoy. Is that your wife? Partner?"

Before Hudson could respond, a yowling noise interrupted us. That's when I noticed a pet carrier on the ground next to the librarian.

Hudson chuckled as he bent down to unlatch the door. A large, fluffy black and white cat raced out, meowing loudly as he inspected his surroundings. Hudson scooped the cat up and presented him to me. "Thea, allow me to introduce you to Why's new library cat—Dr. McCoy."

* * *

After I had quickly run outside to unsuccessfully plead with the security guard not to ticket my car, and returned, Hudson went to check on his missing luggage. He left me to get acquainted with Dr. McCoy. The cat was cuddled in my arms, showing me where he liked to be scratched—behind the ears, please—when my phone rang.

"Hi Grandma," I said, wedging the phone between my shoulder and ear so that I could keep stroking Dr. McCoy. I had a feeling any interruption to my petting services would not be well received.

"Why are you talking on your phone while you're driving?" my grandmother asked. "You know how dangerous that is."

"You're the one who called me," I pointed out. "And besides, I'm not in the car."

"Where are you?"

"At the airport, waiting for Hudson."

"But his plane landed fifty-three minutes ago," my grandmother said. "You should already be on your way back to Why."

"There's been a slight delay," I said. "Hudson's luggage didn't make the connection from Minneapolis. He's trying to sort it out now."

"Uff da," Grandma said, uttering a Norwegian expression of dismay common in these parts. "There aren't any other flights scheduled today, so he won't get his bags until tomorrow."

"I know." I twisted my head to keep Dr. McCoy from batting my earring, but it didn't help. The cat was persistent, snaking his paw around my neck and poking at the silver hoop. "Hey now, enough of that."

"What was that, dear?"

"Nothing," I said to my grandmother while I set Dr. McCoy down. I gave the cat a stern look, warning him to behave. "No wandering off or spitting up hairballs on the floor," I mouthed.

Dr. McCoy gave me the feline equivalent of a shrug, then proceeded to chew the laces on my Sorel boots.

"It sounds like there's some sort of commotion going on," my grandmother said.

I stifled a laugh as Dr. McCoy untied my left boot. "Just the local wildlife."

"Wildlife? What kind of wildlife could there be at the airport? You're not making any sense." Grandma changed the subject, saying, "Since you're running late, just bring Hudson directly to the library. I don't think you'll have time to take him to his lodgings before the reception starts."

"I still don't understand why a reception was scheduled the same day Hudson arrived. Couldn't they have given the poor man some time to settle in first before he meets the library board of trustees and all the other community bigwigs?"

"It wasn't my decision," my grandmother said. "I suggested it take place this weekend. The rest of the board agreed, but Thornton insisted it had to be tonight."

"Oh, I'll bet he did. That man is so full of himself. I don't know how you and the others put up with him."

I glanced down to check on Dr. McCoy. I was relieved to find he had lost interest in my shoes and was now curled up by my feet, napping. Turning my attention back to the ill-timed reception, I said, "What I don't get is why Thornton got to decide when the reception was going to take place. Ivy is the president of the board, not him."

My grandmother chuckled. "I don't think Thornton accepted the fact that he lost this past election. He'd won every election for the past ten years. I think he assumed the board would just keep re-electing him. He thought he'd be president for life."

"He bullied the board into electing him year after year," I pointed out.

"It helped that he ran unopposed in the past. Thankfully, Ivy had the courage to put her hand up this time." Grandma sighed. "But despite the fact Thornton lost, he's still been calling the shots. I hope Ivy can stand up to him going forward."

"Well, I guess there's one benefit to having retired," I said. "Now that you're not the library director anymore, you don't have to deal with Thornton."

There was a long pause before Grandma responded. When she did, her voice sounded wistful. "I'm going to miss it. I know Hudson will do a wonderful job running the library, but it's still hard to . . ." She cleared her throat, then continued, "Never mind that. Let's focus on getting Hudson back here in time for the reception."

I craned my neck, trying to see inside the small office where Hudson was filling out paperwork. "Um, Grandma, we might have another problem."

I could sense her frowning on the other end of the line. "What kind of problem?"

"Hudson did know this job was in North Dakota, right?"

"Of course, he came here to interview in November."

"Hmm. Was it by any chance at the beginning of the month? That was when we had that unseasonable heat spell going on."

"Thea, what's with your sudden fascination with the weather?" my grandmother asked impatiently.

"The man is wearing shorts and flip-flops," I blurted out. "I'm not sure he understands how cold it gets here in the winter. It's like that Seatrina and her entourage. She was wearing a skimpy outfit and the rest of her group were dressed like they were going to spend the day on the beach."

"Seatrina? Who's that?"

"Honestly, I don't have a clue, but everyone else in the county seems to know her."

"Back up a sec," Grandma said. "Shorts and flip-flops. Why is Hudson dressed like that?"

"No idea. We didn't have a chance to discuss it. Hudson wanted to catch the baggage claim guy before the office closed. But the issue is that—"

My grandmother interrupted, saying quickly, "He doesn't have his luggage so he can't change clothes. Okay, I see the problem."

"Yeah, he'll freeze to death the minute he steps outside."

"There's a more serious issue than that. Hudson needs to impress the board, and I don't think shorts and flip-flops are going to cut it."

"Why? They already interviewed him," I said. "They must have been impressed by him, otherwise they wouldn't have offered him the job."

"The board members who were at the interview were impressed," she conceded. "But things have changed since then. Thornton is dead set on firing the poor man, and he's been busy trying to convince the other board members to go along with him."

"But Hudson hasn't even officially started. How can the board fire him already? Why would Thornton even want to do that?"

"It's complicated, and we don't have time to get into it." Grandma took a deep breath, then said, "Okay, here's what we'll do. Go by the farmhouse and have Hudson borrow one of Grandpa's suits. From what I remember, they're about the same size. Then you bring Hudson directly to the reception. I'll try to keep Thornton and the others distracted in the meantime."

The door to the office opened, and Hudson walked out clutching a stack of papers in his hands. "It looks like he just finished," I said to my grandmother. "We'll be on our way soon."

"Thea, promise me one thing," she said. "Don't tell Hudson what I said. I don't want him to worry about his job."

"Sounds like he should be though," I said.

"I'm sure we can fix it," Grandma said. "Hudson will never need to know."

I shook my head at her use of 'we.' My grandmother had a way of roping me into helping with all sorts of unpleasant tasks like cleaning out the garden shed—do you have any idea how many spiders live in there?—canning pickled cabbage, and repairing damaged books. One time, she even had me investigate a murder. At least this time, all I had to do was help save someone's job. How bad could that be?

***

"All set?" I asked Hudson. My tone was a little too chipper, which is typically a sign that I'm trying to hide something. Fortunately, Hudson didn't seem to notice anything was amiss. The last thing I wanted was for him to ask me what was wrong. What would I say? *'It's been nice knowing you,' 'Don't get too comfortable here,' or 'I hope you have a return ticket to Florida.'*

I felt terrible for the guy. Imagine picking up and moving halfway across the country for a job, only to find out your head is on the chopping block upon arrival. How would he feel having to go back home and tell his friends and family that his stint as a library director didn't work out? Would he be humiliated? Dejected?

Actually, I had an inkling of how he'd feel. I'd left a promising career in Minneapolis eight months ago and returned to my hometown of Why. It's a small place, so naturally the rumor mill had kicked into overdrive. Speculation about why I had moved back home was rampant. Most people assumed it was because a guy had dumped me. The reality was far more boring—office politics. But who wants to talk about the cutthroat nature of corporate America when you can gossip about people's love lives instead?

Hudson held up the paperwork. "They said my bags should be on the first flight from Minneapolis tomorrow. They'll deliver them to the library. I'm all set for toiletries until then, but in terms of clothes—"

I held up my hand. "My grandmother already sorted that for you. She's arranged for you to borrow something from my grandfather to wear to the reception tonight."

"Wow, that's nice of her."

"Word of warning, Grandpa isn't exactly known for his stylish clothes. He owns two suits and I think they both date back to the last century. He spent his life working on the farm. So, most of his wardrobe revolves around overalls and hats he picks up at the local feed store."

"I'm not exactly known for my fashion sense, either. My wife used to buy all my clothes for me, and now that she's, um . . ." Hudson's eyes grew moist, then he abruptly looked off into the distance. When he turned back to me, he smiled faintly. "Sorry, it's hard to talk about it."

Dr. McCoy rubbed against Hudson's legs and meowed plaintively, as though he shared his human's feelings. Hudson scooped the cat up, then said to me, "The past few years have been tough. Your grandmother probably told you about it."

I shook my head. "Told me about what?"

"Oh, I thought she would have." Hudson took a deep breath, then exhaled slowly. "My wife died in childbirth. Losing her and our baby was . . ."

Putting my hand gently on his arm, I said, "You don't have to talk about it if you don't want to."

Hudson was silent for a moment. When he spoke again, his voice was more controlled. "One of the reasons I was excited to take this job was to escape Coconut Cove. Don't get me wrong, I love my hometown. But there are so many reminders of my wife and the future we had planned. People mean well, but they're always asking me how I'm doing. It wasn't a casual, 'Hey, how are you?' either. There's always an undercurrent to the question, as though they're assessing my mental state."

"That must have been tough," I said.

"Coming here is a fresh start for me," Hudson's

voice started to crack. "The grief will never go away, but maybe not being in a place where my wife and I had our first date, or going to the beach where we got married, or passing by the hospital where we saw the ultrasound for the first time . . . maybe it will be easier here."

My stomach twisted in knots. Hudson had been through so much already and now he was going to have to fight Thornton tooth and nail to keep his new job. As I watched Hudson press his face into his cat's fur, I knew one thing for certain—I was going to do everything I could to make sure Hudson kept his job and his fresh start in North Dakota.

CHAPTER 2
THE DISAPPEARANCE OF PAUL BUNYAN

When Hudson and I walked into the library a couple of hours later, my grandmother was waiting for us in the foyer. Grandma looked polished and well put together as usual, wearing a charcoal colored skirt, a merino wool sweater in a pretty shade of peach, and one of her trademark silk scarves tied around her neck. She started to greet us, but when we took off our coats, she was rendered speechless.

I gave her a nervous smile, then walked over to the coat rack. After pushing aside a long brown wool coat, a bright yellow puffer jacket, and a poncho, I passed Hudson a couple of hangers. As he hung up our coats, my eye was drawn to the rack of free books on the opposite wall. I was intrigued by a book about seashell identification, but I looked back at my grandmother when she spluttered, “Why is Hudson dressed that way? This isn’t a costume party.”

I couldn’t make eye contact with Hudson, otherwise I’d break out laughing. His getup was pretty comical—a pair of my grandpa’s old overalls and a blue plaid flannel shirt, along with the flip-flops Hudson had arrived at the airport wearing. At least it was warmer than the shorts and t-shirt he had on before.

“Why isn’t Hudson wearing one of your grandfather’s suits?” Grandma demanded.

“Well, slight problem,” I said. “Dr. McCoy must have had an upset tummy—”

Hudson held up his hand. “It’s my fault. I shouldn’t have fed him so many treats while traveling.”

“If I remember correctly, Dr. McCoy is your cat,” Grandma said.

“That’s right. I sent you pictures of him after my interview.” Hudson looked anxious. “Is it still okay if he comes to work with me?”

My grandmother and I exchanged glances. It was a well-known fact that Thornton did not like cats. Actually, ‘not like’ is putting it mildly. He despised them. And since Thornton wanted to fire Hudson, the fact that his cat was going to accompany him to work each day seemed like more ammunition he could use.

“Absolutely. And if anyone says differently, you tell them to talk to me,” Grandma said firmly. Then she turned to me. "What happened to the suit?"

"As soon as we got to the house, Dr. McCoy started exploring. You know how cats are," I said. Grandma nodded, probably remembering Georgie, my childhood tortoiseshell cat. "Before I knew it, Dr. McCoy had dashed upstairs and into your bedroom. Um . . . well, that's when he threw up on the suit you had laid out on the bed."

"I'll get it dry cleaned," Hudson said quickly. "Or buy your husband a new one."

"Don't worry about it," my grandmother said gently to Hudson. Despite the fact she and Grandpa didn't currently have any pets, she'd always had a soft spot for animals. "Where is the good doctor now?"

"He's in your laundry room," Hudson said. "Don't worry. The door is locked. He won't escape."

"Don't be so sure. When cats want to do something, they usually find a way to make it happen." She chuckled, then turned her attention back to me. "Why didn't you lend Hudson your grandfather's other suit? Or at least get something else from the closet?"

"Easier said than done."

My grandmother waved a hand in Hudson's direction. "It shouldn't have been that hard to find him something better to wear than this."

"Even if there had been anything in the closet, it wouldn't have fit Hudson. The suit you laid out wouldn't have worked either. Just look at him."

As Grandma examined Hudson more closely, she

seemed to realize the issue. My grandfather and Hudson weren't exactly the same size. The overalls Hudson was wearing were at least four inches too short and two sizes too big.

"Hmm . . . I must have misremembered how tall you were." Grandma frowned, then snapped her head in my direction. "What's this about there not being clothes in your grandfather's closet?"

"It was completely empty," I explained. "The only clothes of Grandpa's I could find is what Hudson's wearing. And that was tucked away in the back of a dresser drawer."

My grandmother furrowed her brow. "I don't understand. Were we robbed?"

"The only thing missing was Grandpa's clothes. Not exactly the typical loot that thieves are looking for."

"At least not the smart ones," Grandma said. "But it sounds like the type of thing Bobby Jorgenson would do. One of the gals from my book club found Bobby in her kitchen last week, putting a piece of blueberry pie into a plastic container. When she asked him what the heck he was doing, Bobby said that he didn't want to get crumbs in his truck."

"Is your friend okay?" Hudson asked.

My grandmother waved her hand in the air. "She's fine. Bobby does that kind of thing all the time. When my friend threatened to call the police on him, Bobby dropped the pie on the floor and ran out of the house."

I shook my head. "I doubt if Bobby stole Grandpa's clothes. Right now, the idiot is probably camped outside of wherever the celebrity Seatrina is staying like a lovesick puppy."

"You keep mentioning this Seatrina person." Grandma looked perplexed for a moment, then she got back to business. "Never mind all that. What we need to do is get Hudson inside." She pointed at his flip-flops. "Couldn't you have at least gotten him some proper shoes? His toes are blue."

"His feet are at least two sizes bigger than grandpa's."

"Believe me, I tried to cram my feet into a pair of your husband's boots, but it wasn't going to happen." Hudson looked at the double doors which led into the library and frowned. "I can't go in there dressed like this. What are people going to say?"

"That you have a good sense of humor," I suggested. "Imagine what a great story this is going to make later."

My grandmother didn't look convinced. "Well, it is what it is," she said with forced brightness.

Hudson took a deep breath, then held the door open for us. For a moment, I thought he was going to flee the scene once Grandma and I had entered. But instead, he followed us inside with more confidence than I could have mustered if I were in his situation.

While growing up, it had felt like I spent as much time at the library as I did at school or at my grandparents' farmhouse. It was like a second home to me. Now, standing next to Hudson, I tried to see it with fresh eyes.

The main part of the library was known as the 'Reading Room.' It had comfortable seating areas, book displays, and public computer kiosks. A large counter where patrons could check out materials and library staff were available to answer questions was located near the entryway. Behind the counter were two offices—one for the library director and one shared by the reference and youth librarians.

Off to the right was what community members affectionately called the 'Imagination Room.' The bright, cheerful space housed the children's collection, as well as an area for teens to gather. I smiled when I saw the welcome banner hanging over the arched entrance to the room. Based on the crooked letters spelling out Hudson's name, I suspected a group of the elementary kids had made it.

Opposite the Imagination Room was another arched entrance which led to the Collingsworth Wing, a more modern addition to the library dating back to the 1980s. There were rows of bookshelves where the adult collection was housed, racks of periodicals and newspapers, and tables with chairs where you could often find people working. At the back of the Collingsworth Wing was a hallway which led to meeting rooms, restrooms, the staff break room, and a storage room.

I glanced at Hudson and my grandmother. They were talking quietly to each other. From what I could hear, it was a fascinating discussion about the merits of the Dewey Decimal versus the Library of Congress cataloging systems. Fascinating, that is, if you were a librarian, less so if you were a mere mortal.

After the two of them appeared to come to some sort of consensus about how books should be organized, my grandmother led us to the meeting room where the reception was taking place.

"Can I have your attention, please?" she said, her voice carrying across the room with its usual calm authority. After everyone turned in her direction, she continued, "Allow me to present Why's new library director, Hudson Carter. We're lucky to have someone of Hudson's caliber accept this role. He comes to us from Coconut Cove, Florida, where he was the youth librarian. He also has extensive volunteer experience, including serving as a volunteer lifeguard and on the board of the local food bank. He reads widely, but admits to a special fondness for sci-fi books. Please join me in welcoming Hudson to our library and to the community."

As everyone clapped politely, I scanned the room. Some people looked confused by Hudson's attire, while others appeared bemused. Regardless, they were all good-natured about it, smiling at the new library director. Everyone except one man—Thornton Silas.

Thornton was in his mid-fifties, shorter than average with a stocky build. He was one of those guys who took fitness seriously. Not so much because he enjoyed working out, but because the thought of acquiring a beer belly made him shudder. He wore his light brown hair in a mullet, maybe to compensate for the slightly thinning hair on the top of his head or to try to reclaim his lost youth. The bottom half of his mullet was currently covered up by a thick yellow and white striped scarf he had wrapped around his neck. His arms were folded across his chest, his eyes narrowed, and he was shaking his head. If disapproval could drip off someone, the carpet underneath his feet would be soaking wet by now.

Standing next to Thornton was Ivy Gordon. The current president of the library board of trustees was a regal-looking woman in her early forties. She wore her dark brown hair in box braids which she had pulled into a bun. Her hot pink eyeglasses matched her blouse, and a royal blue pencil skirt paired with black high-heeled boots completed the stylish outfit. Ivy was a naturally warm and encouraging woman, traits which made her an effective elementary school principal. Her kind smile in Hudson's direction was a stark contrast to Thornton's glower.

Thornton stage whispered to Ivy, "Is this some sort of joke? The man looks like a cross between a rodeo clown and a surfer."

Ivy took a step sideways, as though to distance

herself from Thornton. Some folks rolled their eyes at Thornton's statement. Others shrugged. These types of arrogant digs from Thornton were par for the course.

To his credit, Hudson didn't react to Thornton. Instead, he turned and gave a slight bow in my grandmother's direction, thanking her for her introduction.

"I bet some of you are wondering why I'm dressed like this," Hudson said. "Well, the airline seems to have misplaced my luggage and then I had, um . . . let's just call it a costume malfunction involving a cat. But Mrs. Olson was kind enough to let me borrow some of her husband's clothes."

Hudson continued with his remarks for a few moments, telling everyone how pleased he was to be in Why. When he had finished, my grandmother invited everyone to enjoy the refreshments, then turned to Hudson. "Why don't I take you around and introduce you to everyone? Some of them you met when you came to the interview. But there will be some new faces. Why don't we start with . . ." her voice trailed off as Thornton stormed toward us, Ivy trailing behind him.

"So, this is the famous surfer boy from Florida," Thornton said, his voice dripping with sarcasm. Hudson held out his hand, but Thornton refused to shake it. "How do you expect anyone to take you seriously if you read science fiction? Librarians should read serious works, like *The Odyssey*."

"I studied the classics in college," Hudson said. "It's interesting how women have a more prominent role in *The Odyssey* rather than what you find in other ancient works, don't you think?"

Thornton looked flustered for a moment, then he jabbed a finger in Hudson's direction. "That's not what *The Odyssey* is about."

"That's the wonderful thing about reading," Hudson said good-naturedly. "Everyone can take away their own meaning from a book."

The other man scowled. He took a step forward, getting in Hudson's face. "I heard about your cat. Bringing that mangy creature to the library isn't going to happen on my watch."

"What's your cat's name?" Ivy asked, ignoring Thornton.

"Dr. McCoy," Hudson said with a smile.

Ivy's eyes lit up. "As in *Star Trek*?"

"Are you a fan?"

"Absolutely."

"Which is your favorite series?" Hudson asked.

"Well, if you had asked me a few years ago, I would have said *Deep Space Nine*, but now—"

Thornton held up his hand. "Enough with the sci-fi babble. This is a library, not one of those conventions where people dress up in ridiculous costumes."

"We do have several *Star Trek* books in the library," my grandmother pointed out. "They're very popular."

Thornton pressed his lips together. "Humph. We'll see about that as part of the review."

"What review?" Hudson asked.

Before Thornton could explain, the youth librarian approached us. Erik Andersen was in his mid-twenties. Although he wasn't originally from the area, Erik had the classic Scandinavian looks that so many of the residents of Why shared, including myself—tall, fair-skinned, blond hair, and blue eyes.

"I'm sorry to interrupt, but there's a problem with the coffee maker," he said.

"Can't you see we're talking?" Thornton snapped. He turned his back on Erik and began telling Hudson why science fiction didn't merit a place on the library shelves.

Erik twisted his hands and tried to interject, but Thornton's loud, non-stop rant about the lack of shelf space for classic books made it impossible.

Grandma intervened, inserting herself in front of Thornton. "We can discuss this later."

Giving my grandmother a grateful look, Erik said, "The coffee maker was working earlier, but now it's refusing to cooperate."

"Is it one of those large urn types you use for parties?" Hudson asked. When Erik nodded, Hudson said, "I used them all the time at my former job. I can help you figure it out."

Erik looked relieved. "Thanks, I'd appreciate that."

"It's nice to meet you formally," Hudson said to the

other man. "Mrs. Olson has said such good things about you."

"Rose, please," my grandmother said to Hudson. "No need to be so formal."

"We could use some more formality around here." Thornton looked down at Erik's jeans and sneakers. "Especially when it comes to the dress code."

Ivy frowned at Thornton, then turned to Hudson. "We're lucky to have Erik on the library staff. Not only is he a fabulous youth librarian, but he also plays a key role in the county-wide literacy program."

"Waste of time, if you ask me. If people can't read or write, it's their own fault." Thornton looked pointedly at Ivy. "Or it's a failure of the school system."

Ivy narrowed her eyes. "It's exactly that kind of attitude that makes people reluctant to ask for help. I'll have you know that the school system works hard to identify children who need additional support, and we have excellent programs and resources in place to assist them. But there are still some people who slip through the cracks—perhaps they have a learning disability that wasn't diagnosed, or English might not be their first language, or maybe they came from a disadvantaged background. That's where people like Erik come in. They provide enrichment programs for children, and classes and tutoring for adults."

"I think it's great that you're a member of the board," Hudson said to Ivy. "Strong relationships between the schools and the library are important." Then he turned to Erik. "I'm looking forward to hearing more about the literacy program."

"Don't waste your time," Thornton said. "Erik, shouldn't you be fixing the coffee maker? And this time, don't make it so strong. Also, I noticed there aren't any napkins on the buffet table. You better get some out there."

Erik's eyes widened as he scurried off in the direction of the staff kitchen.

"You know, Thornton, Erik doesn't work for you," Grandma pointed out.

"We'll see about that," Thornton said ominously. "In any case, he might want to make sure his resume is up to date."

* * *

After his veiled threat about Erik's future employment, Thornton excused himself, saying he needed to speak with some fellow board members about their upcoming meeting. As Thornton strode across the room, I noticed some people avoided eye contact with him, while others smiled at the man as though hoping to curry favor.

Hudson looked rattled by Thornton's treatment of Erik, but quickly regained his composure. "Maybe I should help with the coffee maker," he suggested.

"That's a good idea," Grandma said. "The staff

kitchen is at the end of the hall."

Once Hudson had left, Ivy turned to my grandmother. "Thornton has been bad-mouthing Erik for weeks. I don't know why, but for some reason, he's out to get him."

"Don't worry about it," my grandmother reassured Ivy. "Thornton's bark is worse than his bite."

Her tone was light. However, based on our conversation earlier, I knew Grandma was worried about Thornton. And rightly so. Not only was Thornton looking for an excuse to fire Hudson, he also apparently had it in for Erik. I wondered if the rest of the library staff were in jeopardy as well. But I couldn't figure out why. Thornton had always been a mean-spirited man, but now his behavior was reaching new levels of viciousness.

"Normally, I'd agree with you," Ivy said. "But something is different this time. Did you know he tried to put an item on the board meeting agenda about charging for library cards?"

My grandmother furrowed her brow. "That doesn't make any sense. The purpose of a public library is to provide free access to books and services to the community."

Ivy scowled. "He thinks if people really want to use library resources, then they should pay."

"Next thing you know, he'll want to ban books," I said.

"Uff da," Grandma said. "Over my dead body. Book

banning goes against everything the community of Why stands for."

"I totally agree," Ivy said. "As long as I'm president of the library board, it will never happen."

My grandmother smiled at the other woman. "I'm grateful you're in charge. Even though I'm retired, I'll still always look out for the library."

"You mean meddle in the library," I joked.

Grandma batted back playfully. "Meddling is a form of caring, dear. You know that."

I grinned. "Oh, don't I ever."

Before my grandmother could retort, the library assistant approached us.

"I know this isn't normally one of your volunteer days, but would you mind covering the front desk?" Carol said to me. "I need to help the knitting circle set up some equipment in the other meeting room, and Erik is busy helping with the reception."

"Of course," I said.

As I turned to follow the woman, I heard Ivy say to my grandmother, "I'm surprised Thea didn't follow in your footsteps and become a librarian. Hasn't every woman in your family worked at this library?"

I couldn't hear my grandmother's response, but I knew it would be supportive of my career choice. However, I suspected that Grandma had always been a little disappointed that I had gone into organizational development instead of library science.

Grandma understood why I'd made that choice,

though. Shortly before the car accident that killed both of my parents, my mother had completed her master's degree in library science. I still remember the party my family held to celebrate her achievement. My mom had been so happy that she was now officially a librarian. Then, a few days later, her dreams were extinguished forever and my brother and I were left orphaned. After that tragic event, I had vowed never to become a librarian.

Volunteering at the library, though, was a good middle ground. I got to be involved, but without the full-time commitment that my mother, my grandmother, and the women before them in my family had made.

"I'll try not to be too long," Carol said to me, interrupting my ruminations. "You might get some people wanting to check out books, but if it gets too busy, don't hesitate to come grab me."

As I sat on the stool behind the front desk, a group of high school kids came in. There weren't many places in town where the teenagers could hang out in the dead of winter at night besides the movie theater, the bowling alley, or the pizza place. And since those places cost money, and the library was free, this is where they often ended up.

Standing near a display of new books, the kids joked about who had a crush on whom, argued about who was going to do better on the upcoming chemistry exam, and made plans to 'borrow' a carved wooden statue of Paul Bunyan from the rival high school in the next town over.

I pretended not to hear this last bit. Back in my day, it's possible I may have participated in the 'liberation' of Paul Bunyan one winter night after a basketball game. Sure, it was a prank I probably shouldn't have been involved in, but it's not like I personally carried the statue out of the gym or drove the getaway van. I merely distracted a group of teachers by pretending to faint in the hallway.

Now that he's a police officer, my brother, Leif, likes to joke about how I aided and abetted criminal activity. Fortunately, even to this day, he's never ratted me out to our grandparents. Probably since he knows the dirt I have on him from his high school days is ten times worse.

The kids started to get too loud, so I suggested they hang out in the teen space in the Imagination Room.

"Yes, ma'am," one of them said, immediately making me feel ancient.

The door from the foyer opened again, distracting me from thinking about the fact that I'd attained 'ma'am' status. A short, husky guy approached the desk, clutching a large paper bag in his hands. He was wearing a dark gray sweatshirt with the hood pulled low over his eyes with a scarf covering the rest of his face.

"Is Erik here?" he asked quietly, setting the bag on the counter.

His voice sounded familiar, but without being able to see the guy's face, I couldn't place him.

"Erik is busy with the reception for the new library director," I said. "Can I help you?"

"When will he be done?"

I glanced down and checked the time on the computer monitor. "Let's see, it's eight now. The reception is due to end in about forty-five minutes, assuming they don't run late. The library closes at nine though, so you won't have much time to catch him then. Are you sure I can't help you instead?"

"No," he said abruptly, his deep voice booming out across the room.

The teenagers were standing in the entryway to the Imagination Room and they looked over in our direction as if to ask, 'How come he gets to be loud and we don't?'

The guy tugged at his hood as though trying to make sure it covered every inch of exposed skin. He lowered his voice, and said, "I'll wait."

One of his sleeves got caught on the edge of the counter as he went to pick up his paper bag. As he jerked his arm away, his hood slipped, revealing auburn hair and unique, different colored eyes.

"Logan, sorry I didn't realize it was you," I said.

Instead of replying, he yanked the hood back over his head, then rushed off in the direction of the Collingsworth Wing. I didn't have time to wonder what was going on with Logan as several patrons approached the counter at the same time. After checking out books and pointing people in the direction of the restrooms, I finally had a chance to catch my breath. Realizing Logan had left his bag on the counter, I picked it up and headed to the Collingsworth Wing to give it back to him.

I walked down the aisle between the stacks, finally finding Logan standing with his back toward me in the section which housed books classified in the 500s of the Dewey Decimal system. I wouldn't have guessed that Logan was interested in anything to do with geology, hydrology, or meteorology. But then again, I'd developed an interest in sea turtles earlier this year, something that surprised both me and everyone else to no end, considering the fact that I had never even swam in the ocean.

But Logan and science-related subjects . . . surprising. He had been a popular kid in high school. With an easy-going personality and natural athletic ability, it was no surprise that he had been captain of the wrestling team, not to mention prom king during his junior and senior years. But after Logan had graduated high school a few years ago, he appeared to withdraw, becoming a loner, and bouncing between one dead-end job and the next.

"Hey, you forgot this up front," I said. "It feels like some books. Did you mean to return them?"

Logan spun around to face me, and when I saw what was in his hand, I was so stunned I nearly dropped the bag. He was gripping a hunting knife, its blade glinting in the overhead light. I started to ask him what the heck was going on when something caught my attention on the shelf behind Logan. For a moment, I thought it was a mouse, but quickly realized my eyes were playing tricks on me. It was a leather knife sheath, not some creature making itself at home in the library.

"It's not mine, I swear," Logan spluttered. "I found it behind some books."

"Really," I said dryly. "You just happened to be looking behind some books and found a knife lying there."

"Here, just take it," he said, sheathing the knife, then thrusting it in my hand. Then he grabbed the paper bag and pushed past me, muttering something about waiting for Erik somewhere else.

I looked down at the knife in my hands and shook my head. What in the world was going on? Why did Logan pretend the knife wasn't his, and more importantly, why was he carrying a knife in the library?

CHAPTER 3
FLUORESCENT BANANAS

After my encounter with Logan, I went back up to the front. By this point, the teenagers had moved into the Imagination Room and there were only a few people quietly milling about, looking at the book displays. The only conversations I overheard were in hushed tones, mostly about Seatrina's appearance in the area.

When Carol came back a few minutes later, I showed her the knife Logan had handed me.

"My cousin got her husband one of those for Christmas," she said.

"This knife belongs to your cousin's husband?" I asked.

"No, they live in Minnesota," Carol said. "It couldn't be his."

After I explained that Logan claimed he found the

knife behind some books in the science section, the library assistant furrowed her brow. "That's odd. I shelved books there earlier today. It certainly wasn't there then."

"It has to be Logan's," I said. "He knows we don't allow knives or other weapons inside the library. So, when I caught him, he probably pretended it wasn't his."

"I'm not so sure." Carol pointed at an insignia on the sheath. "This is a custom-made knife and pretty expensive. I doubt if Logan would readily give up something that costs so much. It's not like he would have been in serious trouble. We just would have told him he had to take the knife out of the library."

I thought about Logan's erratic employment history. "How could he afford something like this?"

Carol shrugged, then offered to store the knife in the office. "Maybe he'll come back for it later."

"Maybe. But somehow I doubt it," I said.

After entrusting the knife to her, I rejoined the reception. Ivy was rapping the podium to get everyone's attention.

"On behalf of the library board, I wanted to thank everyone for coming out tonight to welcome Hudson to the community," Ivy said. "I'm excited to announce that one of the new programs that Hudson will be introducing to the library is—"

Before she could finish what she was saying, Thornton interrupted. "I'm afraid Ivy's enthusiasm is getting the better of her. We won't be announcing any new programs at this time."

Ivy gave Thornton a funny look. "We discussed this at our last board meeting."

"I wasn't at that board meeting," Thornton pointed out.

"That's right," she said evenly. "You had an impromptu trip to Hawaii."

"It must be hard making ends meet on a principal's salary. Especially as a single parent," Thornton said, his voice dripping with condescension. "So, I can forgive you for being jealous that I can afford to travel."

"That's not what this is about," Ivy said. "Now, if you don't mind, I'd like to get back to my announcement."

Thornton whispered something in Ivy's ear. She flinched and started to pull away, but whatever he said next caused her to stand still with her shoulders tense and her eyes wide. When Thornton finished speaking to her, Ivy gave him a brittle smile, and then took a step backwards.

"What's going on?" I asked my grandmother.

"I don't know," Grandma said in hushed tones as she adjusted the scarf around her neck. "But I've got a bad feeling about it."

Hudson was standing on the opposite side of the room next to Erik. He caught my eye and gave me a questioning look. I gave him what I hoped was a light-hearted shrug, then turned my attention to Erik. The youth librarian was wringing his hands together as he watched Thornton out of the corner of his eye, waiting to see what was going to happen next.

He didn't have to wait long to find out. Thornton held up his hands to get everyone's attention, then he said something that sent shock waves through the audience. "Ivy has decided to step down from the library board effective immediately. Since I'm vice president, that means I automatically succeed Ivy as president of the board. And, in this new capacity, my first order of business will be to conduct a thorough review of the library budget and staffing."

I turned to my grandmother. "Can he do that?"

Usually an articulate, quick-witted woman, Grandma appeared to be at a loss for words. My stomach churned as I watched her struggle to gain her composure.

I didn't see Hudson come up behind us, so I was startled when I heard him ask, "Should I be worried?"

"We all should be," my grandmother said quietly.

* * *

Thornton's announcement had certainly put a damper on the rest of the evening. Small groups of people clustered together, presumably talking about Ivy's resignation and Thornton's power grab. Ivy stood off to the side, eyeing Thornton warily.

As the reception wound down, Grandma suggested to Hudson that now would be a good time to show him his new office. I wondered how long it would actually be Hudson's office before Thornton forced him out, but I kept the thought to myself.

Erik was visibly shaken. He looked relieved when I offered to clean up the coffee service and other dishes.

"Thanks," he said. "I'll go help out front." What he probably left unsaid was 'anything to get as far away from Thornton as possible.'

As I gathered up empty coffee cups, I noticed Thornton holding court in one corner of the meeting room. Several people, including one of the city councilors and a couple of local business owners, were hanging onto his every word. The snippets of conversation I overheard alarmed me. Thornton was trying to gather support for his plan to slash the library's budget and make staffing cuts. Sadly, he seemed to be succeeding.

At the opposite end of the room, the owner of the bowling alley, Simon Fischer, was huddled up with a couple of his buddies. They were teasing him about the jacket he was wearing.

"Man, that thing is bright," one of them said, shielding his eyes as though he were being blinded. "You look like a fluorescent banana."

The other guy pointed at the embroidered emblem on the front. "Isn't 'Bowling' supposed to have an 'l' in it? That says, 'Bowing.'"

"Yes, I know," Simon snapped.

"Why are you wearing a jacket inside, anyway?" the first man asked. "You must be sweltering to death."

"I'm making a point." Simon jabbed a finger in Thornton's direction. "If that man thinks I'm going to let him get away with producing inferior goods with my money, he has another thing coming. I want everyone to see the shoddy workmanship that came from the factory he hooked me up with. I've got cartons and cartons of crappy products that I can't sell. All because of that man."

Oblivious to the other man's hostile gaze, or perhaps because of it, Thornton gave Simon a cheerful thumbs up. "Looking good, sport."

My tray was full by this point, so I made my way to the kitchen. As I was walking down the hallway, I passed by a group of knitters making plans for their next session. One woman suggested that they make Seatrina an afghan. The others enthusiastically agreed.

Shaking my head at the celebrity mania that had taken over the town, I set the dishes in the sink. After rinsing and loading them in the dishwasher, I went back to the meeting room to get the coffee urn. The library was due to close soon, so I was hurrying back to the kitchen with it when someone jostled my elbow and the urn's lid popped off, splashing coffee onto my top.

"Oh, gosh, Thea," a woman said. "I'm so sorry. I didn't see you there. Did you burn yourself?"

After repositioning the urn in my arms, I looked up and saw Logan's mom standing in front of me. "No, it's okay, Ashley," I said. "The coffee was cold."

As usual, the middle-aged woman looked exhausted. No amount of concealer could hide the dark circles under her gray eyes. Her shoulders were slumped and her dishwater blonde hair was lanky. Her air of fatigue wasn't surprising. In addition to working full time at the bowling alley, Ashley also worked a second job as a cleaner to make ends meet.

"How did the knitting go tonight?" I asked her.

Ashley's expression brightened as she pulled a pair of aqua-colored gloves out of her tote bag. "I just finished these. Aren't they gorgeous?"

As I admired the mohair yarn she had used, Ashley dug through the knitting supplies and projects in her bag.

"You've got a lot crammed in there," I said.

"What can I say? I love knitting. I do it every chance I get—first thing in the morning before I have breakfast, on my work breaks, and while I'm watching TV at night. My knitting tote bag goes everywhere with me." Ashley pulled a tiny pink hat out of her bag. "Here, this is what I wanted to show you. We're making beanies for the children's hospital in Bismarck."

"That's sweet," I said.

"It makes me wish I had a grandbaby," Ashley confided in me.

I tried to keep my expression neutral. Logan was Ashley's only child, so if she was going to have grandchildren, Logan would have to provide them. However, Logan hardly seemed mature enough or financially stable enough to become a father at this point in his life.

"Is Logan seeing someone?" I asked.

Ashley sighed. "No. There was a girl for a while, but she broke it off. What about you? Are you dating anyone?"

"Uh, no," I said, wishing I hadn't brought up this particular topic.

"What about the new library director? I heard he's single." Ashley wagged a finger at me. "I bet your grandmother would approve."

"Hudson and me? Definitely not," I said firmly.

"But he's cute."

I looked down at the coffee urn in my arms. "You know what, this is getting heavy. I better get this to the kitchen."

"Want a hand?"

I knew Ashley meant well, but I really didn't want to continue the discussion of my love life. Before I could decline her offer, Simon spotted us on his way to the men's room. He was dripping with sweat, probably because he still had that ridiculous jacket on. I wondered if he knew that not only was the color unappealing, but also the cut of the jacket didn't do his short, stocky build any favors.

Simon wiped his brow, causing his light brown hair to stand up at an odd angle, then jabbed a finger in Ashley's direction. "What are you doing here? You're supposed to be at work."

I took this as my cue to leave, and said, "I'll let you guys talk."

As I walked toward the kitchen, I heard Ashley claim, "I scheduled tonight off ages ago."

"You're lying," Simon growled. "There's no way I would have approved of that. I'm going to dock your pay for the hours you missed. Now, you better hightail it back to work."

I tried to busy myself in the kitchen and ignore their argument, but Simon and Ashley's voices were so loud I could hear them over the running water.

"Simon, I swear to you, I'm not lying," Ashley said. "I always have the first Tuesday of every month off for my knitting circle. Your wife covers for me."

"Covering for you. Exactly," Simon spit out. "You snuck out of work and my wife had to fill in for you at the last minute."

"Is that what Michelle said?" Ashley said, her voice trembling.

"She didn't have to . . ." There was a pause, then

Simon said coolly, “Maybe I should find someone more reliable.”

“No, Simon, please, I need this job.”

“We’ll talk about it in the morning,” he said. “Now, skedaddle back to work before I fire you on the spot.”

I poked my head out of the kitchen to see if Ashley was okay. The poor woman was leaning against the wall, pressing her fingers against her face as if trying to keep tears at bay. She looked at me sharply, then fled into the ladies’ room. Unsure whether I should follow her, I stood in the hallway for a few moments.

A friendly face couldn’t hurt, I decided eventually. But just as I was about to push the door to the ladies’ room open, I heard a noise behind me. Turning around, I saw Logan slinking down the hallway. Where had he come from? It certainly wasn’t the kitchen—I was just in there. The only place he could have been was the storage room, but why?

Logan stood stock still when he saw me, like he had been caught doing something wrong. I glanced at his hands, relieved to see only his paper bag, rather than a knife or some other weapon that he had mysteriously found behind some books.

Something was going on, though. Logan’s jaw was clenched and his fingers were gripping the bag so hard that some of the paper had ripped on the side.

I took a cautious step forward. “Are you okay, Logan?”

“Fine,” he said through gritted teeth.

"You don't seem fine," I said gently.

"You sound like my mom."

I was pretty sure that wasn't meant as a compliment, but I let it slide. "Erik is at the front desk now. I know you were looking for him."

"Thanks," he muttered, then edged past me.

What was up with that guy? On another day, I might have asked Ashley about it, but she had enough to worry about with Simon threatening to fire her.

My cousin, Freya, had just told me that Mercury was in retrograde this week. "I know you think it's all a bunch of mumbo jumbo, but mark my word, this is going to be a time of upheaval and misfortune," she'd forewarned.

While I certainly didn't believe that the stars and planets were influencing events, something certainly was going on today. It had all started with my parking struggles at the airport, a ticket for leaving my car in the loading zone, Hudson's lost luggage, Ivy's sudden resignation, and Thornton's power grab, not to mention Logan's knife. Just thinking about it all was overwhelming. I took a deep breath and resolved to focus on what I could control.

* * *

As I watched Logan's retreating back, I thought about what I could actually control. How much coffee I drank each day, whether I used dark brown mascara or black, curbing my impulse to buy books—those are all things I had some degree of control over. But the bigger stuff . . . I wasn't so sure. Shaking myself mentally, I decided to stop dwelling on how complicated life could be and go check on Ashley instead.

When I entered the ladies' room, Ashley was standing at the sink, running a brush through her hair. After giving me a faint smile, she set her brush down, then pulled a tube of lip gloss out of her purse. I recognized the brand—it was from a top-end cosmetics line, one that was too pricey for me.

"How's it going?" I asked.

Ashley finished applying her lip gloss, then said, "I guess you overheard Simon."

"He seems like a tough boss." I grabbed a paper towel and wiped some water off the counter. "I used to work for someone like that."

"What did you do?"

I sighed. "Put up with it."

"Yeah, same." Ashley chewed on her bottom lip, mussing up her freshly applied lip gloss. "Simon's wrong about my shift tonight, but there's no way he'd ever admit it."

"Why don't you look for another job? There are plenty of places hiring in town."

Ashley looked at me intently, her dark gray eyes watering slightly. "I've worked at the bowling alley since I moved back to North Dakota. Gosh, it's been almost seven years now. I can't imagine working anyplace else."

"I know what you mean. I went to work for a company straight out of college. I thought I'd retire from there. But then, after what happened . . ." I paused, debating whether to share what had prompted my departure from my last place of employment. It's not like it was a secret, especially in this town. Nothing stayed secret here for long. But still, I wasn't in the mood to rehash things.

"Anyway," I continued. "I did end up leaving and it turned out for the best. Now I have my own consulting company. I can work from home and I have a flexible schedule."

Ashley's expression hardened. "Must be nice."

I felt my face flush. "I'm sorry. I didn't mean for it to come out that way," I spluttered.

"It's fine," Ashley said. "Sometimes, I wish my life had turned out differently, that's all. But I should count my blessings."

"How long has Simon owned the bowling alley?" I asked, changing the subject back to what I hoped was more neutral ground.

"He bought it last year," Ashley said. "Before that, it belonged to the Grangers."

"Oh, yeah, that's right," I said. "Sweet couple."

"They were. They helped me out of a tough situation. I'll always be grateful to them." Ashley slung her purse over her shoulder. "Anyways, I better get back to the bowling alley before Simon fires me."

After she said goodbye, I stared at my reflection in the bathroom mirror and chided myself. It's okay to be grateful for what you have, but maybe keep it to yourself next time. When your good fortune makes other people feel bad about how their life turned out, you need to learn a lesson in humility.

After my little self-lecture, I headed to my grandmother's office . . . correction Hudson's new office.

Wow, it was going to be hard to start referring to it as 'Hudson's office.' For as long as I could remember, the cozy, dark-paneled room had been my grandmother's domain. A large walnut desk took pride of place. Full bookcases lined one wall, and the other was decorated with Grandma's framed needlepoint and family pictures. Next to the window was a tattered, but comfy armchair and ottoman, where I had spent many hours reading after school.

Would Hudson re-decorate the office? If so, I wondered what look he would go for. Being from Florida, maybe he'd go for a surfer vibe. Or was a sleek modern look more his style? Of course, Thornton might end up driving Hudson out of town before he even got a chance to get settled and think about office decor.

As I stood outside the door, I heard laughter coming from Grandma's office. I poked my head through the door. "What's so funny?"

Grandma grinned at me. "I was telling Hudson about the time you buried your mom's jewelry box in the backyard. You were going through a pirate phase and buried treasure was all you could talk about."

I felt my face grow warm for the second time this evening. When you're as pale as I am, bright red cheeks practically glow in the dark. I was too mortified to make eye contact with Hudson. He was gracious enough to sense my discomfort, and said, "That's nothing. My mom is always telling people about how when I was five, I would collect rocks from outside and put them in the fridge. Florida gets hot in the summer and I didn't want them to burn."

Grateful for the shared pain of childhood embarrassment, I turned to look more closely at Hudson. He was a good-looking guy, and I had a feeling the single ladies in town would be making a beeline to his place to drop off muffin baskets and casseroles. Did people know that he was widowed? If so, would it make a difference? Not for some of these single gals—they would play a long game of baked goods and home-cooking in the hopes that once he got out of mourning, he'd look their way.

"I'm going to head home now and have a word with your grandfather about his missing clothes," Grandma said to me. "I'll drop Hudson off on my way. It's been a long day, and he has an early start tomorrow. Erik will close up the library."

"Okay. I won't be far behind." I picked up a dirty

coffee cup from the desk. "I'll just pop this in the dishwasher."

After a final tidy of the kitchen, I was ready to head out. The library was due to close in a few minutes and was pretty much deserted by this point. Even the library assistant had left for the night. Erik wasn't at the front desk, but I could hear him in the office he shared with the reference librarian.

"Don't give up now," Erik was saying to someone. "You've come so far."

"I don't want anyone to find out, especially my mom," replied a man who sounded a lot like Logan.

"You don't have to worry about that," Erik said. "This is confidential. It's just between you and me."

"I don't know, man. I think this is a bad idea."

I heard a chair scraping on the floor, then Logan rushed out of the office. His frantic exit caused me to step back quickly so he wouldn't collide into me.

"Thea, I didn't know you were still here." Erik was standing in the doorway of his office. He looked at me warily. "Did Logan see you?"

"I don't think so. He was in too much of a hurry to notice that I was behind him," I said.

Erik exhaled slowly. "Good. That's good."

"What were you talking with him about? Was it about the knife?"

"Knife. What knife?"

"I found him with an expensive hunting knife. He claims he found it behind some books."

"That's strange." Erik shoved his hands in his pockets and stared at the floor for a moment. When he looked back up at me, he had an earnest look on his face. "I need you to do me a favor and forget what you overheard."

"I didn't hear much. Just you promising that you wouldn't reveal whatever secret he's keeping."

"Oh, so you didn't hear the part about—" Erik abruptly stopped speaking mid-sentence.

I arched an eyebrow. "Well, now I'm curious."

"You have to trust me on this, Thea. Logan's a good guy. If I break his confidence, it will undermine everything we've been working on."

"Sounds like Logan isn't the only one with a secret." Then I held up my hands. "You know what, it's actually none of my business."

"Thanks. I appreciate it. One day, I hope to tell you about it. Then you'll understand."

Erik walked me to the foyer. After I grabbed my coat, he thanked me again, then locked the door behind me.

Once I was outside, I turned and looked back at the library with its original historic architecture and the more modern addition. My eyes welled up as I thought about the changing of the guard today—my grandmother retiring and Hudson taking her place. As I wrapped my arms around myself, I felt a warm presence surrounding me. Maybe it was my ancestors, the women who had built and run this library, telling me not to worry and that everything would be okay. I only hoped they were right.

CHAPTER 4
SO MUCH TWINE

When I came downstairs to the kitchen the next morning, my grandfather was sitting at the table examining a piece of twine. Grandma was standing next to the stove, cracking eggs into a bowl.

"Do you think Hudson likes French toast?" my grandmother asked me.

"Doesn't everyone?" I replied. "Especially the way you make it with cinnamon, nutmeg, and almond extract. Why do you ask?"

"I invited him over for breakfast," Grandma said. "Can you drop him off at the library afterward? I have a doctor's appointment this morning."

"Sure." I poured some coffee into a mug. "But why does he need a chauffeur?"

My grandmother placed a cast-iron skillet on one

of the gas burners, then said, "He's not comfortable driving in the snow yet."

"Humph," Grandpa said.

Although his expression didn't change, I could sense my grandfather's disapproval. People who couldn't drive in a blizzard, tell when wheat is ready to be harvested, or thought watching baseball was a waste of time were people to be pitied.

"Did Hudson think this job was in North Carolina instead of North Dakota?" I asked in a teasing tone. "Cold and snow kind of come with the territory."

"I'm sure he would be fine driving," Grandma said. "But considering the not so warm welcome he got yesterday, I thought he could do without the stress of dealing with it today. We got quite a bit overnight, and it's still coming down."

I peered out the kitchen window at the house across the road. The couple who owned it were spending the winter in Arizona, and had rented it to Hudson until he could find his own place. "Um, is Hudson walking over here in his flip-flops? He might lose a toe to frostbite on the way."

"He was able to find a pair of boots that fit at the Larsens. Ron also said Hudson could borrow some of his clothes. They're about the same size." Grandma turned to stare at my grandfather. "Unlike some people, Ron leaves his clothes in the closet where they belong."

Grandpa studiously ignored her, instead focusing

on tying two pieces of twine together.

She shook her head and said, "Move that stuff out of the way, Thor. We need to set the table."

Grandpa tucked his twine into a large plastic bag, then shuffled over to the coffee maker to refill his mug. While I was putting plates and utensils on the table, I heard someone tapping on the kitchen door. "I think he's here," I called out, then went to let Hudson inside.

"Brr! It's cold out there," he said as he shook snow out of his hair.

"Come on in," I offered, noting his attire with approval–khaki pants, a wool sweater, a warm coat, sturdy boots. Finally, he was appropriately dressed for the weather. "Want some coffee?"

"Sure," Hudson said. "Cream and sugar, please."

I suppressed a smile when I heard my grandfather say, "Humph." Coffee was meant to be drunk black, according to Grandpa's philosophy of the world. Cream and sugar was for wimps, and never get him started on cappuccinos with foam art. Pictures on your coffee were a level of frivolity that he couldn't even begin to understand. He pretended to ignore the fact that my grandmother and I indulged in creamy, sugary coffees from time to time.

"Good morning, sir," Hudson said politely to my grandfather.

Grandpa nodded, then went back to looking through his bag of twine.

"Don't mind Thor," my grandmother said to Hudson. "He's a man of few words. We don't know if it's because he doesn't know that many or if he just doesn't like to use them." She gave my grandfather an affectionate look, then turned back to Hudson. "Now, have a seat. Breakfast is almost ready."

As Hudson pulled out a chair, he noticed a laundry basket full of neatly folded men's clothes by the stairs leading down to the basement. "Looks like you solved the case of the missing clothes," he said.

My grandmother set a plate of bacon on the table. "Thea figured it out."

I chuckled. "It wasn't hard. All I did was look downstairs. All of Grandpa's clothes were in the laundry room."

"Don't sell yourself short," Grandma said. "I would have never in a million years thought your grandfather would try to wash his own clothes."

"Don't like funny smells," Grandpa said quietly.

Grandma rolled her eyes. "Tropical breeze isn't a funny smell. It smells like coconut. And you like coconut."

"In cookies, not clothes."

"You know I got that laundry detergent on sale," Grandma said, a hint of pride in her voice. "I saved quite a bit of money buying that brand."

"Well . . . okay, then," Grandpa said.

I bit back a smile. Grandma knew exactly how to appeal to my frugal grandfather's heart. Tell him something was on sale, and he'd buy it. Even if it was something he didn't need or want, a deal was too good to be passed up. From now on, he would wear his tropical breeze-scented clothes happily knowing that a few cents had been saved in the process.

"Any word on your luggage?" I asked Hudson.

"They said they'll hopefully deliver it to the library today." He grinned at me. "I can't wait to show you the stickers I made. I've got a few packs in my suitcase."

"You make stickers?" I asked quizzically.

"Uh-huh. I started doing them for kids when I was a youth librarian. Now I make all different kinds."

"My cousin will love that," I said. "She's really into stationery supplies. Colorful markers, stickers, washi tape. She loves it all."

"And what about you?" Hudson asked.

I chuckled. "Yeah, I'm more of a ballpoint pen and plain paper kind of gal."

"Shush," Grandma said, placing some French toast on each of our plates. "I don't want you to jinx Hudson's first official day talking about what happened to your cousin Freya."

Hudson poured syrup on his French toast. "Well, now I have to know."

"My grandmother is right. It's not something we should talk about over breakfast." I shivered as I remembered the gruesome discovery I had made during the summer. Trying to shake the feeling off, I asked, "What are your plans for your first day, Hudson?"

"I'm meeting with the staff this morning, then Erik is going to train me on the cataloging system the library uses." Hudson smiled. "But what I'm really looking forward to is sitting in on storytime this afternoon."

"Eat now, before it gets cold. French toast is best hot off the griddle," my grandmother interjected. "And for the millionth time, Thor, twine does not belong at the kitchen table."

"Is the twine for the farm?" Hudson asked politely. "Are you using it to fix something?"

My grandmother and I burst out laughing. When Hudson gave me an inquisitive look, I grinned. "Maybe that should be a surprise for another day."

"I like surprises," Hudson said.

"Humph," my grandfather said.

"Don't mind him. Grandpa thinks surprises are only good if you know what they're going to be ahead of time," I said to Hudson. "But I think you'll like this particular surprise. I guarantee you've never seen anything like it before." Then I dug into my French toast and moaned with appreciation. "It's perfect, Grandma. Just the right amount of nutmeg."

* * *

After breakfast, Hudson and I headed to the library. My grandparents' farmhouse was on a gravel road which didn't get plowed. It was days like this that made me glad my car had all wheel drive.

Hudson was gripping the dashboard, and I'm pretty sure he was pressing down on an imaginary brake on the passenger side floorboard. Dr. McCoy, on the other hand, was totally chilled out catnapping on the back seat.

"Doing okay there, champ?" I asked Hudson.

"This car has airbags, right?"

"Last time I checked."

Hudson twisted his head to stare at me. "When's the last time you checked?"

"Relax," I told him. "I promise to get you there in one piece."

He gave me a wry smile. "That would be preferable to multiple pieces."

As we turned onto the freshly plowed main road which led into Why, Hudson relaxed. Well, by 'relaxed,' I mean he was only using one hand to grip the dashboard instead of two.

"It was nice of the Larsens to lend me their pickup truck to drive until I get a vehicle. But I think I should buy a car sooner, rather than later. I'd hate to damage their truck." Hudson glanced down at his clothes. "I've already got maple syrup on Mr. Larsen's sweater. He'd probably get over that, but crashing his truck into a snowbank might be a lot harder to forgive."

I chuckled. "I'm happy to chauffeur you until you're feeling more comfortable about driving here."

"I appreciate that, but you've got your own life." Hudson sighed. "I think I should look for a place within walking distance of the library."

"There's not a lot available in town," I said. "That's one of the reasons why I live with my grandparents. That and the French toast."

During the rest of the ride, I called out various points of interest. "There's the local grocery store. If you like dill pickles, that's the place to get them."

"I suppose that's why it's called 'The Little Pickle,'" Hudson said dryly.

As we passed a strip mall, I said, "There's the laundromat, pizza parlor, and taxidermist."

When Dr. McCoy started yowling, Hudson whispered, "Probably not a good idea to mention you-know-what again."

I furrowed my brow. "The taxi—"

Hudson interrupted. "Yep, that's the one. The idea of you-know-what freaks him out."

As I turned into the library parking lot, I said, "Well, if I put myself in his shoes, or rather his paws, I can see why he'd be upset."

After Hudson got out of the car, he pointed at the neighboring building. "It's interesting that the bowling alley is next door to the library."

"Do you bowl?"

"Not really. I'm more into tennis." Hudson opened

the rear passenger door and scooped Dr. McCoy up. When the cat meowed, he stroked him behind his ears and said, "It's too cold for you to walk to the library. We need to get you some snow boots."

I smiled. "I've seen those for dogs, but never cats."

When we reached the entrance, Hudson asked if I would hold Dr. McCoy. Then he pulled the key to the library out of his pocket. "This feels like such a momentous occasion."

"Look at the grin on your face. You're like a kid on his first day of school," I said.

"After you," Hudson said, holding open the door.

As soon as I flicked the lights on, Dr. McCoy jumped out of my arms and padded over to a display of books on dogs. After jumping onto the table, the cat promptly knocked one of the books onto the floor. He looked extremely satisfied with himself.

"Not a fan, I take it," I said to the cat.

Hudson apologized as he picked the book back up, then chided his cat. "Hey, what have I told you about dogs? They're our friends, not our enemies."

Dr. McCoy appeared unimpressed with the lecture, deciding now was a good time to wash behind his ears.

"Let's turn up the heat," I said. "The thermostat is in the back by the kitchen. I'll show you where it is."

It took a while to walk from the front desk to the kitchen, because Hudson kept stopping every few feet to examine books and ask me about the library's collection. Surprisingly, I was able to answer most of his questions. I guess growing up with my grandmother and volunteering in the library had paid off.

Hudson lingered by a display of westerns. He picked up a copy of *Lonesome Dove.* "This is one of my dad's favorite books. Does this get checked out a lot?"

"You should probably ask Erik or the reference librarian about that. They'll have all the circulation stats." I jerked my head toward the hallway. "It's cold in here. Come on, let's go."

When we neared the kitchen, I showed him where the thermostat was located. "It's tucked behind this shelving unit."

After we adjusted the temperature, Hudson pointed to where the hallway branched to the left. "What's back there?"

"Oh, that's the storage room. It's where the library stores old books and other stuff they don't know what to do with. It's also where deliveries come in. Here, I'll show you." I opened the door to the storage room, then felt around on the wall until I found the light switch. Once the room was illuminated, I realized that Hudson's first official day on the job was about to take a serious turn for the worse. I quickly spun around and tried to block his view. "You might not want to see this."

"I've seen messy storage rooms before," Hudson joked. Then his expression sobered. "Thea, what's going on? You look white as a sheet."

"It's, um, a, um . . ." As I struggled to find the words, Hudson stepped around me.

When he saw what was on the floor, he sprang into action. "Quick, Thea, call nine-one-one. This man is injured."

As I pulled out my phone and dialed, I said quietly, "I think we're too late. He's already dead."

CHAPTER 5
SIBLING SQUABBLES

The paramedics arrived quickly. While they were busy in the back, Hudson and I waited by the front desk for the police. I was still bundled in my coat with my arms wrapped around myself. The heater had kicked on and the chill in the air had dissipated, but I couldn't stop shivering. Finding a dead body in the library, well, finding a dead body anywhere, has that sort of effect on you. I was desperate for a cup of hot coffee to warm up. Except since the kitchen was next to the storage room where the body was, that certainly wasn't going to happen.

Dr. McCoy was cuddled in Hudson's arms, meowing pitifully. Hudson stroked his fur while saying in a soothing voice, "It's okay, little buddy."

"He probably senses something is wrong," I said.

"Yeah, he's got a sixth sense for sure. I'm just glad he was out here instead of in the back when we found . . ." Hudson looked off into the distance for a moment before continuing, "I still can't believe it. Someone died here in the library."

"It's worse than that," I said. "Someone was murdered in the library."

Hudson locked his eyes with mine. "Murder? Why would you say that?"

"The pool of blood and the way his head—"

"Never mind, I get the idea," Hudson said firmly. "No need to go into details."

"Okay, suffice it to say that the marble bust didn't hit the dead man on the back of his head all on its own." After checking the time on my phone, I said, "The police should be here soon."

"I guess there isn't a hurry, considering the guy's dead."

I watched Hudson as he continued to pet Dr. McCoy. He wasn't shivering like me, nor was he showing any other signs of being freaked out by our discovery. "You're pretty calm and collected."

"I took first aid and CPR," he said. "They train you for these kinds of things."

"They train you to help someone who's injured or unconscious, not coming face to face with a murder victim," I pointed out.

"True." Hudson shrugged, then his expression sobered. "Actually, my stomach is twisting in knots.

How are you holding up?"

"I'm okay. It's not my first rodeo." I tried to sound tough and nonchalant, but I'm not sure I was successful.

He held my gaze for a moment, then blurted out, "Oh, my gosh . . . was that what you didn't want to tell me this morning about your cousin Freya."

I took a deep breath, then let it out slowly. "Yes, I found someone who had been murdered last July. The chief of police wanted to pin it on my cousin."

"What happened?" Hudson asked.

"We found out who really did it."

He furrowed his brow. "Who's we?"

"Me, my brother, and my grandmother. I guess you could say it was a family effort. My brother was taken off the case because it involved our cousin. But he still helped out from the sidelines. I did most of the legwork, and my grandmother, well, she organized everything."

Hudson smiled. "I can see that. Librarians are naturally organized, you know."

"Oh, believe me, I know. Grandma has a card catalog for her spices. If you want to cook something with, say thyme, you have to check it out first."

"Are there late fees if you don't return the spices on time?"

"Yeah, usually payable via extra chores."

After we had a good chuckle about that, Hudson set Dr. McCoy on the counter and said, "There's a woman in Coconut Cove who always seems to find a lot of murder victims. My Aunt Nancy thinks Mollie—that's her name, Mollie McGhie—goes out of her way to find dead bodies."

Dr. McCoy yowled and patted Hudson on his arm.

"I think the good doctor wants me to tell you about Mollie's cat, Mrs. Moto. Whenever Mollie would bring Mrs. Moto to the library, she and Dr. McCoy would hang out together." Dr. McCoy meowed again, then curled up on the counter. "Mollie is a bit of an amateur sleuth, like you."

I put my hand to my chest. "I'm no amateur sleuth. What happened was a one-off. I only got involved because the chief of police wanted to pin the murder on my cousin."

"Do you know who that is back there?" Hudson asked tentatively.

"Well, I couldn't see his face because he's lying on his front. But from the yellow jacket he's wearing, I think it's Simon."

"The guy who owns the bowling alley?" Hudson asked. "I met him during the reception last night. He was . . . um, an interesting character."

"I have a feeling 'interesting character' isn't what you were originally going to say."

Hudson's face reddened. "I don't want to speak ill of the dead."

Before I could probe further, the door opened and my brother, Leif, walked in accompanied by two other police officers. My eyes lit up when I saw he was holding a coffee carrier.

"One of those for me?" I asked him.

"Yep. I was in the drive-through when I got the call. I was picking up coffee to take to the station. Their loss, your gain." Leif passed a to-go cup to me, then looked at Hudson. "I got one here for you, too. Didn't know how you take it, but I assume you're okay with black."

Hudson thanked my brother, then made a slight grimace as he took a sip of his coffee.

"You okay, sis?" Leif asked me.

"Better now," I said.

Leif chuckled. "Is that because I'm here or because I brought you caffeine?"

"Sometimes it's better not to know the answer to questions like that." I took an appreciative sip of my drink, then asked Leif where the chief was.

Leif arched an eyebrow. "Didn't you hear?"

"Hear what?"

Leif asked the other two officers to go check on the paramedics and secure the scene. After they left, my brother lowered his voice and said, "The chief is on administrative leave."

I leaned forward. "Wow. I wonder what happened."

"Don't know. It's all hush-hush. He was pulled off the job yesterday afternoon." Leif looked in Hudson's direction, then said in a more formal tone, "The mayor appointed me as acting chief of police."

My jaw dropped. "You?"

"Geez, sis, you don't have to look so surprised."

"Well, you're pretty new to the force," I pointed out. "I would have thought there were officers with more experience."

Leif looked deflated. "Yeah, I wasn't the first choice. One of the senior guys is off on medical leave, another one's wife is due to give birth this week, and the other person the mayor asked to take over left for vacation today."

"Sounds like the pickings were pretty slim," I joked.

"Well, I did take that course on investigative techniques in Bismarck last month," Leif pointed out. "I aced it by the way."

"Of course you did. You're a smart guy." I squeezed my brother's arm. "But this is a lot to take on right now, especially since there's been a murder."

"You can't assume it was murder, Thea." Leif folded his arms across his chest. "I know you helped when the chief thought Freya had killed someone. But this time, you should leave things to the professionals."

"Go take a look at the murder scene," I said in a snotty tone. "It's pretty obvious he was deliberately killed."

"Fine, I will."

I waved my hand toward the other side of the library. "Well, go ahead. No one's stopping you."

Hudson chuckled as Leif stormed off.

I spun in his direction. “Have something to say?”

He shrugged. “I have a sister, too. Let me guess, you’re older.”

“Good guess.” I ran my fingers through my hair. “Uh, I’m sorry I snapped at you. Leif and I are really close, but sometimes we wind each other up.”

“Don’t worry about it. It’s been a tough morning for everyone.”

We drank our coffee in companionable silence while we waited. After half an hour, the paramedics wheeled a gurney out. Seeing a body covered with a sheet really brought things home. “I think I’m going to be sick,” I said as I rushed toward the bathroom.

When I walked out of the ladies’ room, I tried not to look in the direction of the storage room, but I couldn’t help it. I gulped when I saw the police tape at the end of the hall, sealing off the scene of the crime.

Feeling a bit faint, I leaned against one of the bookshelves lining the hallway to steady myself. As my hands gripped the metal shelf, I swear I could hear a man singing, ‘New York, New York.’ At first, I thought it was one of the officers. Only the voice sounded like someone who was a native of the Big Apple, and, as far as I knew, no one on the police force hailed from there.

I looked around to see if there was someone else nearby, but the hallway was empty, save for me. It had to be my imagination. The stress of finding a dead body was getting to me. I craned my ears, but I couldn't hear the song anymore. Yep, it was all in my head. Nothing that a cup of coffee wouldn't fix. Well, maybe not fix, but it certainly could help.

"Time to get going," I muttered as I pushed myself off the bookshelf. Then I yelped when a book fell on my foot. I picked it up and scrunched up my face when I looked at the cover. Who would want to read a book about chameleons? Okay, that's not fair. Lots of people are into reptiles. I just wasn't one of them.

When I got back to the front desk, my brother was talking with Hudson. Leif gave me a sympathetic look. "Start over?" he said to me.

I nodded, then asked what the next steps were. "I assume you need to interview us since we found the body."

"Yes," Leif said. "Why don't you go down to the station and one of the officers will take your statement?"

As I slung my purse over my shoulder, I asked, "Has anyone told Simon's wife what happened yet?"

Leif furrowed his brow. "Simon? What are you talking about?"

"Don't you think Simon's wife should know that her husband is dead?"

"It wasn't Simon who was back there," Leif said slowly. "It was Thornton."

"Are you sure?" I asked, recalling the bright yellow jacket the victim had on. It looked exactly like the one

Simon had been wearing at the reception yesterday evening.

"One hundred percent." Leif motioned toward the door. "One of the officers will take you to the station now. I'll catch up with you later, okay?"

As I was walking out of the library, I realized that I had left my coffee cup on the front desk. Goodness knows I was going to need every ounce of caffeine to get through this morning. Telling the officer that I'd be right back, I went inside.

"I need to know where you were last night," I heard my brother say to Hudson.

"I was at the Larsens," Hudson said. "Your grandmother dropped me off there after the reception."

"Are you saying you didn't leave the house the entire night?" Leif asked.

I barged in between my brother and Hudson. "Hey, what's going on?"

Leif sighed. "Aren't you supposed to be on your way to the station?"

"It sounded like you're asking Hudson if he has an alibi." I put my hands on my hips. "Why in the world would you do that?"

"Well, if you really must know, it's pretty common knowledge that Thornton wanted to fire Hudson. That would be a pretty good motive for murder, don't you think?"

I jabbed a finger at my brother. "Hah, so you do

think it's murder. I was right."

Hudson cleared his throat. "Um, Thea, do you think you could get me the name of a lawyer? I have a feeling I'm going to need one."

* * *

Later that day, Hudson and I grabbed a bite to eat at Swede's Diner with my grandmother. It hadn't taken too long for me to give my statement at the police station, but Hudson spent several hours answering questions. His lawyer—a local family friend of ours—assured him that everything would be okay, but Hudson was far from convinced.

"I'm trying to stay positive." Hudson pushed his half-eaten cheeseburger to the side of his plate, then drowned his fries in ketchup. "But I'm having a hard time seeing the good in this situation."

My grandmother gave him a sympathetic smile. "Leif will come to his senses and realize he's got the wrong end of the stick."

"Will he though?" I asked. "You know what he's like. When he gets fixated on an idea, he can't let go. Remember when he was obsessed with proving that Hellmann's mayonnaise and Best Foods mayonnaise taste exactly the same?"

"Never heard of Best Foods mayo," Hudson said.

"It's only sold west of the Rockies," I explained. "Leif tried it at a restaurant when he was on vacation in California. He accused the waiter of disguising a bottle of Hellmann's with a Best Foods label."

"Why would they do that?" Hudson asked.

"Exactly. That's my point. A normal person would just eat their BLT and not think there's some sort of conspiracy trying to pass Hellmann's off as another brand." I rolled my eyes. "Do you know how many taste tests he made us participate in? I couldn't eat mayo for months afterward."

Hudson chuckled. "Okay, so your brother is a little obsessed with condiments."

"Yeah, ask me about the summer of ketchup when he was in the seventh grade." I sighed. "Anyway, my point is now that he's acting chief of police, he'll feel like he needs to prove himself. Pinning the murder on you would make everyone happy. Better an outsider rather than someone we know."

Grandma looked me square in the eye and said firmly, "Thea Marie Olson, that's not fair. Your brother is not trying to pin Thornton's death on Hudson. He's just doing his job."

The use of my full name brought back memories of being admonished as a child. I squirmed in my seat. "I'm sorry. You're right."

"Leif needs our support." My grandmother took a sip of her coffee. "We're a family. We stick together."

I nodded, then said, "When I was at the police station, I overheard someone say that the sheriff's office was going to help with the investigation."

Grandma leaned forward and tapped her finger on the table. "That's all well and good, but what Leif really needs is our help. Hudson does too."

Hudson looked up at the mention of his name. "Really? You want to help me? But you don't even know me."

"Nonsense, dear. Of course, we're going to help. That's what librarians do—we help people." Then my grandmother turned to me and said briskly, "Thea, get your notebook out. We need to make a list of suspects."

"My money's on Bobby Jorgenson," a woman said behind me.

I twisted my head and saw Norma, the long-time waitress at Swede's and queen of the local gossip mill. "Why do you think Bobby did it?" I asked the redhead.

As Norma topped up our coffee cups, she said, "Bobby was in here earlier this morning complaining about how Thornton made him take down all the Seatrina posters he had been tacking up around town. When someone told him that Thornton had been killed last night, he suddenly clammed up and high-tailed it out of here."

"Who is this Seatrina person everyone keeps talking about?" my grandmother asked.

Norma's jaw dropped. "You don't know who Seatrina is? Everyone knows who Seatrina is."

"I'm not everyone," Grandma said primly.

"But she won America's Top Talent a couple of

years ago. You must have seen that. Everyone saw it." When my grandmother gave her a blank look, Norma asked, "Don't you remember the uproar when she canceled all her appearances a couple months ago and dropped off the radar?"

"News to me," Grandma said.

Norma was so agitated at my grandmother's lack of pop culture knowledge that she waved the coffeepot around in the air, causing some of the liquid inside to slosh out of the top.

Of course, my knowledge of pop culture was a bit lacking too. That's what came from working practically 24/7 when I was living in Minneapolis. Now that I was back in Why and had my own consulting business, I had a bit more time on my hands. However, reading books and watching the Minnesota Twins during baseball season usually took up my spare time.

"I think someone is trying to get your attention," Grandma said to Norma.

"Be right with you, hon," Norma shouted across the room. Then she pointed at my notebook. "Be sure to write Bobby's name down there. Him and Thornton had a history."

"Bobby's a troublemaker, that's for sure," I said. "But I can't picture him as a murderer."

My grandmother tried again to get rid of Norma, pointing out that Swede had rung the order bell several times.

"Hold your horses," Norma yelled in the direction of the kitchen. "Can't you see I'm busy?"

Swede bellowed back, "What do you think I'm doing in here, twiddling my thumbs?"

Norma rolled her eyes, then continued to list reasons why Bobby was the killer—squinted a lot, drove too fast through the school zone, chewed gum and so on. When someone walked over and grabbed the coffeepot from Norma in order to refill their mug, she finally got the hint and left us in peace.

Grandma pushed her plate to the side, then told me to start writing down suspects. "We have to consider motive, means, and opportunity, right?"

I chuckled. "You'd give Nancy Drew a run for her money."

"I have to confess to being a Nancy Drew fan," my grandmother mused. "Although you always preferred the Three Investigators."

"I loved that series too. I always had my nose in one of those books, even when I was hanging out at the beach as a kid." A smile spread across Hudson's face, but then quickly faded. "I should have never left Florida."

"Personally, I'm glad you're here," I said to Hudson. "Now, my grandmother is right. We need to think about who did this, so that we can clear your name. I think we should start with Ivy."

Grandma leaned back in her chair. "Ivy? Why would you say Ivy? She's a lovely woman and an elementary school principal. Educators don't kill people."

"You saw what happened at the reception last night," I said. "Thornton said something which upset her. I don't know what it was, but it was enough to make her suddenly resign as president of the library board."

"There was something fishy going on there," my grandmother agreed. "But Ivy didn't kill the man, because he forced her out."

I shrugged. "I think it's worth talking to her. Even if you're right that she wasn't involved in the murder, and I hope you are, she may still know something that could point us in the right direction."

"Fine. But don't put her name on the suspect list. Create a separate list . . . I don't know, call it something like 'Friends of the Investigation.'"

That sounded a bit far-fetched to me, but I did as she asked. "Okay, who else do we have?"

Hudson held up his hands. "Don't look at me. I'm new here. I wouldn't have a clue who would have held a grudge against Thornton."

"I hate to say it, but we need to consider Erik," I said.

My grandmother put a hand to her chest. "But Erik works at the library."

"Yes, but Thornton intimated that Erik's job was in jeopardy," I said gently. "That's a possible motive."

Hudson dragged a fry through his ketchup, then

put it back down on his plate. "I guess I'm in good company. The 'People Who Thornton Wanted to Fire' club. Maybe I should make stickers with that on it."

I smiled at his attempt at humor, despite the circumstances. "I still think it's odd that Thornton wanted to get rid of you and Erik."

Grandma nodded. "I think that's a good place to start. What caused Thornton to suddenly want to make changes to the library? I have an idea, but I think the two of you should look at the situation with a fresh eye. Once we know for certain what was motivating Thornton, it could shed some light on our investigation."

"Who would know the answer to that?" Hudson asked.

"Ivy," my grandmother suggested. "The two of you should go see her after school. I think she's at a conference today, so you'll have to do it tomorrow, though."

"I would like to talk with her about partnership opportunities between the school and library," Hudson said.

"And while you're there, you casually turn the conversation over to the subject of Thornton," Grandma said.

I stole a fry off Hudson's plate, then said, "It makes sense that Hudson would go see Ivy, but she'll wonder why I'm there."

"Someone has to drive Hudson," Grandma said, as

though it was obvious.

"I really can drive myself," he said.

My grandmother motioned to Norma for the check, then said, "Nonsense, Thea will drive you."

"I guess that makes me your Worthington." I grinned at Hudson. "But I have to warn you, my English accent is terrible."

When Grandma gave me a quizzical look, Hudson explained, "In the Three Investigators books, Jupiter Jones won a contest organized by the Rent-'n'-Ride Auto Rental Company. The use of a chauffeured Rolls Royce sedan was the prize."

"Well, my car certainly isn't a Rolls Royce, but it can handle the snow and ice," I said. "You need to sit in the front, though. I'd feel weird if you sat in the back."

"Of course," Hudson agreed. "The back seat is reserved for Dr. McCoy. The hired help sits up front with the chauffeur. Speaking of which, thanks again for taking him back to the Larsens while I was still with the police."

"No problem." I cocked my head to one side, remembering the way Simon had been glaring at Thornton the previous evening and complaining about being stuck with cartons of faulty goods he couldn't sell. When I asked my grandmother if she knew anything about it, Norma appeared out of nowhere.

"The two of them were in business together. And,

from what I heard, things had gone sour. Simon claims Thornton ripped him off," the waitress said. When we asked for more details, she shrugged. "That's all I know."

She handed us the check, then hustled over to the kitchen to inform Swede that she was taking a break.

"Who's gonna serve the customers?" Swede yelled, but Norma had already slipped out the door.

"Are they always like that?" Hudson asked.

Grandma chuckled. "Never known them to act any other way toward each other."

"So, we agree that we should add Simon to the list," I said, trying to get back to the business at hand. I jotted his name down in my notebook. "Okay, maybe we can go to the bowling alley tonight and find out more about Simon's dealings with Thornton. We'll see Ivy tomorrow after school. That just leaves Erik."

"Want to do that this afternoon?" Hudson asked me. "When I called him earlier to tell him what had happened and that the library would be closed, he told me that he was going to spend the day at home reading."

"I baked some cookies this morning," Grandma said. "Why don't you take some with you? I just happen to have a tin of them in my car. I was going to drop them off for Pastor Rob, but I think Erik could use them more."

I smiled. "People are more likely to answer nosey questions if there are cookies involved, is that what you're really saying?"

"Can't hurt." Grandma leaned forward and looked me squarely in the eye. "Don't push Erik too hard, okay? I know in my heart of hearts that he didn't do it. My money is on Simon."

"I hope you're right," I said with more confidence than I felt.

CHAPTER 6
CLOWN SHOES

On the drive to Erik's apartment building later that afternoon, Hudson asked me what I knew about the youth librarian.

"Let's see, he's originally from Montana. He moved here after grad school. I think it was because of a girl. But if I remember correctly, that didn't last long."

"He must like it here to have stayed after they broke up," Hudson said.

I stopped the car at an intersection to let a group of school kids cross the road, then pulled into a spot near Erik's building. "I guess so. Although sometimes it's hard to leave a place even when you know it's not right for you. It takes a lot of effort to uproot your life."

"Don't I know it," Hudson said as we got out of the car.

"I know you must have qualms about your decision to move from Florida to North Dakota, but once we clear your name, they'll disappear," I said, trying to reassure him.

"I hope you're right," he said glumly.

"This is a cute neighborhood," I said, trying to distract Hudson. I pointed at an old wood cabin which stood in the middle of a grassy patch between two more modern looking buildings. "That was built in the late 1800s by an eccentric artist by the name of Jasper Collingsworth. He had met Teddy Roosevelt in New York City and was fascinated by his description of the buffalo in North Dakota. But unlike Roosevelt, he didn't want to hunt them, he wanted to paint them. So, he moved out here, built that cabin, set up his easel, and painted buffalo every day for the next forty years."

"It's interesting that you call them buffalo and not bison," Hudson said.

I turned to face Hudson. "I know some people insist that they should be called bison, but people here have always called them buffalo."

Hudson stared at something behind me, his eyes growing wide. "Bu . . . bu . . . bu . . ." he stuttered, his voice getting increasingly more high-pitched.

"Are you okay?" I asked.

Hudson grabbed my arm, then yelled at me to run.

He yanked me, pulling me toward him. But then, all of a sudden, he let go of me and stood stock still. "It's too late," he whispered, the blood draining from his face. "Maybe if we're quiet and don't move, it'll go away."

When I heard a familiar snorting behind me, I grinned. "Let me guess. There's a buffalo standing behind me."

"How can you be so calm?" Hudson whispered.

"It's okay," I said in a normal tone of voice. "This is Bufford, the town buffalo. Well, I call him Bufford. Everyone else calls him something different. No one can seem to agree on what his name is. I guess we're waiting for him to tell us what it is."

Bufford pawed at the ground, then took a step toward Hudson. Hudson took two giant steps backward. The buffalo advanced again, and Hudson retreated again. After a few moments of watching this little dance, I said, "He just wants you to scratch behind his ears. You know, kind of like you do with Dr. McCoy."

Hudson shook his head, saying incredulously. "That's a giant buffalo, not a lap cat."

"Look, I know it's a lot to take in. I felt the same way when I first met Bufford. But he's really harmless, I swear."

After a lot more persuasion, Hudson tentatively put his hand on the buffalo's neck, then gave him a gentle scratch. When Bufford leaned in, Hudson asked, "Is he purring?"

I smiled. "You must have the magic touch."

Eventually, Bufford decided it was time to move on, and we watched as he casually wandered down the street like he owned the place.

"Probably heading to Swede's for some carrots," I said, leading the way to Erik's building. When we got there, the door was wide open. I shut it firmly behind us, saying, "They're letting out a lot of heat."

"I wonder if they have any units for rent," Hudson asked as we climbed the stairs. "This is pretty close to the library."

"It is a good location," I said. "And Bufford likes to hang out around the Collingsworth cabin, so that's a bonus."

After I knocked on Erik's door, he called out, "It's open. Come on in."

When we walked inside, Erik looked at us with surprise. "Oh, sorry. I thought you were my neighbor. How did you get inside the building?"

"The front door was open," I said.

"That's odd. It shouldn't have been. We had a problem with someone stealing our mail, so we've been making sure that the door is always locked. Visitors have to buzz to get in the building." Erik shook his head, then offered us some coffee.

"Please." I handed Erik the cookie tin, then surveyed the cramped studio apartment. It didn't contain much in the way of furniture—a navy blue futon which looked like it had seen better days, a coffee table, and two wooden chairs. There was an alcove with a kitchenette and a door leading to a small bathroom on the far wall. Large bookcases crammed full lined the other walls and piles of books were scattered on the floor and window sills. The excessive amount of books reminded me of my grandparents' house, minus the dust of course. Erik didn't strike me as someone who spent his spare time cleaning.

"Are these Rose's famous rhubarb linzer cookies?" Erik asked as he opened the tin.

"I don't think I've ever had a rhubarb cookie," Hudson said.

"Oh, man, you're missing out. They're delicious. Rose makes the rhubarb jam from scratch." Erik grabbed a plate from the kitchenette, then placed several cookies on it before setting it on the coffee table. He motioned for us to sit down. "I'll get the coffee brewing."

"Um, could I have a glass of water instead?" Hudson asked. "My hands are starting to shake from all the caffeine I've had today."

"Sure thing, man." After he got us our beverages, Erik asked, "How long do you think the library will be closed for?"

Hudson shook his head. "I'm not sure. The police said it could be a few days."

"Haven't they talked to you yet?" I asked Erik.

Erik furrowed his brow. "Why would the police

want to talk to me?"

"Because you were in charge of closing up the library last night," I said. "You'd have critical information that could help them pin down the time of death and how the murder happened."

"Anyone want more coffee?" Erik asked me, despite the fact I'd only had a couple of sips from my cup. Without waiting for a response, he leapt off the futon and darted to the kitchenette. As he started to scoop more grounds into the coffeemaker, he realized there was still coffee in the pot. Fumbling with a filter, he said over his shoulder, "It must have been such a shock to find Simon's body."

I shot Hudson a look, then said, "Simon? You mean Thornton, don't you?"

Erik spun around so quickly that he knocked the coffee canister over on the counter, spilling grounds everywhere. I rushed over to help him clean it up, but he waved me away.

"You okay?" Hudson asked Erik.

"Yeah, fine. Just klutzy."

"Your hands are shaking," Hudson said with a concerned tone in his voice.

"Must be too much caffeine, like you said." Erik finished cleaning up the mess, then poured himself a glass of water. After sitting back on the futon, he grabbed a cookie and munched on it absent-mindedly.

"Maybe you can tell us what happened last night," I suggested.

Erik's eyes widened. "But I don't know anything about how, um . . . Thornton was killed."

"Of course not. No, I meant what happened toward the end of the night. That will help us figure out when Thornton met his demise," I said. "What does the normal closing routine look like?"

This question seemed to relax Erik. He took a sip of water, then said, "Well, whoever closes has a bunch of stuff they need to do. Log off the system, turn off the public computers, walk through the library with a cart and place any unshelved items on it, lock the cash drawer—"

Wondering if robbery could have somehow been a motive, I interjected. "How much cash is there typically in the drawer?"

"Not much," Erik said. "We've eliminated fines, so there's typically just what people pay for copies or printouts. Occasionally, someone owes money, because they have to replace a book or other item. But we're still not talking about huge amounts."

"So, we might be looking for more of a petty thief than a bank robber type," I said.

"Why would anyone rob a library?" Erik asked. "You'd have to be a real jerk to do that."

"Unfortunately, there are a lot of jerks out there."

Hudson looked at me. "Are you thinking that Thornton's death is tied with an attempted robbery?"

"It's a possibility. Maybe Thornton interrupted the thief?" I proposed.

"And Thornton was collateral damage?" Hudson mused. "But his body was found in the storage room, not up front where the cash is kept."

I nodded. "The thief might have come in through the rear door, saw Thornton standing there, and killed him to cover his tracks."

Erik leaned forward. "Maybe Thornton was the thief. Maybe he was there, because he intended to rob the library."

"Why would he do that?" I asked. "Thornton was loaded."

Erik's shoulders slumped. "I guess you're right."

"You raise a good point about Thornton's estate," Hudson said. "Who stood to benefit financially from his death?"

"That's an excellent question." I furrowed my brow. "Thornton never married, and he didn't have children. His parents passed away years ago."

"No siblings?" Hudson asked.

Erik shook his head. "His brother, Reginald, died of cancer a couple of months ago. He didn't have any kids either."

I nibbled on another cookie while I pondered this. Thornton had always been a difficult man, but had grief pushed him over the edge?

As if reading my mind, Erik said, "Thornton's brother wanted to be the library director after your grandmother retired."

"What?" I spluttered. "How come I didn't know that?"

"It didn't get far. He approached her, let's see . . . about six months ago. Your grandma explained to him that he wasn't qualified. When she told him that he needed a master's of library science, he lost interest. Thornton got him a job at the golf course not long after that."

"Thornton's brother flitted between careers a lot," I explained to Hudson. "He would work at a place for a while, get bored, and then quit."

"I guess it helps if you have family money to fall back on in between jobs," Hudson said.

"No, Thornton was a self-made millionaire. But he always bailed his brother out. It was kind of sweet in a way how he always looked out for him." I leaned back in my chair. "It might explain Thornton's sudden animosity toward the library, though. I wonder if that's what my grandmother was thinking when she mentioned having an idea about what motivated his recent behavior."

"But it doesn't explain who killed Thornton and why," Hudson said.

"No, it doesn't." I grabbed my notebook from my purse and jotted down a note. "You did raise a good point about a financial motive. We need to find out who was going to inherit Thornton's estate."

"Isn't that the police's job?" Erik asked.

"Oh, we're just helping out," I said nonchalantly.

"They have their hands full. You said they haven't even had a chance to question you yet, right?"

"Um, no." Erik gulped. "I've never been questioned by the police before. I've never even had a speeding ticket."

"Don't worry about it," I said. "It's just routine procedure. Do you want to practice with us first?" When Erik nodded, I continued, "You mentioned earlier the things you do at closing like turning off the computers, locking the cash drawer, and picking up books. What else did you do that night before you left?"

"We always do a walk around," Erik said.

"As part of that, I assume you make sure there's no one still in the library?" Hudson asked.

"Correct."

I cocked my head to one side. "And was there?"

"The procedure is to check and make sure the library is empty," Erik said stiffly.

"Hmm . . . so that means Thornton and the killer got inside after you left." I started to reach for another cookie, but restrained myself, mostly because there was only one left on the plate. "Did you check to make sure the back door was locked?"

"It's always locked." Erik grabbed the last cookie, then got up and paced around the tiny apartment. "What are you accusing me of? I didn't kill anyone."

Hudson shot me a look, then he said mildly to Erik, "Of course you didn't kill anyone. Thea didn't mean it like that. She's just trying to prep you for when the police speak to you."

As Erik wiped crumbs off his shirt, I asked about access to the library. "Who else has a key besides you? I know my grandmother gave hers to Hudson."

"Just Bonnie, but she's on vacation." Erik looked at Hudson. "She's the reference librarian."

"I met her when I was here for my interview," Hudson said.

Erik frowned. "Right, sorry, I should have remembered that."

"Understandable," Hudson said. "It's been a pretty stressful day for all of us. I can barely remember what I ate for breakfast."

"Ooh . . . better not tell my grandmother that," I wagged a finger at Hudson. "She'd be hurt that you didn't remember her French toast."

He smiled at me, then turned back to Erik. "So, the only people with keys are you, me, and Bonnie?"

"No, the cleaners have a key, too. Someone comes each night around nine or nine-thirty. But they called shortly before we closed last night and said they couldn't send anyone, because of staffing shortages."

Hudson slapped his leg. "Wait a minute. I can't believe we're being so stupid. There must be video footage of who came in and out of the library. The police have probably already checked it and arrested the killer."

"Um, no. We don't have any video monitoring," Erik said.

"It's been talked about," I explained. "But there hasn't been any budget for a security system at the library."

Hudson looked deflated. "It looks like we're back at square one."

"Well, not completely," I said. "Erik confirmed that no one was inside the library when he left and that he checked the back door was locked."

Erik picked up the dishes from the coffee table. As he carried them to the kitchenette, he asked, "So, is that all the police are going to ask me?"

"They'll ask you about your alibi," I said.

The dishes clattered as Erik put them in the sink. "Alibi?"

"Uh-huh, where you were after you left the library and who you were with," I said.

Erik turned on the water and squeezed soap onto a sponge. As he washed the dishes, he said, "I left the library around nine-thirty, then grabbed something to eat at Frank's."

"Frank is a friend of yours?" Hudson asked.

"No, it's an all-night diner in Williston. I had a craving for a patty melt." He rinsed the dishes, then turned back to us. "I don't know why the police would want to know my alibi, though."

"Well, Thornton did seem to have it out for you. Your job was in jeopardy." Hudson spread out his hands. "Both of our jobs, actually. They might see that as a motive for murder."

Erik twisted the dish towel he was holding in his hands. "I know this isn't exactly the right time to tell you this, but I was planning on resigning. So, it didn't really matter to me if Thornton wanted to get rid of me."

Hudson was dumbfounded. "You're leaving the library?"

"I've decided to apply to the Peace Corps," Erik said. "Assuming they accept me, I'll be leaving my job at the library."

"Wow, that's amazing," I said. "I had no idea you were thinking about that."

"It's something I considered doing when I finished grad school, but there was this girl, and well, um . . ." Erik's face flushed. "Anyway, I'm going to go for it now."

"That's fantastic," Hudson said. "I hate losing you, but it's for a great reason."

After chatting for a few more minutes about Erik's plans, Hudson and I said goodbye. As we walked back toward the car, Hudson said, "I guess we can rule Erik out. He didn't have a motive for killing Thornton."

"That will make my grandmother happy," I said. "Leaves us with two suspects—Ivy and Simon."

"Don't forget, we still have to figure out how Thornton and his killer got into the library," Hudson pointed out after we got into the car. "Investigating a murder is more complicated than I thought it would be."

"Yeah, don't I know it," I said.

* * *

"I don't know about this," Hudson said to me later that evening. "I look like a clown wearing these."

"They're bowling shoes," I said. "Everyone looks like a clown."

Hudson scowled as he tugged at his shoelaces. "Tell me again why we're here."

"You want to find out who killed Thornton, right?" I sat on the bench next to Hudson and slipped my boots off. "When we were at Swede's, Norma said that Simon and Thornton had a business dispute. I don't know about you, but if someone was ripping me off, that would be a motive for murder. That's why we came to the bowling alley."

Pointing at the insulated mug I had set next to me, Hudson said, "Let me guess, if someone took your coffee away, that would also be grounds for murder."

I smiled. "Coffee grounds. Grounds for murder. Very clever."

"You've been drinking that stuff non-stop today."

"Today and every day." I held up my cup in a mock toast. "Here's to the elixir of life."

"So, what's the plan?" Hudson asked after he finished tying his shoes.

I pointed at the refreshment stand. "I say we start with Ashley. She doesn't think too highly of her boss, Simon. I bet it wouldn't be hard to get some information out of her."

Hudson patted his stomach. "I'm not really hungry. I had two helpings of your grandmother's scalloped potatoes."

"I think it was three, but who's counting?" I stood and pulled Hudson to his feet. "You can order a pop."

"Pop. That's cute." He grinned. "We call it soda where I come from."

I smiled back. "Some people call it soda here, but I think it's more fun to say pop."

We waited while Ashley helped a family with their order, then approached the counter. "What can I get you?" she inquired cheerfully.

Hudson ordered a drink, and I got a box of Milk Duds. I popped a candy in my mouth and asked Ashley what she thought about the murder.

Ashley frowned. "It's awful, isn't it? Especially for your grandma. Imagine something like that happening at her library."

"Well, it isn't really her library anymore." Remembering that Ashley wasn't a regular patron, I said, "She retired, you know."

"Oh, yeah, I think I saw that in the paper. I can't wait until I can retire." She frowned as she wiped down the counter. "Not that I'll ever be able to afford to stop working."

"That's a tough position to be in," Hudson said.

"It sure is." Ashley set her rag down and gave him an appraising look. "How are you settling in? I'd be happy to show you around sometime."

Feeling irrationally possessive, I quickly said, "No problem. I've got that covered." When Hudson looked at me with surprise, I quickly told Ashley, "My family is looking out for him. He's staying across the road from us at the Larsens' place, you know."

A couple of teenagers came up to the counter and ordered nachos. While Ashley was fixing food for them, Hudson whispered to me, "What do we do now? We can't stand here all day."

"We'll order something else," I said. "Do you like soft pretzels?"

He rubbed his belly. "I do, but I'm not sure my stomach would agree."

"We'll split one then."

While I slathered mustard on our pretzel, I tried to engage Ashley in conversation about Thornton before she got any more customers. I asked general questions like, "What do you know about Thornton?" and "Who do you think wanted him dead?" but it didn't elicit much of a response from the woman. So, I decided to take the direct approach, blurting out, "Do you think Simon killed him?"

Ashley was so stunned that the bag of potato chips she was holding slipped out of her hands. Fortunately, potato chip bags are soft and they don't break after making contact with the ground. I must have also startled Hudson, because he dropped his cup on the counter. The lid came off and pop and ice spilled everywhere.

"I'm so sorry," he said, grabbing a stack of napkins and trying to wipe up the mess.

"I'll get that," Ashley said.

As she turned to get a rag out of the sink, Hudson turned and mouthed to me, "Really subtle."

After Ashley cleaned up the counter and got Hudson a new pop, she turned to me. "Why do you think Simon did it?"

"I heard that Simon and Thornton's business dealings had gone sour."

Ashley looked around to see if anyone was listening, then leaned across the counter. "Sour is an understatement. Simon was livid about what happened."

"What happened?" Hudson asked before taking a sip of his drink.

"You see those graphic t-shirts?" She pointed at a display of equipment and clothing at the entrance to the bowling alley.

"Simon gets them made by a place in Fargo. The designs on them are so cheesy, but I don't dare tell him that."

"Why's that?" Hudson asked.

"Simon drew them himself. Apparently, he got an 'A' in art class back in high school and ever since then he thinks he's some sort of Michelangelo." Ashley rolled her eyes. "He's been selling them for years. But now he wants to create a high-end line of bowling-themed apparel. Not just t-shirts anymore, but jackets, hats, shirts, shoes, and even belt buckles. The fool thinks his designs are going to be the next hot thing. He keeps talking about going viral. The guy's an idiot. Seriously, who's gonna want to buy the tacky stuff?"

"How did Thornton fit in with Simon's plans?" I asked.

"Thornton had connections with manufacturers overseas. He was going to help Simon with the production of the clothing line. All Simon had to do was give him a big deposit, and Thornton would do the rest. He even said that he had a big celebrity lined up to endorse Simon's clothing line."

"Let me guess," Hudson said. "The money disappeared and Simon has nothing to show for it."

"Bingo. At first, Thornton kept talking about shipping delays, then problems with sourcing the fabric and materials, that kind of thing. Eventually, Simon got some cartons of jackets, and nothing else. The jackets look awful, too. You probably saw Simon wearing one of them last night."

"Couldn't miss it," I said.

"Simon wears that jacket every time he sees Thornton," Ashley said. "As if that's going to convince Thornton to do something about the defective jackets.

Do you know what Thornton does? He puts on one of the jackets himself and parades it in front of Simon. It's kind of like he's giving him the finger, saying, 'Look at how stupid you were to give me all your money.'"

I turned to Hudson. "That explains why Thornton was wearing a yellow jacket when he was killed. There were two jackets. Simon was wearing one, and now I remember seeing another one on the coat rack last night. That must have been Thornton's. He put it on toward the end of the evening to antagonize Simon."

"I told Simon he was a fool to give his money to that creep, but he didn't listen to me," Ashley said gleefully. "His wife told him the same thing, but there was no stopping Simon."

I sighed. It wasn't the first time I had heard of people making bad business decisions and it costing them dearly. What was it they say? There were three main motives for murder—jealousy, revenge, and money. It looked like money might have been the driver in this case.

"Did you tell the police this?" I asked Ashley.

"No, why?" She gave me a puzzled look, then it dawned on her. "Oh, my gosh, you're serious. You think Simon killed Thornton."

"He's a suspect, that's all," I said evenly.

"Do you think I need police protection? Do you think I'm going to be next?" Ashley looked around her wildly. "Simon isn't here tonight. Do you think he's off killing someone else?"

"Has Simon threatened you?" Hudson asked with concern. "Do you really think he's going to come after you?"

Ashley's breathing became shallow. "What about my son? Do you think he'd go after Logan?"

"Ashley, please calm down." I walked behind the counter. Taking the woman's hands in my own, I said in a soft, even tone, "Everything is going to be okay. Tell you what, why don't I call Leif? He's the acting chief of police. He can help you."

"I feel sick," Ashley said. She tore off her apron and flung it on the counter. "I need to go home."

After Ashley rushed out the door, Hudson said to me, "Well, that went well."

"Shut up," I muttered, half-joking, and half not. I knew Hudson was only teasing, but he had a point. How had we gone from asking Ashley about Simon to her freaking out that she was going to be his next victim and her running out of the bowling alley? Why in the world had she reacted that way?

Hudson nudged me. "Maybe we should go talk with the third investigator. I have a feeling she'll know what to do next."

"You mean my grandmother?"

"Uh-huh." Hudson walked over to the bench and took off his bowling shoes, then said, "Do you think she'll have any more of those rhubarb cookies?"

I gave Hudson a sideways look. "Weren't you just

complaining about how full you are?"

He grinned. "Yeah, but when it comes to those cookies, I'll make an exception."

CHAPTER 7
KEEPING SCORE

By the time Hudson and I got to my grandparents' place, the windchill had dropped significantly. I was happy to be cuddled up in the warm and cozy kitchen rather than outside, where frostbite was a real danger.

"I might need to whip up another batch of these," my grandmother said as Hudson helped himself to another rhubarb cookie. "Or maybe I should make you some krumkaker instead."

Hudson wiped crumbs from his mouth. "What's krumkaker?"

"They're one of my favorites," I said. "It's a type of waffle cookie. You make them with a decorative iron griddle. The one my grandma uses was handed down from her great-grandmother."

"One day it will be handed down to you." My grandmother smiled at me. "That is, if you can learn how to make krumkaker without setting the smoke alarm off."

I scowled. "That only happened one time."

"She was lost in a book as usual," Grandma said to Hudson.

Hudson showed solidarity with me, and replied, "I've burned a few dishes myself, because I was caught up in something I was reading."

My grandmother got up from the table. "More coffee, anyone?"

"No, thanks." Hudson put his hand over his cup. "I'm not sure if I'll be able to sleep tonight with all the caffeine running through my system."

"It's decaf," Grandma said.

"Well, in that case, I'll take some more." As Hudson stirred cream and sugar into his cup, he added, "Of course, if I do manage to fall asleep, I'm probably going to have nightmares about finding a dead body in the library."

"It's hard to believe that only happened this morning." I looked at the kitchen clock and yawned. It was already after ten, and I was ready to hit the sheets. "Maybe we should call it a night."

"I think we need to figure out our next steps first," Grandma said.

Hudson grinned. "Do we need to formally convene a meeting of the 'Three Investigators?'"

"Motion to convene the meeting," I said, hoping the quicker we could start, the quicker I could get some sleep.

My grandmother seconded the motion, then asked us how it went with Erik.

"He loves your cookies," I said.

"I second that," Hudson joked. Then he said in a more serious tone, "Erik is pretty upset about what happened, and understandably so."

"Didn't you think he seemed nervous?" I asked. "He spilled coffee grounds all over the place when we talked about finding Thornton's body."

"I think anyone would be nervous knowing there's a killer running loose," Hudson said.

"Well, that's why we need to put our heads together," my grandmother said. "The sooner we can help Leif catch the killer, the better."

"Have you talked to him today?" I asked her. "I tried calling to tell him about what happened with Ashley at the bowling alley, but I haven't heard back from him."

"He stopped by after the two of you left. You know what he's like. He can sense my leftover roast beef from miles away."

I leaned forward. "What did he say? Any news on the investigation?"

"This is all off the record, mind you," Grandma warned. "They've pinned down the time of death. It happened sometime before midnight."

"Hmm . . . so it would have happened after nine-thirty," Hudson said. "That's when Erik left the library. He swears no one was inside when he locked up for the night."

"That means Thornton and the killer somehow got in the library after that." Grandma looked over at me. "Thea, where's your notebook? You should be writing this down."

"When did I get elected as secretary?" I grumbled.

"I can do it, if you want," Hudson offered.

"No, it's okay." I opened up my notebook, then wrote down that the time of death was sometime between nine-thirty and midnight. "What else did Leif tell you?"

"The cause of death," Grandma said. "But you already knew that. Unfortunately, the killer wiped the marble bust down. No fingerprints."

I shuddered, recalling the marble bust that was used to clobber Thornton from behind. "Where did that bust come from, anyway? I don't recall ever seeing it before."

"Thornton donated it a couple of months ago," my grandmother said. "I wasn't sure where to display it in the library, so I put it on those storage shelves by the rear entrance."

"Who is the bust of?" Hudson asked. "I didn't get a close look at it."

"The Greek playwright, Sophocles." Grandma took a sip of her coffee, and then added, "Thornton was very fond of the classics. In fact, I'm not sure he read anything else."

"I guess if you find something you like, you stick with it," I said. "Although, in Thornton's case, I bet snobbery had more to do with it than a genuine interest in ancient Greek literature."

"Come to think of it, I wonder if that bust is why Thornton was in the storage room." My grandmother toyed with the silk scarf around her neck. "He had asked me about it the previous week."

Hudson took a sip of his coffee before asking, "What did he say?"

"He was upset that I hadn't put it on display yet. I tried to explain to him that we needed to make space for it," my grandmother said to Hudson. "I also pointed out that you should be involved in deciding where it goes."

"Let me guess, he didn't like your answer," I said.

"Correct." Grandma frowned. "He told me how expensive the bust was and called me ungrateful. I tried to mollify him when he threatened to take it back, but he stormed off."

"I think that explains why Thornton was in the storage room. Somehow, he got into the library after hours to get the bust back or place it where he wanted. At least that mystery is solved." I flipped back a couple of pages until I found the spot where we had listed potential suspects—Erik, Ivy, and Simon. Or 'Friends of the Investigation,' as my grandmother preferred to think of Ivy and Erik. She still couldn't bring herself to consider them as potential murderers.

Tapping my pen on the table, I said, "Based on our conversation with Erik, I think we can rule him out. He was planning on resigning and joining the Peace Corps, so he didn't have a motive to kill Thornton."

"The Peace Corps? How wonderful." My grandmother's eyes lit up. "See, I told you, Erik couldn't have been the murderer. He's too nice of a guy."

"Don't forget, he also has an alibi," Hudson said. "That's two points in his favor."

"Oh, a scoring system. That's a fun idea," Grandma said. "I'm sure Ivy will get two points as well. You're still seeing her tomorrow after school?"

Hudson and I both nodded dutifully. After pushing the plate toward Hudson and telling him to take the last cookie, my grandmother asked us what had happened with Ashley. After recounting what Ashley had said about Simon and Thornton's joint business venture, Grandma said that she wasn't surprised.

"Simon has a reputation for get-rich-quick schemes," she said. "Remember when he was trying to hawk those god-awful Rutamentals supplements?"

Hudson started. "Are you talking about that diet based on rutabagas? That was really popular for a while in Florida, too."

"Don't forget the legwarmers everyone wore, all

because they supposedly sped up your metabolism." When my phone buzzed, I said, "Hang on a second. Leif just sent me a text. Let me call him back."

It was a quick and mostly one-sided conversation. When I ended the call, my grandmother leaned forward. "What is it? You look like you're in shock."

I chewed on my bottom lip. "You're not going to want to hear this."

"Hear what? Go on, spit it out," she said.

"Erik lied about his alibi. He wasn't at Frank's last night."

"What? No, you must have misunderstood," Grandma said adamantly.

"I'm sorry, Leif was very clear," I said. "No one at Frank's saw Erik that night. He wasn't where he claimed to be."

As my grandmother put her hands over her mouth, Hudson said quietly, "I guess that means Erik only has one point now."

* * *

Based on the dark circles under everyone's eyes at breakfast the next morning, I don't think anyone slept well the previous night. My grandmother was in shock that Erik would lie to the police about his whereabouts the night Thornton was killed. Hudson clearly was still anxious that he was going to be charged with murder. I was worried about a client meeting I had later today. And Grandpa was fretting about twine.

"What's with the twine?" Hudson whispered to me.

My grandfather had just handed Hudson a couple scraps of leftover twine from my cousin-in-law's butcher shop and told him to tie them together.

"I can hear you, son." Grandpa got up from the table and told Hudson to follow him to the barn.

When the two of them got back, Hudson was grinning ear to ear. "That was amazing. I can't believe your grandfather has a big ball of twine in the barn."

My grandfather corrected Hudson. "Giant ball."

"I bet the Guinness World Records folks would be interested in seeing it," Hudson said.

My grandmother gasped, and I made a cut throat motion at Hudson. The last thing anyone wanted was for Grandpa to start ranting about how the record for the largest ball of twine should be his, and not those imposters in Kansas.

"Enough twine talk," Grandma said to the two men. "Eat now, before it gets cold."

Everyone scarfed down their eggs and bacon, then Hudson excused himself. "I'm going to head back across the road and check on Dr. McCoy. I think he's feeling restless, because he's been cooped up in the house since yesterday morning."

After arranging to pick up Hudson later in the afternoon, I went upstairs to my room, which doubled as my home office, to prepare for my client meeting. I loved the freedom of owning my own consulting business, but that also meant there was the pressure of getting new accounts. Selling myself and my services didn't come naturally to me.

Fortunately, the meeting went well and the new client emailed back a signed contract shortly before lunch. After a quick roast beef sandwich and corn chips, I drove the short distance to the Larsens to pick up Hudson.

"Thanks for driving me around, Thea," Hudson said as he fastened his seatbelt. Since his suitcase still hadn't shown up, Hudson was wearing another borrowed outfit from Mr. Larsen—black pants, a gray turtleneck sweater, and a puffer jacket.

"That's Worthington to you," I said, affecting a terrible English accent.

Hudson took off his gloves and held his hands in front of the vent to warm up. "I swear I'll get up the courage to drive the Larsens' truck one of these days."

"Well, spring is only a few months away." I glanced at the library director. "It's a beautiful time of year. Come April, the weather seems to change overnight."

For the rest of the ride, Hudson and I chatted about the weather in Florida compared to North Dakota and whether it was better to live in a hurricane zone or deal with snow and ice. I voted for winter weather over the threat of your house being demolished by violent winds.

When we pulled into the parking lot, I felt instant

sympathy for the teachers who were trying to corral the kids into orderly lines to wait for their rides. Despite the chaos, the staff had smiles on their faces. Educators and librarians had a lot in common—they found fulfillment through serving their communities. Sure, there were days when students or patrons drove them over the edge, but helping people was one of their core motivators.

Ivy waved us over. "Sorry, we're short staffed today, so I need to help out with student pickup. Why don't the two of you wait for me in the cafeteria? I'll join you shortly."

As we scrunched down and sat at one of the child-sized tables in the cafeteria, Hudson said, "My mom always packed my lunch in elementary school. I can't tell you how many times I wished I could have bought my lunch instead. For some reason, macaroni and cheese or a sloppy joe always seemed more glamorous than a peanut butter sandwich."

"Leif and I had packed lunches too, except on Fridays," I said. "That was corn dog day."

"Did I hear someone mention corn dogs?" Ivy asked as she perched on one of the plastic chairs next to us. "My daughter loves them. I try to tell her they're an occasional treat, but it falls on deaf ears."

"How old is your daughter?" Hudson asked.

"She's seven," Ivy said.

"That's a fun age." Hudson smiled. "Does she go to school here?"

Ivy chuckled. “I don’t think she can decide if it’s cool that her mom is the principal or just embarrassing.”

“It’s been a while since I’ve seen Tiana,” I said. “Where is she? Waiting in your office?”

“No, my mom picks her up after school.” Ivy smiled. “It’s such a blessing having my mom living with us now. As a single parent, I can use all the help I can get.”

“Thornton made a dig about you being a single parent at the reception, didn’t he?” I asked.

Ivy’s smile faded. “I hate to speak ill of the dead, but Thornton could be really cruel at times. Honestly, I don’t know why he was against people who are trying to raise kids on their own. I think he saw it as some sort of failure.”

“That’s rich coming from a guy who never married or had kids,” I said.

“Yeah, I know.” Ivy took a deep breath. “It hasn’t been easy raising Tiana on my own. Lord knows I wish her daddy was still around.”

I reached over and squeezed the other woman’s hand, then turned to Hudson. “Ivy’s husband was in the Army,” I explained. “He was killed on a mission not long after Tiana was born.”

“I’m so sorry for your loss,” Hudson said, his eyes growing moist. “I know what it’s like to lose your spouse. My wife passed away a few years ago, and it’s still a struggle every day.”

"Grief is a journey, not a destination." Ivy looked off into the distance for a beat, then focused back on Hudson. "There's a local grief support group, if you're interested. I still go from time to time."

"Let me think about it," Hudson said. Then, in a more business-like tone, "Now, could you tell us about the literacy program and how the library can help?"

"Although North Dakota has a high rate of literacy compared to other states, there are still some people who struggle to read or write above a third grade level," Ivy said.

"It just amazes me in this day and age that still happens," I said.

"Unfortunately, it does. There's a number of reasons why, such as learning disabilities or a cycle of family illiteracy." Ivy lowered her voice. "And, I hate to say it, but occasionally teachers ignore the issue. It's easier to give a student a passing grade than to provide the support they need. Fortunately, those types of educators are few and far between."

"Honestly, I can see how that happens," I said. "Sadly, teachers are underpaid and overworked."

"You're preaching to the choir," Ivy said. Then she explained more about how the program operated. "You could volunteer as part of the after school enrichment program, Thea. I think you'd be a great asset."

"Maybe," I said. "But I already have my hands

pretty full with my business and volunteering at the library."

"Your commitment can be as little as an hour a week." Ivy went into full-blown salesperson mode. "Trust me, you'll get a lot out of it. The look on the kids' faces when they master a new skill is priceless."

"I'll think about it," I said.

Before Ivy could press me to sign up then and there, Hudson asked her about the support provided to adults.

"We offer classes when we have enough participants to merit it. Otherwise, we provide one-on-one tutoring. For some people that works better anyway, because they can keep their struggles with reading and writing private."

"I can see how it could be embarrassing," Hudson said.

Ivy nodded. "It shouldn't be, but it is. It takes a lot of courage to admit that you need help, so we try to meet them where they are."

The school secretary poked her head through the door to remind Ivy that she had a meeting starting in fifteen minutes.

"I'll be right there," Ivy said, then she turned to me. "Maybe you should talk to Erik about volunteering for adult classes and tutoring. You might prefer that over the school reading enrichment program. Or you could do both."

"Um, sure," I said, wondering if I could possibly

squeeze a few more volunteer hours into my week. When Ivy started to get up from her chair, I stopped her. "I know you have to get going, but do you mind if we ask you a few questions about Thornton first?"

Ivy frowned as she sat back down. "Sure. What do you want to know?"

"I'm not sure if you know this, but the police are very interested in the fact that Thornton was threatening to fire Hudson and Erik."

"Yes, they asked me about it," Ivy said slowly.

"What did you say?" I asked.

"There wasn't much to tell. It's not like the police aren't aware of how difficult Thornton could be. The whole town knew what he was like." Ivy shook her head. "But the police can't seriously think anyone would kill Thornton over a job."

Hudson smiled at the principal. "I appreciate you saying that."

Ivy nodded, then lowered her voice. "Don't worry. I pointed the police in the right direction."

"What direction is that?" Hudson asked.

"Simon."

"Oh, right, because of their business dispute," I said.

"Hmm . . . I don't know anything about that," Ivy said. "I was talking about the fact that Thornton had hit on Simon's wife. Simon flew off the handle and threatened to kill him."

"How do you know this?" Hudson asked.

"It happened during a party at Simon's house. I'm friendly with his wife. I overheard the whole thing."

Relief washed over me. Truth be told, I had been seriously worried about the fact that Erik had lied about his alibi. But now we knew Simon had two clear-cut motives for wanting Thornton dead—being angry about Thornton's pass at his wife *and* a business deal gone bad. The spotlight would be squarely on Simon, and not on Erik.

"Okay, I really got to go now," Ivy said as she gracefully got up from the child-sized chair. Based on the effort it took me to extract myself from my own chair, I wondered if yoga classes might not be a bad idea.

As Ivy walked us out of the school, Hudson casually asked, "Did the police ask you for your alibi?"

Ivy chuckled. "Yeah, you too?"

"Uh-huh. Only I didn't have one," Hudson said. "I was home all night alone."

The woman shook her head. "That's tough when you don't have anyone to vouch for you."

"Who vouched for you?" I asked.

"My mom," Ivy said. "When I got back from the reception, we had a glass of wine and streamed some shows together."

"I bet you needed a big glass of wine after what Thornton did to you at the reception," I said.

"What do you mean?" the other woman asked.

"Well, it kinda looked like he forced you to resign

as president of the library board," I said.

"Oh, that. No, that was just a misunderstanding." Ivy waved a hand in the air. "Now, I gotta run."

As we watched Ivy walk back into the building, Hudson said, "So, what does that make? One point for Ivy or two?"

"I'm not sure," I said. "She has an alibi, but I still think something is going on with her sudden resignation. The way she denied it feels fishy. What do you say we call it one and a half points until we know more?"

CHAPTER 8
GAME NIGHT

The next day I was busy with work, Grandpa was occupied with his twine, Grandma started a new needlepoint project, and Hudson huddled up with Dr. McCoy at home reading and playing with toy mice. I think we all tried to put the murder out of our minds, but I'm not sure how successful we were.

Later that night we all got into the car and headed to the Prairie Dog Lodge for game night. Well, everyone except Dr. McCoy, that is. Hudson explained to the cat that only service animals were allowed at the lodge. I'm not sure Dr. McCoy was thrilled with that explanation based on the hairball Hudson told me he'd hacked up shortly afterwards.

Game night was a huge tradition in our family. On the second Thursday of every month, all the Prairie

Dogs in Why gathered together to eat game meat—usually venison, pheasant, or duck—followed by playing a variety of board games.

Grandpa had been a Prairie Dog since he was old enough to vote. Shortly after getting married, my grandmother had become a Prairie Dog as well. My brother joined after graduating from college. Now that I had moved back to Why, my family was applying pressure on me to become part of the fold.

My brother mentioned the social events. "There are a lot of parties. You like dancing." When I'd remind him that my idea of a good evening was curling up with a book and cup of cocoa, he said sarcastically, "And that's why you don't have a love life."

"Think of the community service projects you could be involved with," my grandmother said. "Just last year, we raised thousands of dollars for the new children's playground." When I'd pointed out all the hours I already put in volunteering at the library, she tried to guilt me. "Are you saying the kids don't deserve new play equipment?"

Grandpa cut to the chase. "Drinks are cheap."

Despite their attempts at persuasion, I remained steadfastly uncommitted to becoming a burrowing rodent. So, they turned their attention to poor Hudson. Little did he know that these monthly dinners weren't just about eating game meat and playing games, they were about recruiting new members. He had thought Grandma and Grandpa invited him just to be nice.

We were seated at a table near a large woodcut prairie dog statue and had just ordered drinks when my brother rushed in, still in his uniform.

"Sorry, I'm late," he said. "Things have been crazy at the station."

"I'm actually surprised you're here," I said.

"I don't have long, but when I heard pheasant with wild mushrooms was on the menu tonight, well . . ." Leif held up his hands and shrugged.

Hudson eyed Leif warily. Dining with someone who considered you under suspicion for murder wasn't exactly a pleasant way to spend the evening. But given what we now knew about Simon's double motive for killing Thornton, Hudson could probably relax.

"How's the investigation going?" my grandmother asked, totally focusing the evening back on the murder.

"You know I can't talk about it," Leif said.

"Okay, let's play a game instead," Grandma suggested. "I'm going to say a series of statements. If what I say is true, you move the salt shaker. If it's false, you move the pepper shaker."

"Why don't we wait until they break out Monopoly and Clue after dinner," I suggested.

Grandma would not be deterred from her salt and pepper game. "Do you see how many people there are here tonight?"

"Told you everyone comes out for the pheasant," Leif said.

"It's going to be ages before we're served. This will help pass the time." She looked around the table. Her eyes landed on my grandfather. "Why don't we start with you, Thor?"

He nodded, probably thinking this game wasn't such a bad idea. He didn't have to say anything, just move salt and pepper shakers.

"Okay, let's see," my grandmother said. "The biggest ball of twine is in Kansas."

Grandpa frowned as he forcefully moved the pepper shaker forward, and everyone laughed.

"The Minnesota Twins have a chance of winning the World Series this year."

My grandfather was torn. On the one hand, he was a huge fan of the Twins and wanted to believe they could win it. On the other hand, I knew he didn't think much of the changes they were rumored to be making to their lineup before the season started. He stared at the shakers for a long time before finally pushing the pepper one forward. When in doubt, go with pessimism—that way you might be pleasantly surprised. That pretty much summed up my grandfather's philosophy of life.

"Okay, let's try Hudson," Grandma said. "*Dune* is set on a desert planet inhabited by giant sandworms."

"That was too easy," I said as Hudson pushed the

salt shaker forward. “You should try something harder like, ‘The main character in Janet Evanovich’s Stephanie Plum series is a hairdresser.’”

Hudson didn’t hesitate in selecting the pepper shaker. “Wrong, she’s a bounty hunter.”

“Hmm, you didn’t strike me as a Stephanie Plum fan,” I said.

“I have to confess that I haven’t read any of them,” Hudson said. “But my mom is a big fan of the series. She loves Grandma Mazur, the feisty grandmother character.”

Leif chuckled. “Does she bear any resemblance to our feisty grandma?”

“Okay, smarty pants, it’s your turn,” Grandma said. She looked off into the distance as if formulating the perfect statement for my brother. Then she leaned forward and abruptly said, “Simon is the prime suspect in the murder investigation.”

Leif almost choked on his cola. “Uh . . . That's not fair. I told you I can’t discuss it.”

“No one is asking you to say anything.” Grandma gave him an innocent look. “We’re just curious if you prefer sodium or a little heat sprinkled on your food.”

My brother and I exchanged glances. When our grandmother was fixated on something, there was no stopping her. Realizing he wouldn’t hear the end of it, Leif reached his hands out, letting them hover over the shakers. After a dramatic pause, he pushed both the salt and the pepper shakers forward.

"What's that supposed to mean?" I snapped. "Either Simon is your prime suspect or he's not."

"Make of it what you will," Leif said before taking a drink of his cola.

"You know, you were a lot easier to deal with when you weren't the acting chief of police," I grumbled.

"Who knows, sis," Leif gave me a cocky grin. "Maybe the mayor will appoint me as the permanent chief of police."

"Not if you botch up this investigation," I snapped.

"Children, enough," our grandmother said. "What do we Prairie Dogs always say?"

We both put our hands under our chins, mimicking a prairie dog surveying its territory, then said obediently, "We stand by our burrow mates through thick and thin. Yip, yip, yip!"

* * *

After Leif had given us his ambiguous salt and pepper answer about the prime suspect in the investigation, he ate his dinner quickly, and then excused himself. The rest of us lingered over dessert and coffee, talking about baseball. Although my grandfather still wasn't impressed that Hudson put cream and sugar in his coffee, he appeared to be warming up to him over a shared love of baseball.

We paid the bill, then my grandfather said that he would pull the car up to the entrance. Before he could go out to the parking lot, he got caught up in a debate with some fellow Prairie Dogs about the best timing for spring planting this year. While Hudson and my grandmother waited in the lobby, I made a trip to the ladies' room. On my way back, I noticed Simon sitting by himself at the bar.

Well, if Leif wasn't going to give us a straight answer about the investigation, I'd have to do my own digging. I sidled up next to Simon at the bar and ordered a ginger ale.

Simon nodded at me, then went back to sipping his drink.

"Where's your wife?" I asked him.

Simon frowned. "She left today to go visit her sister in Wisconsin."

"You didn't go with her?"

"Someone has to manage the bowling alley," he grumbled. "With Michelle away, I'm having to put in a lot of extra hours."

"It's stressful being a small business owner, right?" I asked. "I just started my own company. I know how it feels."

"Yeah, I heard about that," Simon said. "You don't have any employees, do you?"

"No, just me."

"And you don't have customers that come into your premises?" Simon drummed his fingers on the bar. "In fact, you don't have any sort of premises at all, do you?"

"Uh, no. I work from home."

"Then you have no idea what it's like to run a business," he scoffed. "All you do is sit and type on your computer. A trained monkey could do that."

"There's more to it than that," I said.

"Sure." He motioned at the bartender for another drink, then said, "Do you know what it's like to find out at the last minute that the person scheduled to work didn't show up? No, you don't."

"Are you talking about Ashley?"

"You betcha. The other night, she was supposed to be working while I was at the reception for that library fellow, but instead she was hanging out with her knitting friends."

"Ashley told me she scheduled time off."

"She told you a big fat whopper." Simon fished a piece of lime out of his drink and flung it onto the bar. "My wife tried to cover for Ashley. You gals always stick together, don't you?"

I arched an eyebrow. "Are you saying your wife lied too?"

"I don't want to talk about my wife," Simon said glumly.

After taking a sip of my ginger ale, I said cautiously, "Rumor has it that Thornton had made a play for her."

"Where did you hear that? I bet it was at Swede's, wasn't it? That Norma can't stop flapping her gums." Simon slammed his fist onto the bar. "Michelle would have never had anything to do with that jerk."

"Of course not." We sat quietly for a few moments, then I asked Simon about the night Thornton was killed. "Did you go back to the bowling alley after the reception?"

"Yeah, Tuesday nights are crazy. Even more so cause Ashley didn't show up after her stupid knitting thing." Simon downed the rest of his drink, then he leaned toward me and said, "She killed him, you know."

It took me a minute to digest this. "Ashley? Killed Thornton? But why?"

"She's a gold digger." Simon was slurring his words at this point. I think the bartender noticed as well, since he put the rum bottle back on the shelf and brought Simon a plain cola. "When Thornton dumped her, Ashley was angry."

"They were dating?"

"Well, if you want to call what they did together 'dating,'" Simon said, making air quotes. "Thornton was just using her. Then when he got tired of her, it was goodbye."

Before I could pump him for more details about Ashley and Thornton's relationship, one of Simon's buddies ambled over to the bar and interrupted us.

As I went back to the lobby to rejoin the others, I wondered what to make of this latest revelation. Being a jilted lover was a classic motive for murder. And the fact that Ashley didn't go back to the bowling alley after the knitting circle meant she might have very well had the opportunity to kill the man who'd dumped her.

* * *

The next day, Hudson got the all-clear from the police to reopen the library. Grandma offered to drop him off so that I could work. We all agreed to meet that evening over dinner and discuss the investigation.

When I came into the library later that afternoon for my volunteer shift, it felt like everything was back to normal. Erik was leading a storytime in the Imagination Room, a couple of the regulars were reading newspapers, and teenagers were giggling while they did their homework. It was hard to believe that only a few days ago someone had been murdered here.

Hudson was busy helping patrons at the front desk. So, I said a quick hello, then grabbed the cart with books to be shelved, and got to work. I started with the fiction books, chuckling when I picked up *Death by Pantyhose*. Laura Levine's mysteries always cracked me up. Unfortunately, death in real life wasn't nearly as funny as when you read about it on the pages of a cozy mystery.

After clearing the top shelf on my cart, I started on the non-fiction items. It looked like someone was considering some home renovations based on the number of books I had reshelved on the topic. It was always interesting to see what books were popular and circulated often, and what books stayed on the shelves—sad and lonely, desperate for someone to take them home.

When I picked up the next book on the cart—*The Fundamentals of Bowling*—a shiver went down my spine. My conversation with Simon the previous night came flooding back to me. Simon claimed he had been at the bowling alley after the reception, but was that the truth? The bowling alley was crowded, especially on Tuesday nights when they ran their 'two for one' special. Simon could have snuck out unnoticed and headed to the library—the two buildings were next door to each other. But that meant he would have known Thornton was there in the storage room at the time.

Just thinking about it was making my head hurt, so I pushed it out of my mind for the moment. As I started placing the bowling book on the shelf, I heard a man's voice with a thick New York City accent say gruffly, "You're on the wrong track, lady."

I looked around me, but didn't see anyone. Assuming the guy was on the other side of the bookshelf and speaking to someone other than me, I went back to putting the book in the correct place. I sighed when I realized that a book on hairstyling had been shelved in the wrong place. This section was for the 700s—arts and recreation. Thanks to my grandmother's quizzes on the Dewey Decimal system when I was a kid, I knew that books related to hairstyling should be found in the 600s. As I placed the book on my cart, I smiled at the photo on the front cover of a man sporting a mullet. Not exactly my favorite look, but it seemed to be popular with some guys.

Backtracking to the correct section, I made space to put the hairstyling book on the shelf. Then I yelped as something swatted my hand.

"What the heck?"

I pulled back and heard that same New Yorker's voice again. "Don't you get it, lady? Check out the book."

Darting around the bookshelf, I looked for where the voice was coming from, but this section of the library was quiet. Not a soul was around.

Mentally shaking myself, I went back and picked up the hairstyling book from the floor where I had dropped it, then firmly placed it on the shelf.

"Seriously, lady. You are dumber than a box of rocks."

What was going on? Had something happened to the acoustics in the library that was causing people speaking in another part of the library to sound like they were right next to me? I shook my head. No, it was more likely that I was overtired and imagining things.

I ran my finger along one of the shelves, noting

that it was dusty. Making a mental note to tell Hudson to speak with the cleaning service, I inspected the shelf below it. Not only was this one dusty, but it also looked as if someone had spilled a drink on it. It was frustrating that some patrons ignored the no food and drink rule despite several warnings.

Scanning the other shelves, I spotted other issues—more misshelved books, a Lego piece, and . . . was that a chameleon? I rubbed my eyes, then looked again at where I thought I had seen a reptile. No, it was just the book about chameleons. The same one that had fallen on my foot the day of the murder. How in the world did it end up over here?

I stuck the chameleon book on my cart, then took a deep breath. I really needed a good night's sleep. Getting back to the task at hand, I shelved a couple more books, then pushed the cart over to the next bookshelf. I blinked hard. A chameleon was sitting on the shelf staring at me with its odd eyes.

"Okay, it's real," I muttered to myself. "Some kid must have thought it would be hysterical to let his pet loose in the library."

"Who are you calling a pet, lady? Do you think I'd let some stupid human take care of me?"

I stumbled backward when I realized the chameleon was talking. In English. To me.

"Close your eyes. Deep breath, deep breath, deep breath," I said to myself.

"You're going to hyperventilate if you keep that up."

I snapped my eyes open. The chameleon hadn't disappeared and was still talking away. What baffled me was that he sounded like a chain-smoking old guy from New York. It's not like I'd ever imagined what a chameleon would sound like if it spoke, but I certainly never expected it to sound like that.

"There you are," I heard Hudson say behind me. At least I thought it was Hudson. Who knew? It could have been an elephant with a voice that sounded similar to Hudson. When I spun around to check, I was relieved to see a human looking at me with concern.

"Hey, are you okay?" Hudson asked. "You look like you might faint."

"Um . . ." I turned back around, searching for the mysterious chameleon. Part of me wanted to find him to prove to myself that I wasn't crazy. Yet the other part of me didn't, also to prove that I wasn't crazy. But all I saw were books. Not a single reptile in sight.

I looked back at Hudson and smiled brightly. "I'm fine. What's up?"

"Do you have a minute? Erik says that he needs to talk to us."

When we walked into Hudson's office, Erik was sitting in one of the chairs in front of the desk. He was digging his nails into the palm of one of his hands so hard that I thought he might draw blood. I had never seen Erik in this kind of state before, and it worried me.

I sat across from Erik and asked gently, "Hey, what's going on?"

"I don't know who to talk to," he said quietly.

I inched my chair closer. "You can talk to us."

Hudson perched on his desk. He kept just enough distance so that Erik didn't feel penned in, but close enough he could still hear the other man. "We're here for you, buddy."

Erik looked down at the ground, his eyes fixed on a worn section of carpet. "I lied to you about where I was the night Thornton was killed."

"We know," I said simply. "But you came clean, and that's the important thing."

"It was a pretty stressful situation," Hudson said. "I can see why you did it. To be honest, I might have done the same thing."

"Really?" Erik looked sharply at Hudson.

"Sure, we're both in the same boat. Neither of us has alibis for the night of the murder."

Erik appeared to relax a bit. He unclenched his fist, then slowly rubbed his palm where he had dug in his fingernails. "There's something else I need to get off my chest. Something big."

Hudson and I waited patiently until Erik summoned up the courage to continue.

"I saw Thornton lying there dead on the floor in the storage room," he confessed, so faintly that we could barely hear him.

"But you couldn't have," Hudson said. "The

murder happened after you left the library."

Erik took a deep breath, then exhaled slowly. "When I left the library that night, I was almost home when I realized I had forgotten my book on the front desk. I only had a couple more chapters left to read, so I went back to get it. I let myself in, and that's when I realized that I hadn't locked the front door."

"But it was locked when we came in the next morning," I said.

"I locked it when I left the second time." Erik looked at me. "Could I get a glass of water?"

"Sure," I said.

When I started to get up, Erik held up his hand. "Wait . . . I need to tell you what happened before I chicken out."

"Okay, take your time," Hudson said.

"I heard a noise in the back. I rushed back to see what was going on. But when I got there, the back door was blowing in the wind, banging against the file cabinets. I started to walk over to close it. That's when I saw Thornton lying on the ground. I stared at him for the longest time." Erik started digging his fingernails into his palm again. "I could tell he was dead from all the blood on the floor and the way the back of his skull had been . . ." he slumped in his chair as his voice trailed off. Then he said defensively, "And before you say it, I know I should have called nine-one-one at that time."

"Why didn't you?" I asked.

"Because . . . because I panicked when I saw what had happened to Simon."

"What do you mean? Was Simon there too? What happened to him? Where did he go?" I asked rapid fire.

Erik shook his head. "I originally thought it was Simon who had been killed, because of how he was dressed in that yellow jacket."

"Hmm . . . I made the same mistake." I rubbed the back of my neck, trying to ease the tension in my muscles, then I looked back at Erik. "The hair confused me too. It was short, like Simon's."

"Thornton got his hair cut earlier that day," Erik explained. "I heard him telling someone about it. But he was upset with how it looked. He thought the mullet had made him look younger. That's why he was wearing that scarf around his neck."

I leaned back in my chair. "Why would anyone think a mullet would make them look younger?"

"Thea, that's probably not important right now," Hudson declared. Then he looked intently at Erik and said, "What I want to know is why you didn't report what had happened? Were you protecting someone?"

"No, I told you. I panicked." Erik bolted out of his chair. "I shouldn't have said anything. Please, just forget what I said."

"I don't think we can do that," I said. "You need to go to the police and tell them everything you told us."

"No, I can't do that." Erik's breath was ragged and

his eyes darted around the room, as though trying to figure out an escape route.

"The information you have might help solve the case," I said. "You want the murderer to be caught, don't you?"

This seemed to get through to Erik since he nodded. "Okay, I'll talk to them."

"Great, let me call Leif. He'll come here and you can tell him exactly what you told us."

"Can we do it at my apartment? Please?" Erik put a hand to his chest, trying to calm down his breathing. "I need to get out of here."

We tried to persuade Erik to stay at the library, but he kept insisting that he wanted to go home. As if sensing the youth librarian's anxiety, Dr. McCoy got up from the armchair where he had been napping, padded over to Erik, and jumped on his lap.

As Erik stroked the cat, I said, "Well, you can't leave now."

"We used to have a black and white cat when I was a kid. That one wasn't this fluffy, though." A faint smile crept across Erik's face when Dr. McCoy started purring loudly. Then the youth librarian looked at me. "Okay, you can have Leif come here. But only him, okay? Not a bunch of other police officers."

It only took my brother a few minutes to get to the library. I tried to stay in the office while he spoke with Erik, but he was obstinate as usual. "Wait outside, Thea. Go read a book or something."

"As if I could read a book at a time like this—" I retorted, but Leif had already closed the door in my face.

Hudson and I sat on the stools behind the front desk in stunned silence for a while.

"Wow, just wow," I eventually said.

"Yeah, wow," Hudson echoed.

I rubbed my temples, then said, "You know what this means, don't you? This investigation has gotten way more complex."

Hudson cocked his head to one side. "How so?"

"Well, before Erik's confession, we were looking for someone who wanted Thornton dead. But now, we should look for someone who wanted Simon dead." Hudson looked confused, so I added, "Don't you see? Thornton and Simon looked similar from behind—yellow jacket, short brown hair, and a stocky build. The murderer might not have known it was Thornton he was killing. He might have thought it was Simon."

Hudson thought about this for a moment, then he said, ". . . Wow, just wow."

CHAPTER 9
TATER TOT HOTDISH

While Leif was talking with Erik, Hudson and I perched on the stools at the front desk. We sat in silence, but it wasn't a calm, peaceful silence I'd usually associate with the library. The atmosphere was tense and the quiet surrounding us was strained. Hudson stared off into space, chewing mindlessly on his fingernails, while I tried to calm my nerves by rearranging paper clips.

Feelings of doubt, mistrust, and even fear flooded my mind. I thought I had known Erik. I believed he was a good guy. But after one brief conversation, where he confessed to seeing Thornton lying dead in the storage room and not doing a single thing about it, I was shocked to my core.

The sudden noise of Carol rushing through the

door startled me and I dropped the paper clips I had been assembling into an elaborate chain on the floor.

"Sorry, I'm late," she said breathlessly. "There's a big traffic jam on Main Street. I had to take the long way around."

"What happened?" I asked.

"Seatrina turned up downtown." Carol's eyes were bright with excitement as she showed us photos on her phone. "Look, here's one of Seatrina coming out of Swede's. Isn't her coat fabulous?"

"Well, I'm not sure I would call it a coat," I said, peering at the sheer purple garment Seatrina was wearing over her hot pink jumper. "It looks more like a beach cover-up."

Looking through the seemingly hundreds of photos the library assistant had taken of the celebrity sighting distracted me momentarily from thinking about Erik. Yet again, I couldn't help but be fascinated by Seatrina's beehive hairdo and her iridescent body make-up. How long did it take her to get ready in the morning? My make-up routine was pretty simple—powder foundation, neutral eyeshadow and eyeliner, mascara, and a clear coat of lip gloss. I usually wore my long blonde hair down, but still that took me a good fifteen to twenty minutes overall. Seatrina must spend hours in the bathroom.

Carol gazed at her phone, clearly star-struck. "I wonder if Seatrina will visit the library. That would be awesome, wouldn't it?"

"Sure," Hudson said absentmindedly. "Awesome."

As Carol turned to look at her new boss, she seemed to clock that something was off. "I thought Erik was scheduled to work the front desk. Why are you here?"

"Oh, um, he's busy in my office," Hudson said. "I'm covering for him."

The woman furrowed her brow. "Busy with what?"

Realizing he should somehow explain why Erik was in his office and he was at the front desk in his place, Hudson gave a lame excuse. "The acting chief of police is giving Erik some career advice. He's thinking about becoming a cop."

At first, the library assistant was dumbstruck. "A cop? Erik?" Then she started laughing. "Oh, I get it. That was a joke."

"Why don't we get some coffee in the kitchen?" I suggested to Hudson before he dug a bigger hole for himself.

"Sure thing. More caffeine is just the ticket to calm my nerves," he muttered.

"Don't worry, we'll get you decaf," I said, motioning for him to follow me.

As we walked through the Collingsworth Wing, I looked around nervously, worried that the mysterious chameleon was going to make another appearance. That was the last thing I needed now. If you're going to imagine something, it should be a cute kitten or a fluttering butterfly, not a grumpy reptile.

When we reached the end of the hall, Hudson and I both hesitated. To our right was the kitchen—the room where we could spend a few peaceful moments enjoying some coffee. But if we turned to our left and walked a few feet, we'd find ourselves at the entrance to the storage room where Thornton's body had been found.

Coffee or the place where someone had been killed? You'd think I would have chosen the former. But even to my surprise, I pointed to the left. "What do you say? Should we check it out?"

"Okay." Hudson turned sharply to the left and briskly marched toward the storage room. Then he held open the door and motioned for me to go through. "Ladies first."

I gave him a wry smile. "Are you being polite, or are you nervous about seeing the crime scene again?"

"Maybe a bit of both."

Taking a deep breath, I turned the light on and entered the room. The place was so thoroughly cleaned by a specialist company from Bismarck that you wouldn't have known someone had been murdered here. Metal storage shelves held neatly stacked old books and magazines, cardboard boxes, spare equipment, and other odds and ends. Two file cabinets stood near the back door. A colorful poster which proclaimed, 'Read something new today!' was tacked to the wall. Everything was as it should be except . . . wait, no, it wasn't. Something was different about this place.

Squeezing my eyes shut, I tried to mentally recall how the room had looked before someone had been murdered here. After a moment, I figured it out. The carpet runner Thornton had been lying on was removed, exposing the linoleum floor underneath. But when I opened my eyes again, I realized that wasn't the answer either. Sure, the lack of a carpet was different, but it wasn't what my subconscious was trying to bring to my attention. But if it wasn't the carpet, what was it?

I startled when Hudson said gruffly, "It's right in front of your nose, dummy. Do I need to paint you a picture?"

"What?" I asked, spinning around to look at him.

Hudson was standing in the doorway, clearly reluctant to enter the room. He shook his head. "I didn't say anything."

"No, you said something," I insisted. "What was it?"

"Seriously, I didn't say a peep." He held up his hands. "Promise."

Then it dawned on me. The male voice I heard hadn't been Hudson. He wouldn't call me a 'dummy' or speak with a thick New York accent. It was that darn apparition again. My mind was playing tricks on me.

I rubbed my temples. "Sorry, I'm a bit jumpy."

"Understandable," Hudson said. "This place is kind

of creepy now. Maybe we should go get that coffee instead."

"Just a sec." I turned back around to survey the storage room. What was different about this place? I hated it when my subconscious was secretive. "If you know something, just spit it out," I mentally screamed at that part of my brain which was withholding important facts from me. Of course, it just ignored me and went back to doing whatever it was that a subconsciousness does.

Eventually, I gave up. Letting out an exasperated sigh, I followed Hudson to the kitchen. As we sat at the table with our drinks—coffee for me, herbal tea for Hudson—we talked about Erik's stunning revelation.

"I still can't get over the fact that he didn't call for help," I said. "Sure, I can see how he panicked. Who wouldn't when confronted with a dead body? But we called nine-one-one when we found Thornton. We just didn't close the door, go home, and pretend nothing happened."

"Maybe it was easier since there were two of us," Hudson suggested. "Moral support and all that."

I shrugged, remembering how I had found another body last summer. Even though I had been all alone, I still had called 911. I ran my fingers through my hair. Was I being too hard on Erik? Perhaps.

Hudson blew on his tea to cool it down, then said, "You obviously know Erik better than I do. But I was wondering if he's trying to protect someone. That might explain why he didn't tell anyone what he had seen until now."

"Protecting the murderer? Interesting theory. You could be onto something." I furrowed my brow. "Let's think this through. When Erik returned to the library, he mentioned he heard a loud noise and rushed back here to investigate."

"What do you think the noise was?" Hudson asked.

"Erik said the back door was banging against the file cabinets," I recalled. "When the killer rushed out, the door didn't latch, and the wind kept blowing it back and forth. It means that by the time Erik got to the storage room, the killer would have been long gone."

"I guess that blows my theory that Erik was protecting someone," Hudson said.

"Not necessarily," I said slowly, as my mind processed an alternative explanation. "How about this —suppose the killer came in through the rear door, surprising Thornton?"

"It might not have been a surprise. They might have arranged to meet there," Hudson pointed out.

"True. But either way, in this scenario, while the murderer and Thornton are talking, the wind is banging the rear door back and forth against the file cabinets."

"Why wouldn't one of them have shut it?" Hudson asked.

"They might have been having a heated argument and the door was the last thing they were thinking about."

"Huh. If it was an argument, I wonder what it was about," Hudson said.

I got up from the table and paced around the room, thinking about that question. Did the other person come to the library intending to kill Thornton? Or had it been an impulsive murder, one that happened in the heat of the moment after their argument escalated? I continued pacing as I pondered this. The kitchen was so small that I could walk five steps forward, reach the fridge, do a quick pivot, and take five steps backward to the sink. I was turning back and forth so quickly that I started to get dizzy.

"Uh, Thea, maybe you should sit down?" Hudson suggested.

"It's just so much to wrap my head around." As I joined Hudson at the table, I said, "Okay, let's think about the position of the body. The way Thornton was lying, someone had clearly hit him from behind. He fell forward and his head ended up near the back door with his feet pointing toward the entrance of the storage room from the library, right?"

"That means the killer probably didn't enter the library from the back door. Otherwise, when they hit Thornton on the head, he would have fallen the other way with his feet closer to the back door." Hudson paused for a beat, then said, "Meaning they probably came in through the front door of the library. Remember, Erik said that he had forgotten to lock it. Then they walked down the hall and entered the storage room through the door over there. The one next to the kitchen."

"Okay. That would mean the rear door was open, because the killer left that way." I leaned back in my chair and looked up at the ceiling. "Remember those bloody marks leading out of the rear door?"

"Wish I didn't," Hudson muttered.

"Our mystery person killed Thornton, then ran around him through the pool of blood, and out the door." Lowering my eyes to look back at Hudson, I said, "So, if Erik saw the killer—and that's still a big if—then he probably only saw their back. The killer might not have even known Erik was standing in the storage room entrance."

"In that scenario, Erik figured out who the killer was from what they looked like from behind. He could tell from their height or build or the clothing they were wearing, something like that."

"Uh-huh. And it was someone Erik wants to protect. Someone he felt sympathetic toward, someone he doesn't want to go down for murder."

Hudson contemplated his cup of tea. "Here's something else to throw in the mix. What if the killer turned around and saw Erik? What if that person isn't someone Erik wanted to protect, but someone Erik's terrified of? What if Erik didn't call nine-one-one or come forward before now, because he thought the killer would come after him next?"

I grabbed our mugs and put them in the sink.

"Hey, I was drinking that," Hudson said.

"Not anymore. I'm tired of waiting around. We need to go see Leif and tell him your theory about Erik having seen the killer. Erik's life could be in jeopardy."

I hurried through the library, not even bothering to check and see if Hudson was following me. When I reached the office where Leif and Erik were talking, I quickly knocked on the door and then pushed it open.

Leif frowned at me. "Not now, Thea."

Erik twisted in his chair to look at me. "It's okay. I don't mind if she joins us."

My brother locked eyes with me, but a stupid staring contest wasn't going to make me budge. Not with Hudson's theory front and center in my mind.

Leif sighed, then turned back to Erik. "I think we should go to the police station, so that I can take a formal statement."

I was stunned when Erik didn't protest. At first, I thought Leif must have had a calming influence on the other man, but then I realized it was all due to Dr. McCoy. The fluffy black and white cat was still sprawled on Erik's lap, kneading his paws while Erik stroked his fur. Studies had shown that the purring noises cats make could lower a human's blood pressure and stress levels. It looked like this situation proved it positive right here.

Dr. McCoy yowled when Erik lifted him off his lap and set him on the desk.

"Can he come with us?" Erik asked my brother.

"Not this time." Leif gave a wry smile before escorting Erik out of the office. Hudson nodded at the two men, then turned to help a harried mom and her two toddlers check out a stack of books.

I wasn't sure what to do next–go back to shelving books, get another cup of coffee, or call my grandmother and let her know about the latest turn of events. As I was pondering this, I overheard a group of people standing near the entrance to the library talk about what had just happened.

"Did you see that police officer hauling Erik away? Do you think he's the killer?" an older gentleman asked.

A woman wearing a sweatshirt with Seatrina's face emblazoned in sequins on it said, "I can't believe the library employs a murderer. What has this town come to? Next thing you know, we're going to have serial killers working at the dry cleaners and grocery store."

"Someone should call the mayor," another person said. "The police chief should be fired for allowing this to happen."

"His head is already on the chopping block," the older gentleman pointed out.

"Good riddance." The Seatrina fan pressed her lips together as she stared in the direction of the front counter. "And they should fire the new library director, too. This happened on his watch."

The others turned to follow the woman's gaze. Hudson finished checking the stack of books out, then gave the group a quizzical look.

When the crowd started booing, I lashed out. "How dare you blame Hudson. He didn't have anything to do with the murder. Don't you have anything better to do with your time, like maybe read a book?"

After my outburst, Hudson ushered me into his office. At first, I thought he was going to call me out for creating a scene. Instead, he walked over to his desk, opened the top drawer, and pulled a die-cut sticker out. "My luggage finally came. I don't know what I'm more excited about. Being able to wear my own clothes or getting my stickers back. Anyway, I know it's silly. But I thought maybe you could put this on your notebook as a reminder."

I smiled when I read the saying on the colorful sticker, 'It's okay to not be okay.'

"None of us are okay right now, Thea," he said gently. "We're all on edge and I don't think it's going to get easier anytime soon."

"Why do you say that?"

"Because I think there's another potential explanation for why Erik lied about everything."

"What's that?" I asked. But as the words slipped out, my stomach twisted in knots. I knew what Hudson was about to say, so I said it first. "The only other person in the storage room with Thornton was Erik."

Hudson nodded. "That's right. Erik might be the killer. We should consider the possibility that Erik's story about finding Thornton dead is just that—a story designed to distract us from the truth."

* * *

"Uff da. No, I don't believe it." My grandmother refused to accept the new theory later that evening after I had returned to the farmhouse. She turned the coffeemaker on, then sat at the kitchen table while the coffee brewed. "There's no way Erik could have killed Thornton."

"Grandma, I know you don't want to believe it, but the fact of the matter is that Erik isn't who you thought he was. Don't forget he didn't tell the truth about where he was the night of the murder. Then when he realized his fake alibi wasn't going to hold water, he came up with a new plan—tell us that he came back to the library, heard a noise, went to the back, and found Thornton's dead body. We'd be so distracted by his supposed 'confession' that we'd overlook the fact that he was the person who killed Thornton."

"But there's no logical reason why Erik would do that," my grandmother said adamantly. "He was planning on joining the Peace Corps. He didn't have a motive."

"He might have lied about the Peace Corps," I said. "You always look for the best in people, especially library people. It's a great trait, but maybe this time you're wrong about Erik."

Grandma smoothed imaginary wrinkles from the tablecloth while she pondered this. "I hope you're wrong."

"For your sake, I hope so too." I patted my grandmother's hand, then got up to pour the coffee and grab the last of the rhubarb linzer cookies.

"Can you get the half-and-half out of the fridge?" my grandmother asked. When I gave her a questioning look, she smiled. "I think we could all do with a little cream in our coffee tonight. If we had some Bailey's, I might even have suggested that."

"Good thing Grandpa is out in the barn with Hudson," I said. "He'd give us a hard time about ruining perfectly good coffee."

After I sat back down at the table, I chewed on a cookie and mulled over the state of the investigation. "I'm not ruling Erik out, okay? But I do agree that we need to consider other suspects. The tricky thing is that we have to look at this from two angles—who would have wanted to kill Simon and also who would have wanted to kill Thornton."

"This could get confusing," Grandma said. "I think you're going to need your notebook."

"Already on it." I flipped it open, then drew a line down the center of a blank page. "Okay, in the Thornton column, we have Simon, Erik, Ivy, and Ashley."

"I still can't believe Ashley had an affair with Thornton," my grandmother said.

"Remember, that was according to Simon. We don't have any proof it's true." I looked back down at my notebook. "In the 'Who Wanted to Kill Simon' column, the only person I can think of is Ashley. Simon laid into her that night at the library. He's not exactly 'boss of the year' material. Maybe that was enough to push her over the edge."

"It's interesting that Ashley is on both lists," my grandmother pointed out.

I doodled on the bottom of the page while I considered this. "We don't really have any other suspects for who wanted Simon dead."

"No, we don't." Grandma walked over to grab the sugar container. After she stirred a generous spoonful into her coffee, she glanced over at my doodle. "What is that? A lizard?"

"It's nothing." I felt my face grow warm as I pulled the notebook away from her.

"Don't be embarrassed," Grandma said. "It's a perfectly fine drawing. I'm just surprised. You've never been that interested in art."

"I'm not. It's just this . . ." My voice drifted off as I realized what I was about to say. If I told my grandmother that I had seen a talking chameleon in the library, she'd think I was nuts. Heck, even I thought I was nuts.

Grandma's a patient woman. I'd give her that. She sat there quietly for a good fifteen minutes, sipping her coffee, waiting until I was ready to spill my guts. She had used the same approach successfully when I was growing up. We'd sit at this same kitchen table, and Grandma would do needlepoint or work on a crossword puzzle. She'd wait while I got up the courage to tell her what was bothering me.

When I was a young kid, it was things like Bobby Jorgenson teasing me in school or that I had accidentally broken one of the china plates. In my teenage years, being rejected by a boy I liked or getting a 'C' on my algebra exam were the types of things that tormented me. Now that I was an adult, my worries were usually career or finance related. Never in a million years would I have thought that I'd be concerned over the possibility I was seeing things.

Knowing that I'd feel better once I confided in my grandmother, I finally told her what had happened to me in the library from the initial appearance of the rude chameleon to his unhelpful commentary.

"Hmm . . . that's interesting," she said. "I didn't think you'd get a guide."

"A what now?" I spluttered.

Grandma smiled at me. "We call them guides."

I rubbed my temples. Why was my grandmother so

calm about my mental delusions? "Want to tell me who 'we' is?"

"Me, your mother, your great-grandmother, and your great-great-grandmother . . . all the women in the family since we settled in North Dakota."

"So, you're saying that everyone in the female line in our family has all had these delusions?" I shook my head. "Why didn't anyone warn me this was going to happen?"

My grandmother took my hand in hers and squeezed it gently. "It's not your imagination, it's real."

"No way." I pulled my hand away. "This has got to be some elaborate joke."

"I pretty much had the same reaction when it happened to me. Oh, and so did your mother." Grandma chuckled while shaking her head from side to side. "I can't believe your guide is a chameleon."

"You mean you see something different?" I held up my hand. "Not that I still don't believe this is some elaborate practical joke."

"Fair enough. It'll take time for you to process this. But as you do, keep in mind that each guide is specific to each individual." My grandmother took a sip of coffee. "Mine is an angora bunny rabbit with a southern drawl."

"That's a lot cuter than what I'm stuck with," I grumbled, still unsure it was real. "What exactly do these so-called guides do?"

My grandmother got up to check the oven. “They help you. Sometimes with small stuff, sometimes with big stuff.”

“He called me a dummy,” I said. “Super helpful.”

“I think these tater tots need to brown a bit more,” Grandma said. After putting the casserole back in the oven, she continued, “Are you sure he didn’t help you with anything? Maybe you weren’t in a receptive state of mind. What were you doing at the time?”

“I was shelving a book about bowling when he said, ‘You’re on the wrong track, lady.’”

“Maybe he was trying to give you a message about Simon.” My grandmother stirred even more sugar in her coffee, then asked, “Is that all that happened?”

I shook my head. “No, the little monster smacked my hand when I was holding a book about hairstyling.”

My grandmother made a tsking sound. “It’s not nice to call your guide a monster.”

“But he struck me,” I said petulantly.

“Maybe he was just trying to get your attention?”

“Whose side are you on?”

“I’m not on anybody’s side.” My grandmother laughed. “Listen to yourself. This sounds exactly like when you and Leif start squabbling.”

After telling me to get the salad dressing out of the fridge and set the table, my grandmother asked me to describe the hairstyling book. I nearly dropped the placemats when it dawned on me. “The picture on the cover of the book–it was a man with a mullet. It happened right before Erik told us about finding the dead body and thinking it was Simon."

"That's because Thornton was wearing a yellow jacket like Simon had been earlier, right?" Grandma asked.

"Uh-huh, but also because the two men had similar builds and hair color. Thornton had his mullet chopped off earlier that day, so his hair kind of looked like Simon's from the back." I smiled. "Maybe that infuriating chameleon was predicting what Erik was going to say."

"Could be."

"That's not the only thing," I said. "When Hudson and I were in the storage room earlier today, I had this sense that something was different about the place, but I couldn't figure out what it was. Then I heard the chameleon say that it was staring me right in the face."

"That's odd. Why don't we check it out tomorrow? Maybe I'll be able to figure out what's different. Something could have been moved. It could be as simple as that." Then my grandmother pointed at the table. "We need more placemats than that. Hudson is coming to dinner. I'm making hotdish."

"Does Hudson even know what hotdish is?" I asked.

Grandma chuckled. "No, I had to explain that it's the quintessential type of casserole up in these parts."

"They sure don't know what they're missing in

Florida," I said. "I hope you're making the one with sloppy joe meat and tater tots on top. That's my favorite kind."

"Don't worry. I am." My grandmother smiled. "Actually, better set one more place. Your brother always senses when I'm making sloppy joe hotdish."

"I know why. It's delicious." When I finished setting the table, I turned to my grandmother. "Do you remember when Freya was accused of murder back in July? Well, I was in the library and there was this book that kept falling off the shelf. When I think back on it, it was a clue to who the killer really was."

"I think that could have been your guide at work," Grandma said. "He just wasn't ready to reveal himself to you yet."

"Earlier you said that you didn't think I'd get a guide. Why's that?" I asked.

"Because you're not a librarian," she said simply.

Before I could ask her to explain, my grandfather and Hudson walked in the door.

Hudson had a huge grin on his face. "Thor let me tie some twine on."

"Need to work on your knots, son," Grandpa said before going to the sink to wash his hands.

As my grandmother set the salad bowl on the table, Leif burst in the door. He sniffed the air, then asked hopefully, "Hotdish? With sloppy joe meat?"

Grandma smiled and motioned for everyone to sit down. Then she turned to Leif. "How's the investigation going?"

My brother gave me a sideways glance. "Well, I was hoping Thea could help me out."

I arched an eyebrow. "Me? You want my help? Is that your way of saying you're in over your head?"

Before Leif could retort, my grandmother intervened. "Tell your sister what you need."

Leif poured an unhealthy amount of ranch dressing over his salad before saying, "I need Thea to ask Ashley who Logan's father is. Unofficially, of course."

"That's a strange request." I tried squeezing some dressing out of the bottle, but Leif had drained it. "Why me?"

"You're a woman."

"Uh, duh."

Leif speared a tomato, and then admitted, "Well, it makes you qualified to do that girl-talk thing with her."

"It's not girl-talk, it's nosey talk," I said. "I don't know Ashley that well. You just don't go up to someone and casually ask them who the father of their child is."

Hudson scooped some of the hotdish onto his plate. "Is it a secret who Logan's father is?"

"Ashley got pregnant a couple of years after she graduated high school," my grandmother explained. "She never said who the father was, and then she moved out of state to be with her parents. When Logan got older, Ashley and he moved back to the area. By that time, no one cared that much anymore who Logan's dad was. Too much time had passed."

Hudson nodded, and said, "By the way, tater tots on top of sloppy joe meat, genius."

"If you think that's good, you should try my grandma's chicken and wild rice hotdish," Leif said. "She puts sour cream and cream of mushroom soup in it."

"Can we swap recipes some other time, guys?" I asked. "Now Leif, why is it so important that we find out who Logan's dad is?"

"We got an anonymous tip," Leif explained. "Apparently, if we figure out who the dad is, we'll figure out who killed Thornton."

CHAPTER 10
PLASTIC WRAP

The next day, I dropped Hudson off at the library in the morning, did a bunch of errands in town, met a friend for lunch, and then headed back home to pick up my grandmother.

When Grandma got into the car, she was holding two travel mugs. “You’ve been running around all day, so I thought you could use some coffee.”

“Thanks, that was sweet of you.” I took a sip, then scrunched up my face. “Whoa, this is sweet, too.”

“Oops, that one must be mine,” Grandma said as she exchanged our mugs.

“What’s with all the sugar?” I asked as I pulled out of the driveway. “You put a ton of it in your coffee last night, too.”

“I guess it’s just my way of coping, I suppose.” She

took a sip of her coffee and sighed. "A little extra sugar helps soothe the nerves."

"Are you worried about checking out the storage room?" I asked. "You don't have to go with me if you don't want to."

"No, that's fine. It's not like I can avoid going in there for the rest of my life." My grandmother sighed. "Actually, that's not true. Since I'm not the library director anymore, I don't have a reason to go to the storage room or any other place that's restricted to staff. The only reason I need to go to the library now is to check out books. I'm just an ordinary patron now."

"Hardly," I said. "You're far from ordinary."

For the rest of the ride, we were both lost in our thoughts. After we pulled into the parking lot, my grandmother said, "Do you mind if we pop into the Imagination Room first? I want to see what they're doing at the Saturday Crafternoon session today."

"The kids love those," I said.

"Why wouldn't they?" Grandma said. "What could be better than spending the afternoon reading books and doing crafts?"

When we walked into the library, Carol handed us eyepatches and hats adorned with skulls and crossbones. "Ahoy, there. Want to join in? The kids are making pirate-themed Valentine's Day cards."

"Pirates and Valentine's Day—that's a great combination," I said.

Carol smiled. "Arrr, matey."

My grandmother put the eyepatch and hat on, then motioned for me to do the same. Once we were suitably disguised as pirates, we poked our heads inside the Imagination Room.

Children of all ages were sprawled on the floor listening to Hudson read *Magic Marks the Spot* by Caroline Carlson. Laughter broke out when Hudson reached the section with the talking gargoyle. A few days ago, I would have told you that gargoyles or chameleons only talked in books. Now, I knew better. I wish I didn't. But I did.

"Why is Hudson leading the session?" I whispered to the library assistant.

"Erik is on medical leave," she said. "It's stress-related, you know. Of course, I can't blame him. I'd be a nervous wreck if the police were going to charge me with obstruction of justice."

"Where did you hear that?" I asked.

"When I was picking up coffee at Swede's this morning. Norma told me all about it."

Carol excused herself to hand out construction paper and other card making supplies. I caught my grandmother's attention and pulled her aside. "Did Leif tell you Erik is facing charges?"

She frowned. "No. I'm going to have to have a talk with that boy. He shouldn't be keeping secrets from his grandmother."

"Maybe it's just one of the usual rumors at

Swede's," I mused. "You know what Norma is like."

"I think we should stop by there when we're done here," Grandma said.

I smiled. "Fine by me. They serve knoephla soup on Saturdays."

"Perfect. You and I can have a girls' night out while your grandfather eats leftovers."

"There's leftover hotdish? I thought the guys polished that off last night."

"Hmm . . . that's true. Thor can have a sandwich then. He likes sandwiches."

"He likes it when *you* make him sandwiches," I pointed out. "When he has to make his own, he grumbles and ends up having toast and peanut butter."

"He'll be happy with peanut butter on toast. I got peanut butter on special the other day. Two for one."

"Grandpa does like a bargain," I admitted.

We watched the kids make cards for a while, and then waved goodbye. As we walked out of the Imagination Room, I said, "I feel bad for the cleaners. All that glitter and paper scraps everywhere."

"Crafting can be messy, especially glitter," Grandma agreed. "But they're having such a good time."

"Wait a minute." I stopped in my tracks. "The cleaning company has a key to the library. Do we know if Leif ever checked to see if someone used that key to get in through the back entrance?"

"But Erik said that he forgot to lock the front door that night," my grandmother remembered. "Didn't the killer come in that way?"

"Maybe, maybe not," I said. "Erik locked the front door after he came back that night to pick up his book, so it wouldn't have been unlocked for that long."

"Hang on a minute. I'm going to call your brother." When Leif didn't answer, Grandma left a message telling him to call her back as soon as possible. As she tucked her phone back into her purse, she said, "You know who works for the cleaning company, don't you?"

"Ashley," I said. "Sounds like I have two things to talk with her about. Logan's dad and her cleaning gig."

My grandmother pursed her lips. "Leif shouldn't be asking you to get information out of Ashley. It could be dangerous."

"It'll be fine. I just need to make sure she thinks I suspect Simon, and not her. Which is kind of the truth, anyway. Simon is still a suspect." I nodded at a woman sitting on one of the couches. "Speaking of suspects, isn't that Ivy's mom?"

Like her daughter, Janelle Simpson was a regal-looking woman with an impeccable fashion sense. The outfit she was wearing would be considered casual wear on any other woman—dark jeans, a plum-colored merino sweater, and suede boots—but on

Janelle, it looked like she had stepped straight off the fashion runway and into the library. Her cropped curls accentuated her high cheekbones and slender neck, while her jewelry was tasteful and elegant.

Some women use their beauty as a weapon against other women, but not Janelle and her daughter, Ivy. They were down-to-earth ladies who believed in supporting and lifting up other women, not stepping over them or pushing them down to get ahead. So, when I saw the way Janelle gave us a warm smile and beckoned us over, my stomach lurched. It would be awful to find out her daughter was the murderer. I shook my head, aware that I was struggling to remain objective. I was falling into the same trap as my grandmother, not being able to believe that people I like could do horrible things.

"Are the two of you setting off to sail the high seas?" Janelle asked as we walked over to join her.

Realizing that we were still wearing our eyepatches and hats, Grandma and I both laughed. After removing my pirate gear, I smoothed down my hair, and then grinned when I saw that my grandmother was still sporting her eyepatch and hat. The woman did love a costume. I think if she had to pick only one holiday to celebrate, it would be a tie between Halloween and Christmas.

As we sat down across from Janelle, I said, "I saw your granddaughter in the Imagination Room."

"Tiana loves coming to the Crafternoon sessions," Janelle said.

"Is Ivy here too?" my grandmother asked.

"No, she's at home lying down."

"Everything okay?" Grandma asked.

"She's got one of her migraines," the other woman said. "They run in the family. I hope Tiana doesn't get them."

"My cousin Freya gets migraines occasionally," I said. "They wipe her out."

"Isn't that the truth." Janelle gave a sympathetic look as she sat the cookbook she had been looking at down on the coffee table. "Does your cousin take anything for them?"

"Uh-huh. But she doesn't like taking it," I said.

"I don't know why she's so stubborn about it," my grandmother said. "It takes the pain away."

"Yes, but then it makes her sleepy," I explained. "She crashes and doesn't wake up for hours."

"Sounds like the one I take. It knocks me out. Thankfully, I only get a migraine once a month or so. I had one earlier this week . . ." Janelle tapped her lips with her finger. "Let's see, when was that? Oh, of course, it was on Tuesday. How could I forget? It was the day Thornton was killed. That's a day I don't think any of us will forget anytime soon."

We chatted for a few more minutes, mostly about some new recipes that Janelle wanted to try. Then Tiana rushed up to us, waving a card in her hand.

"Grammy, I made this for you."

After admiring the young girl's artistry—pirates wearing t-shirts with purple hearts on them was pretty creative—my grandmother and I took our leave.

"Okay, let's go check out the storage room," Grandma said to me. "Then we can get you a bowl of knoephla soup."

I tensed as we walked past the bookshelf where the mysterious chameleon had first made his appearance. Although I had felt oddly relieved when my grandmother told me that seeing a personal 'guide' in the library was normal for the women in our family, I wasn't in the mood to deal with the rude reptile again anytime soon.

"Get the light, will you, Thea?" Grandma asked me as she opened the door to the storage room.

A shiver ran down my spine as I flipped the switch. "Please don't let me find another dead body," I whispered to myself. When I opened my eyes, I breathed a sigh of relief. No dead bodies, only my grandmother inspecting the room.

"I'm not sure what's missing. It would have to be something in plain sight." Grandma examined the shelving units. "Not something in the boxes or in the file cabinets."

"Correct." I surveyed the area, turning to check each part of the room. "I don't know. I was pretty unnerved after what happened with my so-called guide. In fact, I'm not sure I knew what was real and what was my imagination."

"Well, I don't see anything different other than the rug being missing," my grandmother said. "What do you say? Should we head to Swede's? Maybe your subconscious needs more time to process everything."

As I followed Grandma out of the storage room, I whispered a warning message to my subconscious, "Hurry up and figure things out. I have a feeling it's important." As usual, my subconscious ignored me. It was starting to remind me of some cats I've known—always wanting attention when it wasn't convenient and then completely ignoring you the rest of the time.

"What was that, dear?" my grandmother asked over her shoulder.

"Nothing."

She turned and looked at me. "I thought I heard you say something. Were you talking to your guide?"

"Thankfully, no." I smiled. "Though maybe this is worse. I was talking to my subconscious. It's starting to give me a headache."

"I have some ibuprofen in my purse," Grandma offered. "Hmm . . . a headache."

Then we both said at the same time, "Janelle's migraine."

"If she took a migraine pill the night of the murder and it knocked her out, then—"

My grandmother finished the sentence. "Then Ivy could have left the house without her knowing. That means she doesn't have an alibi."

"Time to update the scoreboard," I said. "Ivy just lost a point."

* * *

When we got to Swede's, the place was jam-packed with the senior set, which was not really a surprise. If your hair was graying, the diner was the place to be on a Saturday night. Everyone loved the early bird special—knoephla soup and dinner rolls, followed by rice pudding. I made a mental note to bring Hudson to Swede's some Saturday night to try the special. Odds were that he hadn't sampled the traditional German dumpling soup before. It was popular in the Dakotas and Minnesota, but not widely known elsewhere in the States.

"I think we'll have to wait for a table," my grandmother said to me.

My stomach rumbled, making me all too aware that the salad I ate for lunch hadn't satisfied it. "Look, Ashley and Logan are sitting at a table by themselves. Maybe they'll let us join them."

Grandma frowned. "I don't think asking questions about the murder during dinner is a good idea."

"Don't worry. I'm not going to interrogate the woman right now, especially not with Logan sitting next to her. I'm hungry, that's all."

Ashley appeared surprised when we walked up to

her table and asked if we could sit with them. "Um, sure."

Logan looked uncomfortable when I slid into the booth next to him, no doubt remembering the knife incident from the other day. Imagine if he knew that I had overheard part of his conversation with Erik later that same night. I still wondered what secret the two of them were keeping, but in comparison to solving a murder, it wasn't that important. I'd leave the 'Case of the Mysterious Knife' to my subconscious to chew on.

My grandmother sat next to Ashley. After setting her purse on the floor, Grandma turned to the other woman and asked, "Are you still working for Clean Me Up?"

Ashley nodded as she tore off a piece of her dinner roll.

I shot Grandma a look which clearly said, 'Are you kidding me? We weren't going to ask murder-related questions, remember?'

My grandmother gave me her best 'innocent as a lamb' expression before waving Norma down. "Can we get two of the specials, please?"

"Sure, hon," the waitress said. "Whaddya have to drink with that?"

My grandmother arched an eyebrow. "Do you even need to ask?"

Norma chuckled. "Couple of cups of coffee coming up."

"So, remind me," my grandmother said to Ashley.

"Is the library one of the buildings you clean?"

"It depends," she said. "Sometimes it's me, sometimes it's one of the other girls."

"Pass me the sugar, will you, dear?" Grandma asked Logan before turning back to Ashley. "How do you get the key?"

For some reason, Ashley didn't find this to be an odd question. In fact, she appeared eager to discuss the subject, especially how disorganized the supervisor at Clean Me Up was.

"She constantly changes the schedule on us," Ashley said. "One week, I get one of the office buildings in town, and the next week it's the dentist or an apartment building. You never know where you're going to be working until that day. I've told her that it would be more efficient if we worked at the same place each time. That way, we wouldn't have to go into the Clean Me Up office first to get our assignments and pick up the keys."

Grandma stirred sugar into her coffee. "Oh, so you don't keep the keys on you?"

"Nope. We pick them up, do our shift, and then drop them back off," Ashley grumbled. "I spend half the night driving back and forth."

Well, that answered that. Ashley didn't use her key to gain access to the library via the rear door that night, because she didn't have one. If she did enter the library, it would have been through the unlocked front door.

I smiled at Logan. "How's the soup tonight?"

"Fine," he mumbled as he swirled his spoon in the creamy broth.

"I don't know what I love more about knoephla soup—the potatoes or the dumplings. What about you?"

Logan shrugged. "Don't know."

I turned to Ashley. "Your family is German, isn't it? Did you eat knoephla soup growing up?"

"I'm only German on my dad's side," she said. "My mom was of Norwegian descent. She did the cooking, so knoephla soup wasn't on the menu."

"Same here," I said. "I tried making it once, but I couldn't get the hang of the dumplings."

"Oh, there's a trick to it," Ashley said. "My grandmother taught me how to make them before she passed."

"Really?" I leaned forward. "Would you mind teaching me?"

Ashley looked pleased by my request. "Sure. I've got some time tomorrow after my shift at the bowling alley."

I cocked my head to one side. Just a few days ago, Ashley had run out of the bowling alley, terrified Simon was the killer and that he might come after her and Logan. Had something changed and she no longer suspected Simon? Or did she need the money so badly that she was still working for the man despite her fears? Those weren't exactly the types of questions I could ask her now, especially not with her son sitting here. Instead, I said, "Great, I can buy the ingredients and bring them over to your place."

After making arrangements to meet the next day, the conversation ceased while everyone concentrated on their soup. Once our bowls were scraped clean, Norma was over in a flash to clear the dishes and set rice pudding down in front of us.

Norma was writing up our bill when Bobby Jorgenson pushed through the crowd of people waiting for a table. "Hey, wait your turn," Norma barked at him.

"Don't worry, babe. I'm not here for dinner," Bobby said, waving a stack of papers in Norma's direction.

"I'm not your babe. Never will be." Norma put her hands on her hips. "In fact, the odds of you getting anyone in town to be your 'babe' are less than zero."

Bobby sauntered over to our table. He grinned at Norma, then pointed at his cheek. "See this here? This is where Seatrina kissed me. You know what that means, don't you? She wants to be my babe."

Someone at a neighboring table called out, "It was a pity kiss."

When Bobby spun around to see who had heckled him, I was able to see the side of his face that he had shown Norma. My eyes widened. "Is that plastic wrap?"

"Yep. I'm persevering Seatrina's kiss," Bobby said gleefully.

"I think you mean 'preserving,' you moron," Norma said.

"Let me see that," my grandmother said. Then she made a tsking sound when Bobby bent down to give her a closer view of his plastic wrapped face. "I think your cheek is infected."

Bobby touched his cheek and winced. "Is not."

"Your cheek is red," Grandma said.

"That's Seatrina's lipstick," Bobby said.

"That's not lipstick. You need to see a doctor," my grandmother insisted. "Your cheek is red and inflamed. How long have you had that plastic wrap on there?"

"Since Tuesday."

"Uff da." Grandma shook her head. "I don't know what's worse—the plastic wrap or the duct tape you have holding it down."

"How long are you planning on keeping your cheek wrapped up?" I asked Bobby.

"Until I see Seatrina again and she can give me another kiss." Bobby slapped his stack of papers down on the table. "And that's where you all come in. I was thinking we could organize a party for her, you know, to make her feel welcome here in Why. We can do a potluck kind of thing. All you have to do is mark down what you're going to bring and I'll sort out the rest."

"Seatrina is a celebrity," Norma snapped. "She's

not going to come to some silly potluck."

"You're just jealous that she's stolen my heart." Bobby gave Norma a cocky grin, and pushed the papers in front of Logan. "Why don't you start? I've got a page for each type of food—drinks, appetizers, main dishes, and desserts. Pick one and write your name down."

Logan looked bewildered as he shuffled the pages. "I don't really cook."

"Then write your name on the drinks page." Bobby handed Logan a pen, then turned back to Norma. "What are you going to bring?"

"How about a slap to the back of your head?" Norma sneered, then she snatched the papers out of Logan's hands. "Take these and get out of here."

"Consider yourself uninvited." Bobby sorted through the papers, then turned to Logan and grinned. "Nice one, man."

"Did you really sign up to bring drinks?" Ashley said to her son.

"Guess so," Logan muttered.

"No, he did way better than that," Bobby said. "He signed up to donate the grand door prize."

Logan's eyebrows shot up. "I did?"

"Yep. A thousand smackeroos." Bobby gave Norma a triumphant grin. "See what you'll be missing out on? A chance to win some big bucks."

After Norma yanked Bobby away and steered him toward the exit, Ashley whispered to Logan, "We don't have that kind of money."

"I know, mom," Logan said peevishly. Then he slumped down in his seat, pulling his hood over his head as though he could hide under it.

Grandma and I exchanged glances. "We should get going, Thea. The library will be closing soon. We told Hudson we'd pick him up."

"You sure are spending a lot of time with that guy." Ashley gave me a knowing wink. "You'll have to give me the scoop when we get together tomorrow. He's a hottie, don't you think?"

I smiled at the other woman, but it was one of those smiles that didn't quite reach my eyes. Leif would be happy—Ashley and I were going to have girl-talk tomorrow—but I certainly wasn't. The last thing I wanted to discuss with her, or with anyone actually, was whether or not Hudson was a 'hottie.'

CHAPTER 11
DID SHE OR DIDN'T SHE?

The next day was hard for me. The anniversary of my parents' death had always been tough, but this year it was more brutal than it was in a long, long time.

Emotional trauma has a way of toying with you. Rough, raw emotions course through your body and soul like a raging river threatening to flood over the banks. Sadness, anger, denial, self-loathing . . . all the dark feelings you have names for, as well as the ones you don't. They haunt you, twisting you into sharp, agonizing knots that feel like they're made of barbed wire.

Then suddenly, without warning, the pain ebbs. You're lulled into a false sense of security. *At last, I'm moving on from my grief*. You tell yourself, *I'm letting go. I'm not broken with a million shards of glass slicing me from the inside out. I'm finally whole.*

Wrong. The peacefulness that had surrounded you, the lightness you felt, the joy that filled your soul . . . it was only temporary. The pain's back, surging through you with a vengeance, striking deep into your heart, and worming its way into all those places where you'd locked up the painful memories. Then it would shake them loose, so that they could haunt you once again.

At least, that's how it was for me on this particular Sunday morning as I lay huddled under my floral duvet, curled up in a tight ball. I wondered if emotional trauma affects other people the same way. My family didn't talk about how the loss of my parents had affected us, not the deep stuff anyway. That was the Olson way, I guess. Keep difficult, hard to process emotions bottled up inside. If you didn't talk about them, then they didn't exist, right?

As I sniffled into my pillow, thoughts of Hudson filled my mind. How did he cope with the pain of losing his wife and child? Did he struggle to get out of bed on the anniversary of their death too?

Then my mind turned to Thornton. Unmarried, childless, and friendless—there was no one to mourn him. The only person who would have felt the loss of Thornton would have been his brother. But Reginald had preceded him in death, and left Thornton all alone.

Enough of this, I finally told myself, poking my head

above the covers. The bright winter sun streamed through the windows, trying to convince me that I should get out of bed and join the living.

I shoved the covers aside and got to my feet. Not because I had any desire to face the world. The fact of the matter was that I had run out of tissues on my nightstand. Apparently, I hadn't yet sunk to the depths of despair that would lead me to wiping my nose on the duvet cover.

As I was rummaging through the linen closet in the hallway for another box of tissues, I heard my phone beep. When I read the text Leif had sent me, my eyes welled up.

Sorry I can't come to the cemetery with you today. The investigation is at a critical point. Promise I'll come by the house after dinner. Love you, sis.

I was about to reply, when another text came through from Leif that left me utterly perplexed.

Pretty sure A didn't do it. More later.

Did the 'A' stand for Ashley? Did that mean I didn't need to go to her house later this afternoon for the knoephla soup making session? I texted my brother back to clarify. But he never responded, obviously caught up in the investigation.

A few minutes later, Ashley sent me a text with her address and a list of ingredients I needed to bring. I hesitated before replying. Should I cancel? No, that would be rude. Besides, learning how to make knoephla soup would be a good distraction. And goodness knows, I needed all the diversions I could get on this particular day.

After I texted Ashley a thumbs up emoji, my stomach grumbled, reminding me that I hadn't had breakfast yet. When I went downstairs, I found a note on the kitchen table from my grandmother.

You were sleeping so soundly; I didn't want to wake you. I figured you could use the rest. Grandpa and I have gone to church, then we're heading into Williston. There's a grand opening for a new outlet store today. Grandpa wants to see what kind of deals they have. We'll see you later tonight.

Hugs and kisses - Grandma

PS. The more I think about it, the more I'm convinced Ashley is guilty. When you see her today, ask her about the money she was flashing around town a couple of months ago.

PPS. Can you pick up some tater tots when you're at the store?

Great. Two contradictory messages about Ashley. Leif thought she didn't kill Thornton, but my grandmother was convinced that she had.

Shaking my head, I scrounged in the fridge for something to eat, finally settling on a strawberry yogurt and a glass of orange juice. Somehow, I mustered up the energy to get showered and dressed.

After a quick stop at the florist for a bouquet of my mother's favorite flowers—pink carnations and daisies—I made the drive to the cemetery. It was situated ten miles outside of town, near the old reservoir. When I crossed over the train tracks which ran along the edge of the reservoir, I smiled remembering stories of how my grandfather and his friends would 'hitch a ride' on the side of boxcars, and then dive into the water as the train got close enough.

When I reached the cemetery, I parked next to a gray sedan. As I walked past the other car, I noticed a sticker from a local car rental agency on its rear window. People moved away from the area all the time, but most of them still had strong ties to the community and family they had left behind. They would fly in, rent a car, and reconnect with their loved ones—alive and dead.

Scanning the cemetery, I spotted a woman wearing a black jacket standing near one of the graves over by the old maple trees. Naturally, I was curious about who she was, but I respected her privacy. After giving the woman a wave, I pushed open the wrought-iron gate and entered the cemetery. The wind kicked up, blowing a light dusting of snow across the stone path. Adjusting my scarf and pulling my wool hat down over my ears, I made my way toward the far side of the cemetery where our family plot was situated. I paused at the places where my great-grandparents, great-aunts and uncles, cousins, and other ancestors were buried. Before long, I found myself standing in front of my parents' grave marker.

My father's name was inscribed on the left side and my mother's on the right. Despite the tears welling up in my eyes, I smiled at the stack of books carved into the dark granite. By all accounts, both my parents had been avid readers. My grandmother would often tell me how delighted she was that my mother had married a fellow bookworm.

I bent down to lay the bouquet on the snow covered grass, then traced my mother's name—Alice Olson Olson. It always cracked me up that her maiden name had been the same as her married name. Apparently, her friends had found it hilarious too, giving her the nickname 'Oxygen,' after the chemical symbol for O2. A perfectly geeky moniker for a geeky girl.

Honestly, you might think that the chances of my mom falling in love with someone who had the same last name were remote. But if you knew how many Olsons lived in the area, you wouldn't be surprised. My mom's family and my dad's family weren't related at all, except maybe in the very distant past back in Norway. Yet both Olson clans had somehow ended up in the same small town in North Dakota, destined later to intertwine their families.

After snapping a picture of the gravesite and sending it to Leif, I turned to head back to my car. When I reached the gate, I heard someone cry out in pain. I whipped around and saw the woman in the black coat lying on the ground clutching her ankle.

"Are you okay?" I called out as I rushed over. When I reached her, she was struggling to her feet. "Here, let me help you."

The woman thanked me as I helped her hobble to a nearby bench. "I'm glad you were here. I can't believe I slipped and fell like that."

"The path does have some icy patches. They really should do something about that," I said.

"I blame my klutziness." The woman adjusted her position, then grimaced when she bumped her leg on the bench.

"We should get you to a doctor," I said. "You might have broken something."

She reached down and felt her ankle. "I think I just twisted it. It'll be fine in a few minutes. Go on, I'll be okay."

I shook my head. "No. I'm not leaving until I'm sure you can walk."

"Really, it's okay." She gave me a faint smile, then tucked her shoulder-length reddish brown hair behind her ears. "I can take care of myself."

As she adjusted the collar of her coat around her neck, I examined the woman's face. She had freckled skin, a pierced nose, and dimples. Perfectly groomed eyebrows accentuated her striking eyes—one was blue and the other was hazel.

"You're shivering." I unwrapped my scarf and handed it to her. "Here, take this."

She started to refuse, but then grabbed it from my hands. "Thanks, you're really sweet."

"It's fine. I'm used to the cold. Besides, I have a hat

and gloves, and you don't."

"Yeah," she said with a chuckle. "I didn't really pack the right clothes for this trip."

"You're not from the area, are you? I noticed you're driving a rental car."

"No, I came to pay respects to . . . um . . . a family friend." As she looked off into the distance, she stated, "It was all so sudden. I had just started getting to know him when he passed away."

"I'm so sorry for your loss." I gave her a sympathetic look, knowing all too well the pain of losing someone you were close to.

"He was such a wonderful man. So creative. The paintings he did were out of this world. Such intense colors and symbolism."

Thinking of the small gallery that had just opened up in town, I asked, "Did he exhibit his work?"

"No, *certain* people thought his paintings were too edgy and modern. 'Art should be classic and uplifting,' they told him." The woman's voice was heavy with disdain. "If you're not strong enough to stand up to controlling people, they end up wearing you down. It's easier to give in than fight."

"That's what happened to your friend?" I asked.

"That's just the tip of the iceberg." She sighed. "Sorry, I don't know why I'm spilling my guts to you."

I shrugged. "Sometimes, it's easier to talk to strangers."

"Probably. They don't have a hidden agenda when

they listen to you." The woman's eyes welled up, and she reached into her cross-body bag. "I thought I had a pack of tissues in here."

"Don't worry, I have plenty for the both of us. I came prepared." I handed her some tissues, then added, "I'm Thea, by the way."

"Ceely." She dabbed her eyes. "Who are you visiting?" After I told her about my parents, she squeezed my hand. "How awful to lose both your parents when you were so young. Losing one parent is hard enough, but your mom and your dad . . . that would be devastating."

As she squeezed my hand, I asked, "You lost one of your parents?"

"Um . . . my mom is still alive." She pulled her hand away, then felt her ankle again. "I think it's better. I should probably get going."

"Alright. I'll walk you to your car just to make sure you're okay." When Ceely started to protest, I held up my hand. "I don't want you to slip again."

She nodded, then let me help her to her feet. When she put weight on her injured leg, Ceely winced. After testing her weight on the foot again, she swore that she was good to go. I stuck close by her side in case she needed support, but she was able to walk to her car under her own power.

"Thanks again." The woman carefully climbed into the front seat, and then turned on the car. She grinned when music blasted from the speakers, turning the volume down quickly. “Sorry about that. I told a friend I’d listen to his demo track. He needs to rework that bass line, if you ask me.”

We exchanged a few more pleasantries before Ceely closed the car door. The gray sedan sped off down the road, kicking up snow and gravel in its wake.

I groaned when I realized Ceely still had my scarf. Although we had exchanged first names, I didn’t have a clue where Ceely was staying, or if she was even staying in town. How was I going to track her down? Then I remembered the car rental sticker. I knew the company in Williston. Could I persuade the owner of the rental agency to give me Ceely’s contact information? No, probably not.

Normally, the loss of a scarf wouldn’t bother me. But this particular one had sentimental value. My cousin Freya had knitted it for me out of a soft purplish yarn. Maybe Ceely would try to find me. There were only a couple of other Theas living in Why. If she asked around, someone might point her in my direction. All I could do was hope, though.

I tugged at the zipper on my jacket, pulling it all the way up to the top of my neck and turned toward my car. As I was pulling the keys out of my purse, a thought occurred to me. Ceely had been visiting the grave of a family friend. If I could figure out who, maybe that would be enough of a clue to track her down.

I walked over to where I had seen Ceely earlier, being careful to watch my step and avoid icy patches. It wasn't hard to figure out which gravesite she had been visiting—there was only one new grave marker in that section of the cemetery. When I got close enough to read the name inscribed on it, I gasped. Ceely's family friend was none other than Reginald Silas, Thornton's brother, who had passed away two months ago.

* * *

Wow, I didn't expect that Ceely was friends with the Silas family. However, it was interesting that she hadn't mentioned Thornton's recent death when she was talking about Reginald. Now I had more than one reason to hope our paths would cross again—get my scarf back and see if Ceely might have any insights into who'd wanted to kill Thornton.

I hurried back to my car, turning the heater up to full blast once I was inside. When my phone rang, I picked it up right away. "I thought you were too busy to talk until tonight," I said to my brother.

"When I saw the picture of the flowers at mom and dad's grave you texted me, I stepped out of my meeting. I needed to hear your voice." Leif sounded gruff, like he was trying to control his emotions. "I wish I could have been there with you today."

"I wish you could have been too." I wiped away a

tear from my eye. "Leif, I'm so glad I have you in my life."

Leif's answer was only one word, "Ditto." There was a depth of meaning layered underneath it, reminding me that no matter how often we squabbled, we would always share an unbreakable sibling bond.

I took a deep breath, then and changed the subject. "I got your text earlier about not suspecting 'A' anymore. What was that about? Did you mean Ashley?"

"After you told me about Ivy's mom not being able to provide an alibi for her, we did some checking. One of the neighbors was out walking their dog when they saw Ivy leave her house that night." While I processed this information, Leif quickly added, "This is all off the record, got it?"

"Uh-huh," I said. "Do you have proof that Ivy went to the library after that?"

"No, but we do know that she withdrew a large sum of money from a nearby ATM."

"Oh, that's interesting," I replied. "Maybe it was hush money for Thornton. He must have known something about her, some secret from her past that she didn't want to get out. That could be what he whispered to her that night at the reception."

"That's what we're thinking," Leif said.

The car was getting warm, so I turned down the heat and unzipped my jacket. "Have you questioned

Ivy yet?"

"No, we're still getting our ducks in order. But we will."

I shook my head. "Poor Tiana. I hope you're wrong for her sake."

"Don't forget Grandma. She'd also be happy if I was wrong," Leif pointed out. "You know how fond she is of Ivy."

"Have you told her yet?" I asked.

"No, I'll wait until tonight. Something like that is better in person."

"It's a tough situation. On the one hand, she'll be disappointed about Ivy. On the other, she'll be glad that Erik and Hudson are in the clear." I drummed my fingers on the steering wheel. "Are you still going to charge Erik with obstruction of justice?"

"I'm afraid we don't have a choice."

"There goes his dream of joining the Peace Corps," I said. "Funny how one mistake can change your life completely."

"I feel for the guy, I really do," Leif said. "He obviously panicked when he saw Thornton's body. Then the lies snowballed from there."

"Gosh, it all makes sense now," I said. "When Erik went into the storage room that night, he must have seen Ivy running out the back door. He was trying to cover for her. That's why he didn't call nine-one-one."

"Sorry, sis, I think you're wrong. It would make our job easier if we had an eyewitness, but Erik swears he didn't see anyone in the storage room that night."

"And you believe him?"

"I do," Leif said simply. "Listen, I gotta go."

"Hey before you hang up, are you positive that it's Ivy? After all, you did get that tip about Ashley."

"I think it was just a crackpot. Or maybe Bobby Jorgenson thinking he was being funny," Leif said. "You don't need to talk to Ashley."

After we hung up, I started to text Ashley, saying that I couldn't make it. Only then I remembered how her eyes had lit up when I suggested getting together. I got the feeling she could use a friend. It brought to mind the C.S. Lewis quote. I whispered it aloud, "Friendship is born at that moment when one person says to another, 'What! You too? I thought I was the only one.'" Now I was curious. Was there something I might find out about Ashley that would surprise me? Something only the two of us shared?

* * *

After swinging by the grocery store to get the ingredients for the knoephla soup—potatoes, milk, onion, chicken broth, flour, butter, and eggs—I drove to Ashley's place. The small ranch house looked like it had seen better days with peeling paint, missing shingles on the roof, and a cracked balustrade on the porch. But when I walked inside, it was a totally different story—the environment Ashley had created was warm and welcoming. Colorful afghans and throw pillows brightened up vintage furniture, crisp white curtains framed the windows, whimsical floral paintings drew your eye, and the flickering fire made me want to curl up in front of it with a book.

"Watch your step," Ashley said to me as I tripped over a canvas tote. "That's my latest knitting project. I'm making a hat out of this gorgeous aqua mohair. The yarn cost an arm and a leg, but it's totally worth it."

"I've never been a knitter," I said.

"You should try it. Come to the knitting circle next month." Ashley grabbed one of the grocery bags I was holding. "The kitchen is this way. Do you want a glass of wine while we cook?"

I glanced at the clock hanging on the wall. It was only three in the afternoon. I didn't normally drink this early, but it had been a rough day. "Are you having some?"

"Yeah, I got some bad news today." Ashley pulled a bottle of white wine out of the fridge and unscrewed the cap. "Maybe this will help."

"That's terrible. What happened?" I asked.

"Simon fired me. Can you believe it?" Ashley's hands shook with rage as she poured a generous serving of wine into a glass. "He couldn't even be bothered to tell me face to face."

"Things like that are so hard over the phone," I said. "You can't read the other person's body language while they're talking."

"Oh, no, you're giving that man too much credit. He didn't have the guts to call me either. The jerk sent a text." Ashley took a swig of wine, then grabbed her phone. After unlocking it, she thrust it at me. "Here, look. Can you believe the gall?"

I tapped on Simon's name, then read the text he had sent Ashley.

I know what you did. Consider yourself fired.

"What is he thinking you did?" I asked.

"Other than work my butt off at the bowling alley? Nothing." Ashley leaned against the kitchen counter and gulped down her wine. "Have you ever had to clean bowling shoes? Those things stink to high heaven. But did I ever complain about cleaning them? Nope. Well, what about getting dried-up nacho sauce out of the carpet? Have you ever had to deal with that? It's not easy, let me tell you."

Ashley drained the rest of her glass, then filled it right back up. This time, she took a more moderate sip of her wine before belching loudly. "Oops, sorry about that."

"Happens to all of us," I said, waving it off.

"You seem way too proper of a lady to belch. Guess we'll have to get some more wine in you and see if it happens." Ashley grinned at me, then inspected the bottle. "Wow, I can't believe we've gone through nearly half of this already."

"Really?"

Ashley placed her finger to her lips. “I’ll let you in on a little secret. I had a glass before you got here. But it’s more fun now that you’re here to share.”

Oblivious to the fact she hadn’t actually served me any wine yet; Ashley topped her glass back up. After taking a sip, she unpacked the grocery bags.

As she set the bag of potatoes on the kitchen table, I asked, “Seriously though, what does Simon think you did?”

She placed the other ingredients on the counter, then got out a cutting board, vegetable peeler, and knife. “He said I was flirting with the customers.”

“That hardly seems like a fireable offense.”

“Exactly,” Ashley said, slurring her words slightly. After telling me to peel the potatoes and cut them into cubes, she continued. “Did you know that a couple of weeks ago, he accused me of having an affair with Thornton?”

I actually did know this, but decided now was probably not the time to bring it up. Not that I would have been able to since Ashley didn’t let me get a word in edgewise. She ranted about Simon for a few more minutes, and then added, “As if I would ever have slept with Thornton, especially not after what he did to me.”

When Ashley paused to down more of her wine, I quickly asked, “What did Thornton do to you?”

“I don’t want to talk about it.” Ashley belched again, and started giggling uncontrollably. “Even if I did want to talk about it, I couldn't. At least that's what the lawyers said. Isn't that funny?"

"Is that one of those lawyer jokes?" When I glanced up from my potatoes expecting a punchline, Ashley wasn't laughing anymore.

"Thornton's dead, right?" she asked, her eyes scrunched up as if she was having problems seeing me.

"Last I heard."

Ashley sat down at the table, leaned forward on her elbows, and looked at me intently. "If he's dead, then the lawyers can't tell me what to do anymore, right?"

I gave the other woman a confused look. "What are you talking about?"

Before she could explain, Logan walked into the kitchen holding a sketchbook. He nodded at me, and opened the fridge. "Mom, did you get any iced tea when you were at the store?" he asked over his shoulder.

"They were out," Ashley said absent-mindedly.

"Now, what am I supposed to drink?" Logan asked sullenly.

"I think there's milk."

He slammed the fridge shut. "Milk is for kids."

I wanted to tell Logan that he was acting like a kid, but I bit my tongue. I waited for Ashley to remind Logan he was an adult and could stock up on his own iced tea. Instead, she kissed him on the cheek. "You're such a good boy."

Logan tried to pull away, but Ashley pulled him into a hug.

"Okay, enough." Logan squirmed out of his mom's arms. "I'm going back to my room."

"Not before you show Thea your drawings." Ashley yanked the sketchbook out of Logan's hands and plopped it on the table, narrowly missing the pile of potato peels.

After I wiped my hands and flipped through the sketchbook, I looked at Logan with surprise. "These are good. Really good. I had no idea you were so talented."

"Thanks," he muttered, looking down at the floor.

"Did you do those floral paintings in the living room?" I asked.

"Aren't they amazing?" Ashley swayed slightly, then grabbed hold of the counter to steady herself. "He takes after his—"

"She doesn't want to hear about all that," Logan said, cutting his mom off. He snatched the sketchbook out of my hands and stormed out of the kitchen.

Ashley let out a loud sigh before she polished off the rest of the wine in her glass. "I'm going to run to the bathroom. You keep working on those potatoes. If you finish with those and I'm not back yet, the recipe is on the counter."

Once the potatoes were cubed, I set them in a bowl. Next, I picked up the cutting board with the potato peels on it and walked toward the trash can. As I was opening the lid, an animal streaked past me, causing me to lose my balance. I groaned as the cutting board landed on the floor, scattering the potato peels in all directions.

As I was picking the peels back up, Logan walked into the kitchen. "Have you seen Henry?"

"Does Henry have gray fur?" When Logan nodded, I pointed toward the laundry room. "Something matching that description went that way."

"Thanks," he said.

While Logan went to collect his wayward pet, I dumped the potato peels in the trash and wiped down the floor with a rag. I was washing the cutting board in the sink when Logan came back in, clutching a large gray cat. He set the cat on the floor and then poured some crunchy nuggets into its bowl.

"Can you do me a favor?" I squeezed some dish soap onto a sponge. "Your mom left the soup recipe over there. Could you read it to me so I know what I'm supposed to do next?"

Logan hesitated for a moment, then picked up the index card. "You cut up some potatoes."

"I already did that. What's after that?"

"Um . . . you add dill. Sprinkle it on the potatoes."

"Dill? Okay, where does your mom keep her spices?"

"Over there." Logan pointed at a drawer near the stove. He then scooped up the empty cat bowl and deposited it in the sink. "Come on, Henry. Time to play laser pointer."

Henry's meows made it very clear that he was down for a game of laser pointer. As the cat rushed out of the room, Logan turned to me. "What time's dinner going to be ready? My mom's taking a nap, so I can't ask her."

I looked over at the nearly empty wine bottle and shook my head. "No idea, Logan. No idea."

CHAPTER 12
CATS JUST GOTTA HAVE FUN

After checking on Ashley—her thunderous snoring had convinced me that she wasn't getting up anytime soon—I covered the potatoes, and tidied up the kitchen. As I was putting the milk in the fridge, I noticed the knoephla soup recipe lying on the counter. It was clearly a treasured recipe handed down to Ashley from her grandmother. I loved how the ingredients and steps were written in a precise script in blue ink on the yellowing index card. Strange, though—there was no mention of the dill Logan had said needed to be sprinkled on the potatoes. I'd have to ask Ashley about that later.

I grabbed my coat and purse before I stopped by Logan's room to let him know I was leaving. I had to knock a few times before he opened the door.

After removing his headphones, Logan gave me a wary look. "Yeah?"

For some unknown reason, I tried to engage him in conversation. "This is a good sized room. You have plenty of space for a bed and desk." Noting the canvases stacked next to the doorway, I added, "I see it doubles as your art studio."

"Yep."

"That one with the large yellow dots and small reddish brown splotches on that one edge looks interesting. Do you do much in the way of modern art?"

Instead of gracing me with another one-word answer, Logan simply shook his head. It was such a scintillating conversation. Despite that, I felt compelled to keep talking to the guy. And it really was talking *to* him, because he wasn't doing a lot of talking back.

"What kind of laptop is that?" I asked. "I think I'm going to need to replace mine soon."

Logan scratched his head, then shrugged.

Noticing Henry pushing a pencil off Logan's desk, I chuckled. "Cats are so cute, aren't they? Uh-oh, looks like he's going to go after your glass next."

Logan turned around and clapped his hands sharply. But if this was meant to deter the cat from his entertainment, it wasn't very effective. Instead, Henry locked eyes with his human and pushed the glass a few inches toward the edge of the desk.

"Henry, stop it," Logan said in a pleading tone of voice.

I bit back a smile as I watched the power struggle play out. Cats just gotta have fun, especially if it's at their human's expense. I was making a mental note of the things Henry might shove off the desk next—sketch books, markers, napkins—when my eyes landed on that expensive hunting knife I had found Logan with at the library.

When Logan noticed me staring at the knife, he quickly shoved it into a desk drawer. Henry took advantage of the distraction, knocking the glass off the desk. Fortunately, it landed on Logan's bed and didn't break. Unfortunately, whatever was inside spilled all over the comforter and pillows.

Logan threw up his hands and let loose a few swear words. Satisfied that his work was done, Henry jumped down from the desk and padded out the door.

"Looks like you got your knife back," I said once Logan had calmed down.

"Um, yeah." He averted his eyes, and muttered something about dinner. "Tell my mom I'm not hungry, okay?"

I arched an eyebrow as he closed the door in my face. Then I headed out of their house, feeling sorry for Ashley.

* * *

By the time I got back to my grandparents' house, I was mentally and physically exhausted. The combination of not sleeping well the night before and dealing with the emotions that accompanied the anniversary of my parents' death left me wanting to climb back into bed so that tomorrow could come sooner.

When I walked through the kitchen door, my grandmother looked at me with surprise. "I thought you'd be eating knoephla soup at Ashley's."

"It's a long story," I said. "Suffice it to say that Ashley needed a nap more than she needed to teach me how to cook."

"You look like you need a nap, too." Grandma motioned at the kitchen table. "Sit down. I'll get you some coffee."

I smiled my thanks as she set a steaming mug in front of me. "Is Leif here?"

"He's watching the game with your grandfather." Grandma sat down opposite of me and fidgeted with the tablecloth. "Your brother told me about Ivy."

"I'm sorry it turned out to be her," I said.

"Me too . . ." She let out a deep sigh, then said, "They brought her in for questioning this afternoon. According to your brother, she wouldn't say a word, not even with her lawyer there. They're keeping her in custody overnight."

I put a hand to my mouth. "How awful. Does Tiana know what's happened?"

Grandma shook her head. “I talked with Janelle earlier tonight. She told Tiana that her mom is at a conference.”

“The truth is going to come out sooner or later,” I said.

“I know.” My grandmother pressed her hands together. “Janelle is adamant that Ivy is innocent.”

“She’s her mom. If your mom doesn’t stand by your side, who will?” As I said the words, I felt a stabbing pain in my heart. At least Ivy had a mom to stand by her. I bit my lower lip, willing myself not to cry. I changed the subject. “I never got around to asking Ashley about the money.”

My grandmother shrugged. “It doesn’t matter anymore.”

“I’m still curious as to why you were interested in that.”

“Oh, I ran into one of the gals in my book club, and she was telling me how she went to the casino before Christmas. Well, apparently, Ashley had waltzed in and started placing huge bets on the roulette table. Now you gotta ask yourself, given her circumstances, where did she get that money from?”

I thought back to the pricey lip gloss I had seen Ashley using the other day, not to mention the expensive mohair yarn she was using for her knitting project.

“You’re right. There’s no reason why Ashley’s finances should concern us now.” I took a sip of my coffee, glad I was drinking that instead of wine. I'd probably be in trouble if they ever came up with a coffee-flavored wine. "I'm surprised Hudson isn't here. You always seem to be inviting him over."

"Pastor Rob and his wife asked Hudson to join them for dinner," my grandmother said.

"Did they pick him up?"

Grandma grinned. "No, Hudson drove there."

"Good for him." I mentally crossed my fingers that he didn't have any issues on his drive. If he was going to lay down roots here in North Dakota, he was going to need to drive in all sorts of weather conditions.

"Did you pick up the tater tots?" my grandmother asked. "I was thinking of making that chicken and wild rice hotdish tomorrow night."

I jumped up from the table and grabbed my purse. "Oh, no, I forgot. I can run back out to the store now and get them."

"No, don't worry about it." Grandma pushed her chair back, got up, and pulled me into a hug. "I'd rather spend time with you."

As I rested my head against my grandmother's shoulder and breathed in her lavender scent, feelings of warmth, security, and comfort washed over me, pushing the grief and pain away . . . at least for now.

* * *

I felt more like my normal self the next day. Spending

time with my family the previous night had lightened my spirit and being busy getting ready for my business trip to Denver had kept my mind occupied.

"Where are you off to?" my grandmother asked when I rushed into the kitchen after dinner carrying my coat and purse.

"Hudson called. He needs me to pick him up."

"But he drove the Larsens' truck to work today," Grandma said.

"Yeah, but it won't start," I said. "Hudson called roadside assistance, thinking the battery was dead. But apparently, that's not the problem. The roadside guy said it might have something to do with the starter. They're going to tow it to a service station in the morning."

Grandma chuckled. "Guess you're back to being Hudson's personal chauffeur."

"At your service, ma'am," I said in an English accent as I bowed.

When I arrived at the library, it had already closed for the night. Before I could call Hudson to let me in, he pulled the door open.

"Ready?" I asked, jiggling my car keys in my hand.

"Do you mind hanging out for a bit? I'm waiting for the Larsens to call me back about the truck."

"Can't they call you on your cell?"

"Ron wants me to check something in the engine first."

I bit back a smile. "And you know how to do that?"

"Well, no . . . but I do know where I can find a book about auto repair," Hudson said with mock indignation.

I stuck out my tongue. "You're not the only one, smarty pants. They're classified under six-twenty-nine."

"Six-twenty-nine what?" Hudson prompted.

I thought about it for a minute, then said triumphantly, "Point two-eight-seven."

"I'm impressed." Hudson gave me an appraising look. "Why didn't you become a librarian? According to the staff, you know your way around library operations and clearly know the Dewey Decimal system."

"A trained monkey could do all that." When Hudson arched an eyebrow, I laughed. "You know what I mean."

"Well, you have something that can't be trained too," Hudson said. "You care about people and you want to help them."

I was taken aback by his assessment. Nurses, educators, librarians—people drawn to those professions all wanted to help people. I was just an ordinary gal who'd worked in a corporate office for years, and now owned my own business. "I'm not sure I would describe myself that way."

"All you've done is help me from day one," Hudson said. "You stood up for me against your own brother when he thought I killed Thornton. You've been driving me everywhere, you've made me feel welcome in town, and you even bought Dr. McCoy those cat treats he goes nuts for. Sounds like someone who likes to help."

"Did you ever think that maybe it's *you* I wanted to help, and not the whole world?" I shrugged. "What can I say? You bring out the best in people."

Hudson gave me a funny look—one I couldn't read. "We have quite the mutual admiration society going on here, don't we?"

"Should we get badges?"

"No, stickers. Always stickers." Hudson smiled at me, then flicked his gaze over to the door behind me. "Oh, Erik's here."

Erik held up the cardboard boxes he was carrying. "Is now an okay time to pick up my things?"

"Um, sure. Wait, no . . . I mean, what things?" Hudson spluttered.

"The stuff in my desk," Erik said. "And I also have some personal books here. I swear I won't take any library property."

"I didn't think you would," Hudson said quickly. "What's going on, Erik?"

Erik gave a nervous laugh. "You're going to fire me, so I thought I'd get ahead of the game."

"Fire you? Why would I do that?"

"Because . . . because . . ." Erik looked at Hudson helplessly, struggling to find the words.

"Let's talk about this in my office," Hudson suggested.

I jerked a finger in the direction of the kitchen. "Why don't I get some coffee while you guys talk?"

"No, stay please, Thea," Erik said. "I could use the moral support."

After we settled in Hudson's office, there was an uncomfortable silence while Erik stared at the floor.

Finally Hudson asked, "Why do you think I would fire you?"

"The District Attorney is going to charge me with obstruction of justice." Erik turned to me. "I'm sure you know that already from your brother."

"Actually, I heard it from . . ." my voice trailed off, not wanting to let Erik know that the town was gossiping about his predicament. Instead, I asked about the legal proceedings. "If you're charged, there still has to be a hearing, right? You haven't been convicted of anything yet."

"Thea's right," Hudson said. "There's no reason why you can't be employed by the library, at least until the matter is settled."

"I don't understand. Why would you want me to work here, especially after how I lied to you? And even if you were okay with it, some parents might be concerned about having a youth librarian who's facing criminal charges."

Hudson leaned back in his chair while he considered this. "I need to talk to HR and find out if there are any employment issues we need to take into account. But listen, you're innocent until proven guilty."

"But I'm not innocent. I'm going to plead guilty," Erik said firmly. "Look, if I were in your shoes, I'd fire me. I left the library without checking to see if anyone was still here that night. Somebody is dead because of that."

"I thought you said you had checked the library before you closed up." I leaned forward and looked Erik in the eye. "You were positive that no one was here."

Erik shook his head. "I was really upset about what Thornton said that night. I took shortcuts in the closing procedures. All I did was turn off the systems before rushing out. I didn't even lock the front door when I left."

My eyes widened. "But that changes everything."

Hudson looked at me. "How so?"

"It affects the timing of the murder. Thornton could have been killed *before* the library closed. The only reason we thought the time of death was after nine-thirty was because that's when Erik said he left. Everyone assumed the library was empty at that time." I chewed on my bottom lip, then turned to Erik. "Did you tell the police this?"

Erik frowned. "I think so. Actually, I'm not sure. I was so confused when they questioned me."

"They must have asked you about the closing process."

"They did, just like you did that day when you came over with the rhubarb cookies. I told them what I normally do."

"What you *normally* do," I said slowly. "But that wasn't what you actually did that night, was it?"

"No," Erik said softly.

Hudson took a deep breath. "Why don't you tell us exactly what happened that night?"

"Well, first I helped get everything ready for the reception. I set up the folding tables, put the food out, made coffee—"

Hudson held up his hand. "How about if you start with what happened after the reception was over?"

"Um, okay. It's a blur." Erik rubbed his temples. He looked at Hudson hopefully. "Is Dr. McCoy here?"

"No, sorry, buddy. He broke into the jar of cat treats last night and he's at home sleeping it off."

"When the reception was over, I offered to clean up and you went to cover the front desk," I said.

"That's right," Erik said.

"So, you were up at the front desk the entire time?" Hudson asked.

Erik frowned. "No, I went to find a book on wind turbines for a patron."

"Books on wind turbines," I mused, unable to remember how they were cataloged. "Wait a minute, those would be shelved with engineering books, right?"

"Assuming it was a non-fiction book," Hudson said.

"It was. She wanted to know more about how they work," Erik said.

"So, you would have gone to look for it on the overflow bookshelves that line the hallway by the restrooms," I proposed.

"Correct."

"Was the patron with you at the time?" I asked.

"No. She has mobility issues. I suggested she wait on one of the couches while I found it for her."

I tried to imagine Erik standing in the hallway, looking for a book on the shelves. "Did you see anyone walk past you?"

"Yes, I did. There was someone in the hall that night."

When he didn't elaborate, I eventually said, "Can you describe them?"

Erik thought about this for a few moments, then said, "An elderly gentleman went into the men's room. But other than that, I was the only one in the hallway."

"An elderly gentleman." I looked at Hudson. "Doesn't really fit the bill."

"Ivy could have already been in the storage room when Erik was in the hallway," Hudson said.

Erik's jaw dropped. "Ivy? You think Ivy killed Thornton? No, that's not possible."

"Good people sometimes do bad things," I pointed out.

"You're right. Of course you are. That's why I thought—" Erik clamped his hand over his mouth as he rocked back and forth in his chair.

I glanced at Hudson, wishing Dr. McCoy was here to comfort Erik. After a beat, I turned back to Erik. "Who did you think killed Thornton?" I asked in my most soothing voice.

"Logan." Erik spat out the name as though it physically hurt him to utter it. "I thought Logan did it. That's why I didn't say anything initially."

"You were trying to protect Logan," I said. "I get that."

"Why do you think Logan wanted to kill Thornton?" Hudson asked.

Erik shook his head. "Not Thornton. Simon."

"Oh, it all makes sense now. When we were at your apartment, you initially thought it had been Simon who was killed. I made that same mistake when I first saw the body." I felt a shiver go down my spine as I remembered the pool of blood on the storage room floor. "Why would Logan want to kill Simon?"

"Logan hated how Simon treated his mom. He told me that he overheard Simon bullying her earlier that night. Logan was so angry about it I worried he might have snapped. You have to understand, he even said that he wished Simon was dead." Erik looked down at his hands, realizing that he had been digging his fingernails into his palms. "You don't understand. Logan has had a really tough life, especially over the last several months. I just wanted to help him, that's all."

"That's the kind of thing the police need to know," Hudson said gently. "It could help your case."

"Oh, my gosh, it all makes sense now." I slapped my hand on the armrest. "Remember when I overheard that conversation between you and Logan?" When Erik nodded, I said, "That was the part you were worried I'd overheard, that Logan threatened to kill Simon."

"No, I never said that," Erik said forcefully. "I said that Logan wished Simon was dead. There's a big difference."

"You're right," Hudson said. "There is a difference."

I leaned back in my chair, thinking about my recent interactions with Logan. "Are you by any chance tutoring Logan?"

"What do you mean?" Erik said with a guarded expression on his face.

"I get the feeling he struggles with reading." I explained how Logan had accidentally signed up to donate a thousand dollar prize for Bobby Jorgenson's potluck for Seatrina. "And when I asked him to read his mom's recipe, he mentioned an ingredient that wasn't listed."

Erik sighed. "Logan has dyslexia. It wasn't

diagnosed when he was in elementary school, so he didn't get the help he needed during those formative years. When he moved back to North Dakota during high school, he had learned how to hide it. He managed to get by. Cheating on exams, getting friends to help with homework, teachers looking the other way because he was a star athlete, that kind of thing. But once he graduated from high school, things got harder."

Thinking about how Logan had become a loner after he graduated and went from one dead-end job to the next, I said, "That explains a lot. Poor guy. It couldn't have been easy."

"You have no idea. If that's all, I'm going to go ahead and pack up my stuff." Erik grabbed his cardboard boxes off the floor, then looked at Hudson. "I appreciate you trying to make it work, but I'm going to make it easier on you. I'm officially resigning."

CHAPTER 13
SO MANY BOOKS

After Erik announced he was going to resign from his youth librarian position, Hudson shook his head vehemently. He tried his best to talk Erik out of quitting, but Erik was steadfast in his decision.

"Sorry, man," Erik said, staring blankly at the wall behind Hudson. "But it's for the best."

After Erik walked out of the office, Hudson turned to me, a look of utter dismay on his face. "When I moved to Why, I was hoping for a fresh start. This isn't exactly what I'd imagined."

I gave Hudson a sympathetic look. "It'll get better, I promise."

"It certainly can't get any worse," Hudson snapped. "Maybe I should go back to Florida. At least there, I don't have to deal with driving in the snow, buffalo roaming the streets, and people turning up dead in the library."

"North Dakota isn't all bad," I said evenly.

Hudson clenched his fists, then slowly uncurled them. "I'm sorry, Thea. I shouldn't be taking my frustrations out on you. What's wrong with me? Why am I being such a jerk?"

I pulled my notebook out of my purse and flipped to the page where I had placed the sticker Hudson had given me earlier. Holding it up in front of him, I said, "What does this say?"

A smile tugged at the corners of Hudson's mouth. "It's not fair to throw that back at my face."

"Go on, read it out loud," I coaxed.

Hudson sighed as he took the notebook from me. "It's okay not to be okay," he said quietly.

"Cut yourself some slack. The world is throwing a lot of tough stuff your way." I gave Hudson a considered look. "I think this is the first time I've seen you react like this. It's pretty impressive, actually."

"Not really. I bottle stuff up inside," Hudson admitted. "It's not healthy."

"Well, that's something we have in common," I said.

"We have—" Hudson glanced down at his phone ringing. "I have to get this. It's Ron calling about the truck."

"I'll go look at books," I mouthed as Hudson answered the phone.

I wandered aimlessly through the stacks, pulling out a book here and there to check out the cover and blurb. This kind of random bibliophile exploration was one of my favorite things to do. You never knew what kind of treasures you were going to stumble across. That's the beauty of libraries—all the possibilities that lay within the pages of books.

The stack in my arms started to get heavy. I had pulled books on project management, art history, and even one on automotive repair that I thought Hudson might be interested in. As I was about to add a copy of *Dyslexia is My Superpower* to the pile, I felt something sticky land on my hand.

My arm jerked and the books I was holding tumbled to the floor. "Gross," I muttered as I examined the glob on the back of my hand.

I was searching for a tissue in my purse when a familiar raspy voice called out, "Hey, lady. Why'd you get in my way?"

"Did you do this?" I scanned the area for my reptilian nemesis. When I didn't see him, I called out, "Show yourself."

"Use your eyes," he said snarkily. "I'm right in front of your big mug."

"I *am* using my eyes," I snapped. "Where are you hiding?"

I yanked books off the shelves, my eyes darting back and forth as I searched for the chameleon's hiding place. Just as I was about to give up, there was a sudden whooshing noise, followed by a flash of light.

"Over here, princess," the voice quipped.

I rubbed my eyes, then scowled when I saw the chameleon casually lounging on the bookshelf like he owned the place.

"Sorry. Guess I forgot to turn my camouflage mode off."

Noting that his apology didn't sound the least bit sincere, I jabbed a finger in his direction. "Feel free to keep it on permanently. And hit the mute button while you're at it."

"Yeah, not gonna happen."

"Great," I muttered. As I wiped the back of my hand with a tissue, I glowered at the chameleon. "Did you spit on me?"

"I was aiming for a fly," the chameleon said. "You got in the way."

I wrinkled my nose. "Why are you spitting at flies?"

"Duh. To catch them. Flies are the only decent thing to eat around here. Do you see any hot dog stands nearby, lady?" The chameleon stared at me with his peculiar eyes. "No, because this godforsaken place is a million miles away from the center of the universe . . . New York City."

"Okay, first of all, it's more like eighteen-hundred miles and, second of all, we eat hot dogs here, too."

"First of all," the chameleon said in a mocking tone, "if you want to be precise, it's one thousand eight hundred and fifteen point six miles. Second of all, what you try to pass off as a hot dog in North Dakota doesn't even begin to compare to the genuine article which you can only find in the Big Apple. A little sauerkraut and some spicy brown mustard on top of a one hundred percent beef frank grilled on the streets of the city that never sleeps . . . heaven."

I chuckled when the chameleon made a chef's kiss emphasized with a flourish of his claw-like toes. "Maybe I could bring you some mustard and sauerkraut to put on top of your flies."

The chameleon scowled. "What? Do I look like a heathen? Mustard and sauerkraut on flies? Please."

"Fine." I held up my hands. "I was just trying to help."

"I think you got that the wrong way around. I'm here to help you and from the looks of it, you need all the help you can get."

"Okay, let's get this 'help' thing of yours out of the way." I folded my arms across my chest. "What do you have for me?"

"You might want to get that precious notebook of yours out," he said.

I arched an eyebrow. "Just tell me already."

The chameleon turned one of his beady eyes in my direction, then said dramatically, "KIAA0319." After a beat, he said, "Sure you don't need to write that down?"

I wanted to strangle the loathsome reptile, but I

got my notebook out instead. “Okay, give that to me again, and slower this time.” When I had finished jotting it down, I asked, “Is that a license plate number?”

“Do all people have the same license plate numbers?”

I shook my head. “You’re talking in riddles.”

“Let’s try something easier. What’s twelve divided by two?”

“Right,” I said slowly. “So, we’ve moved on to math problems now?”

The chameleon smirked. “Are you stalling cause you don’t know the answer? I’ll wait if you need to pull the calculator app up on your phone.”

“You are the most infuriating, cold-blooded creature I’ve ever met.” As I stamped my foot, I heard the cleaner vacuuming in the other room. They were probably grateful that the library’s resident chameleon only ate flies rather than messy hotdogs. Cleaning mustard and sauerkraut out of a carpet was probably a nightmare. Not that they had ever encountered him. Nope, that pleasure seemed to be all mine.

The chameleon inched forward on the shelf and cocked its head to one side. “Give up?”

“No, I don’t give up.” Realizing that the vacuum cleaner had been turned off, I lowered my voice so I wouldn't be overheard. “Twelve divided by two is six.”

The chameleon bobbed his head up and down. Then I heard a 'whoosh' and quickly closed my eyes to shield them from the flashing light I instinctively knew would follow. When I opened my eyes back up, the pesky reptile had disappeared.

"Hey, where did you go?" I whispered toward the bookshelf. When no one answered, I shook my fist. "Some help you are."

* * *

After checking out my stack of books, Hudson turned off the computer system, then did a final walk around the library. When he returned, he gave me a thumbs up. "The only person left here is the cleaner. Let's head on out."

As Hudson grabbed his coat and messenger bag from the office, I noticed a cardboard box on the front desk. My heart sank when I saw what was lying on top of the books crammed in there—Erik's library nametag.

"I think Erik forgot some of his stuff," I said to Hudson as he locked his office. "Let me text him. We can drop it off on the way."

After exchanging a few texts with Erik, I tucked my phone in my purse. "He said he's already in bed. I'm going to pop by his apartment tomorrow morning. I need to check my post office box anyway, and it's nearby."

On the drive home, Hudson and I had an unspoken agreement—no discussion of anything related to the murder or Erik's resignation. We chatted about our favorite comfort foods (grilled cheese and tomato soup for me and beef stew for Hudson), which movie in the Indiana Jones franchise was the best (we both were fans of *Raiders of the Lost Ark*), and whether you should put dill pickles in potato salad (Hudson was a firm no, but I told him he needed to try my grandma's).

When I pulled up to the Larsens' house, we lingered in the car for a few minutes talking about nothing much. It was the good kind of 'nothing much,' the kind of chit-chat that you have with someone you're comfortable around. In some ways, it felt like Hudson and I had been friends for ages. Had it really only been less than a week?

"I should go," Hudson eventually said. "Dr. McCoy doesn't like it when I leave him alone too long."

"You going to take him to the library tomorrow?"

"Uh-huh. We have an event for homeschool kids. Dr. McCoy loves those sorts of things."

After promising to give Dr. McCoy a few pets from me, Hudson got out of the car. As he walked inside, I thought about how upset he had been earlier, even saying he should move back to Florida. I crossed my fingers, hoping Hudson would give North Dakota a chance. If he did, I was sure he'd come to love it as much as I did.

The rest of the evening was quiet, including some dessert with my grandparents, followed by a couple of episodes of *Masterpiece Theater*. When I woke up the next morning, I felt ready to face whatever came my way.

After stopping by the post office and picking up my mail, I drove to Erik's apartment building. The front door was locked this time, so I rang the buzzer. When Erik didn't respond, I dug my phone out of my purse and sent a text.

I shifted the cardboard box while I waited for a reply. Hopefully, Erik was just in the shower and not fast asleep with his phone turned off. As I was about to head back to my car, the door was flung open. A man bundled up against the elements rushed past me, and I stuck my foot out to catch the door and keep it from closing behind him.

As I climbed the stairs to the second floor, I debated what to do. If Erik didn't answer when I knocked, should I leave the box in front of his door? Erik had said that there were issues with someone stealing the mail, but that was outsiders. Was this the kind of building where neighbors also 'helped' themselves to people's packages and belongings?

When I reached Erik's apartment, I frowned. The door was slightly ajar and something felt off. Time seemed to slow down, my senses heightened, and adrenaline coursed through my system as though my body was preparing itself for a fight.

My first instinct was to rush inside and confront what was waiting for me on the other side of the door. Instead, I willed myself to slow down my breathing. Recent events were making me paranoid. My imagination was in overdrive.

I exhaled slowly, then knocked gently on the door. "Erik, are you there? It's Thea. I've got your box."

After knocking several more times without a response, my stomach twisted in knots. Maybe my paranoia was justified? I held my breath as I slowly pushed the door open. The hinges creaked as the scene inside was revealed. I realized then why Erik didn't buzz me in, or respond to my texts, or answer the door . . . he couldn't, because he was dead.

* * *

After calling 911, I slumped to the ground and put my head in my hands, trying to avoid looking at Erik's body. But there was nothing I could do. The poor guy had likely been dead for hours, his skull crushed in from behind by a bowling ball. Erik didn't deserve this. He was a good man, someone who had dedicated his life to helping others. Who would do this? Who would callously snuff out another human being's life?

The answer was obvious, right? The bowling ball pointed at Simon. First, he had killed Thornton. Then, worried that Erik would point the finger at him, he'd murdered him as well.

When loud music started blaring from the next-door neighbor's apartment, I jumped to my feet. Banging my fist against the wall, I yelled for them to turn it down. Eventually, I gave up, realizing they couldn't hear me above the heavy metal music they were playing. I slowly rubbed my hand while I steeled myself to survey the crime scene. Maybe there was something I could see that would help convict Simon. A bowling ball by itself wasn't enough, especially if he had been smart enough to wear gloves or wipe his prints off it.

As I glanced around the small studio apartment, I let out a few swear words. Killing Erik had been pointless. Erik hadn't seen Simon go into the storage room. He wasn't an eyewitness. So, why did Simon think he was? And if he was worried that Erik could pin Thornton's murder on him, why wait until now to kill him?

I looked around Erik's apartment, trying to spot evidence that would tie the murder to Simon. It was probably a hopeless task. This was only the second time I had visited the apartment. How would I know if anything was different or out of place? One thing I knew for sure though, there were a lot of books. What would happen to all of them? Would their next owner love them as much as Erik had?

As my eyes traveled around the small studio apartment, I spotted an abstract painting propped up against a bookshelf. I walked carefully across the room, and then bent down to examine it. When I saw the artist's name, I drew in a breath—Reginald Silas. Why did Erik have a picture painted by Thornton's brother? Then I sighed, realizing with Erik dead, I'd likely never know.

When I took a step back, I stumbled over a pile of books. As I regained my balance, I saw the bowling ball that had killed Erik out of the corner of my eye. Pink felt like the wrong color for a murder weapon. Instruments of death should be a dark color—black, gray, dark red, or maybe a deep maroon—not a cheerful, bright pink hue.

The door to the apartment opened, interrupting my thoughts about the aesthetics of murder weapons. "Hey, sis," Leif said. "Fancy meeting you here."

"Yeah, I'm beginning to think I'm bad luck. That's the second dead body I've found in less than two weeks."

"Let's get you out of here." Leif motioned for one of the police officers to join us. "Officer Cho will take —"

I held up my hand. "Yeah, I know the drill. Station, coffee, statement. Hopefully, in that order or coffee first."

Leif smiled, then turned to Officer Cho. "Do me a favor, swing through the drive-through first and get Thea a coffee before you take her statement, would you?"

As I turned to leave Erik's apartment, I thought of

something. “Leif, can you check on a license plate number for me?” I scrawled out the string of numbers and letters the chameleon had told me the night before on a piece of paper and handed it to my brother.

“Where did you get this from?” Leif asked.

“Let’s just say it was an anonymous source.”

“Huh . . .” Leif examined the piece of paper. “Is this related to the murder?”

“You mean murders? There’s been two now.”

Leif frowned. “Yeah. My job just got a whole lot more complicated.”

CHAPTER 14
GLEEPS!

Despite drinking several cups of coffee at the police station while giving my statement, I still ordered another coffee while waiting for my grandmother and Hudson to join me for lunch at Swede's.

"It feels like we just did this." Hudson waited, standing by as my grandmother got situated in a chair by the window, then he sat down opposite me.

"What do you mean?" I asked.

"Have a Three Investigators meeting at Swede's," Hudson said.

"This time there's nothing to investigate," I said. "It's pretty cut and dry. Simon came over to Erik's apartment last night on some sort of pretext. Then, when Erik turned his back, he clobbered him over the head with a bowling ball."

"Shush, lower your voice," my grandmother said. "Do you want the whole town to hear?"

"You're too late. Norma already knows," I said wryly. "While I was waiting for a table, Swede came out of the kitchen to ask me about the pool."

"Swede wants to build a pool?" Grandma shook her head. "It's winter. Who thinks about swimming pools when the windchill is twenty below?"

"No, not a swimming pool," I said. "A betting pool. The odds are seventy to one that I'm going to find one more dead body by the end of the month."

My grandmother tsk-tsked. "It's not polite to gamble on murder."

"Only if you don't win," Norma said as she handed us menus.

"You have an odd definition of politeness," Grandma murmured as she looked at the menu.

"What's the special?" I asked Norma.

"Nacho dogs. Comes with a side of coleslaw."

"What's a nacho dog?" Hudson asked.

"Just what I said." Norma's eyes flicked upward. "A hot dog with nacho toppings. Cheese sauce, diced onion, jalapenos, salsa, sour cream, and green onions."

"Sounds good to me," Hudson said. "Extra jalapenos, please."

"Make that two," my grandmother said. "But instead of extra jalapenos, can I have extra sour cream?"

Norma nodded, then looked at me. "Well, hon?"

I hesitated, thinking about how much the chameleon liked hot dogs. He was kind of a snob about it, though, insisting that they had to come from the Big Apple. But I'm sure if he tried one of Swede's nacho dogs, he'd quickly realize his precious New York dogs were no match.

"Earth to Thea." Norma tapped her pen against her order pad. "I don't have all day."

"Sorry. I'll take the special as well." As I handed the menu back to Norma, I added, "Actually, make that two nacho dogs. One to go, please."

"Are you dropping a nacho dog off at the station for your brother? That's sweet of you," my grandmother said.

I gave my grandmother a knowing look. "It's actually for a certain friend of mine. The one I told you about before. You know with the . . . um . . . colorful skin."

Grandma did a double take. "Oh, right."

After Norma deposited our drinks on the table, Hudson pointed at the entrance. "Hey, isn't that Janelle and Ivy over there?"

"It sure is." My grandmother waved at the other women. "Want to join us?"

"Such a gentleman." Janelle smiled warmly at Hudson as he pulled an extra chair from a neighboring table. "When I heard they had nacho dogs today, I told Ivy we had to come here for lunch."

"No school today?" Hudson asked Ivy.

"I took the afternoon off." Ivy looked down at the table, avoiding eye contact with Hudson. "I have a meeting with my lawyer after lunch."

There was an uncomfortable silence at the table. Norma bustled over to ask Janelle and Ivy what they wanted to eat. After jotting down their two orders of nacho dogs on her pad, the waitress leaned in, her eyes gleaming, eager to share the latest gossip. "Did you hear about Simon? The police are at the bowling alley right now asking him all sorts of questions about a certain bowling ball," she said, giving us a knowing look.

"How do you find this stuff out?" I asked. "Do you have cameras all over town?"

Norma grinned. "That's not a bad idea. I'll have to look into that."

"Why would they be asking Simon about a bowling ball?" Janelle asked.

"Well, it's gotta be about Erik's murder, doesn't it?" Norma noted. "Well, unless the police are thinking about starting their own bowling league."

Ivy's eyes shot up. "Erik is dead?"

"Yep, rest his soul," Norma said. "He was a nice guy. Used to come in here and order the grilled cheese."

"Is this related to Thornton's murder?" Ivy asked.

"Did Simon kill Thornton and Erik? Seems likely."

Norma pointed at me. "But you should really ask the expert."

I put a hand to my chest. "What? Me? I'm not an expert."

"You found Thornton and Erik, didn't you? That pretty much makes you an expert on dead bodies, as far as I'm concerned."

"I don't know. The coroner might have some sort of claim to expertise in those matters," Hudson said wryly.

Norma cocked her head to one side. "Hey, weren't you there when Thea found Thornton's body?"

"Um, yeah," Hudson said reluctantly.

"Guess that makes you an expert, too." Norma waved her pad at us. "Gotta run and put these orders in."

Janelle shook her head as she looked at her daughter. "If they think Simon killed Thornton and Erik, then that means . . ."

Ivy pressed her lips together. "That means what I went through was for nothing."

"You mean with the police?" I asked.

"Yes, because of them, my daughter . . ." Ivy's voice choked up. After dabbing her eyes with her napkin, she continued, "This isn't how I wanted her to find out about her father."

"Honey, the truth needed to come out sooner or later," Janelle said. "Keeping that secret locked away has been twisting you in knots for years. Maybe what happened was a blessing in disguise."

Ivy slammed her fist on the table. "A blessing? Thornton threatening to blab my private business around town was a blessing?"

"Honey, everyone is staring at you," Janelle said to her daughter.

Ivy's expression hardened. "Let them stare. It's better than them whispering behind my back."

"Maybe we should go someplace else," Janelle suggested.

Ivy sighed. "We already ordered, Mom."

"Okay, if you're sure," Janelle said. "But let's at least change the topic."

"No," Ivy said firmly. "Let's talk about it. People are going to ask questions, anyway. I might as well get used to discussing it."

My grandmother gave Ivy a gentle smile. "Whatever it is, just know that we're here to support you, not judge you."

Ivy leaned forward and squeezed my grandmother's hand. "Thanks, Rose. That means a lot to me." Then she took a deep breath as she looked at Hudson and me. "Okay, here it goes. Tiana's dad and I weren't married."

When she didn't elaborate, I furrowed my brow. "That's it?"

Hudson chimed in, "Lots of people who aren't married have kids."

"Yes, but I lied about it," Ivy said. "It was one tiny

little lie that snowballed until it got a life of its own. I couldn't backtrack, no matter how much I wanted to."

Janelle cleared her throat. "Well, that's not exactly true. You could have told the truth at any time. You were just embarrassed."

"Of course I was embarrassed, Mom. Do you have any idea what it's like to admit that you've done something wrong?"

"Yes, I do," Janelle said. "Here's the thing, though. I believe in forgiveness. It doesn't change the past, but it does affect the future. Acknowledging what you did wrong is going to change your future for the better. I know you can't see that now, but you will."

Ivy looked out the window. She muttered, her voice faint, "I hope you're right."

"For what it's worth, I don't think having a kid out of wedlock is wrong," Hudson said.

"Plenty of people do. They judge you for it," Ivy said. "It certainly wasn't how I wanted it to happen. Anthony and I had been together for three years. Right before his last deployment, he proposed. We were going to get married when he got back. I didn't have any idea I was pregnant when he left."

Ivy looked down at the table for a few moments, wiping tears from her eyes. "Sorry, it's hard to talk about. Anthony was killed before I could tell him about the baby."

"You don't have to continue," my grandmother said.

"No, it's okay. I want to tell you what happened." Ivy nodded in Janelle's direction. "Thankfully, I had temporarily moved in with my mother when I found out I was expecting. It was such a scary time in my life. Alone and pregnant, then getting the news that Anthony would never be coming home."

"I'm so sorry," Hudson said to Ivy. "I know what it's like to experience that kind of loss."

Ivy gave Hudson a gentle smile. "I know you do."

Janelle hushed us as Norma walked up to the table.

"Don't mind me," the waitress said as she set our nacho dogs down. "Just pretend I'm not here."

When it became apparent she wasn't going to overhear any juicy gossip, Norma shrugged and went to clear a distant table.

Ivy toyed with the coleslaw on her plate, and then continued her story. "It all started with my first visit to the doctor. You know how they make you fill out a bunch of forms when you see a doctor for the first time? When I got to the section about marital status, I checked 'married.' It was crazy, I know. But in my mind, I felt like Anthony and I were married. I was carrying his baby. After that, the lie took on a life of its own. People would ask me about the baby's daddy and I'd tell them I was a widow. After a while, I started to believe it myself."

"Did you know she wasn't married?" my grandmother asked Janelle.

"No, not initially," Janelle said.

Ivy hung her head. “That’s the worst part of it. I even lied to my own mother. I told her Anthony and I had gotten married at the courthouse before he deployed.”

“The important thing is that you did tell me after Tiana was born,” Janelle said.

“Yeah, but I lied to you for months,” Ivy said. “And then you ended up lying on my behalf when your friends would ask about Anthony.”

“It’s okay, honey. What’s done is done,” Janelle said.

“How did Thornton find out about your past?” I asked.

“That’s where it gets complicated,” Ivy said. “I had never tried to collect survivor benefits from the Department of Defense when Anthony died. It’s not like I could have since we weren’t married. In fact, I completely distanced myself from all of Anthony’s military buddies and their wives and girlfriends. It was like I started a new life.”

“I can see why you did that,” Hudson said. “They would have reminded you of Anthony.”

“It worked to some extent,” Ivy said. “But a few months ago, I started thinking about Tiana, wondering if she would be eligible for anything since she was Anthony’s daughter. It was a long shot. I wasn’t sure if too much time had elapsed, but I had to try. You have no idea how many letters I drafted to the Department of Defense. I’d write one trying to explain my situation, but when I got to the part about not having been married to Anthony, I deleted it."

Ivy took a sip of her iced tea, then she leaned forward, anger flashing in her eyes. "About two months ago, I was at the library, waiting for our board meeting to start. I had my laptop open, working on yet another letter when one of the library assistants asked me to help with something. Stupidly, I left my laptop open and unlocked."

"Thornton saw the letter," I said.

Ivy nodded. "I didn't realize it at the time. But when I went back into the meeting room, Thornton was sitting in a chair next to mine, innocently looking at his phone."

My grandmother furrowed her brow. "I wonder why he didn't say anything then."

"He was biding his time. Waiting for the perfect opportunity," Ivy said.

"You said he saw the draft letter a couple of months ago, right?" When Ivy nodded, my grandmother said, "That would have been in December when Thornton's brother passed away. The poor man."

"Thornton's brother?" Janelle asked. "Yes, it was tragic that he died from cancer so young."

"Well, yes, him too. But I was talking about Thornton." My grandmother shook her head. "Reginald's death hit him hard. His grief turned into rage and he lashed out at everyone."

"He always lashed out at people," I pointed out.

"This was different," Grandma said. "He took it to a whole new level."

"The library was one of his prime targets," Ivy said.

"In a way, I think he blamed the library for his brother's death. Blamed me, really." My grandmother cleared her throat. "Reginald approached me about taking over my job when I retired. It surprised me, actually. Reginald had never been a big reader as far as I knew. I explained to Reginald that he needed a master's degree in library science in order to run a library. That's when Reginald realized that the job was more complicated than he had thought. He'd have to get his GED, then go to college."

Grandma took a sip of coffee, then continued. "Reginald was sweet about it. He thanked me for taking the time to talk to him. Even gave me a painting for the library." She looked at Hudson. "Come to think of it, we never did get around to finding a permanent place to hang it. It's still in storage. Something to add to your to do list."

"I didn't realize Reginald didn't have a high school diploma," I said.

"He had a hard time in school. I talked with one of his old teachers about it once. She tried to help him, but with one failing grade after another, Reginald dropped out." My grandmother sighed. "Anyway, when Reginald and I discussed this, he had already been diagnosed with cancer. Thornton felt like I had taken away one of his brother's last chances at happiness."

"But that's ridiculous," I said. "Reginald bounced around between jobs his whole adult life. He didn't really want to be a library director. He just wanted to try something new."

"When you're scared that you're going to lose someone close to you, you don't think straight," my grandmother said gently.

"You're almost making me feel sorry for the man. Almost." Ivy pressed her lips together. "I still remember how shocked I was that night at the reception when he whispered in my ear, 'I know you lied about being married.' I tried to pull away from him, but then he said, 'It'd be a shame if Tiana found out what a liar you are.'"

"That bastard," I said.

"I completely agree," Ivy said. The man was a vile piece of work. Did I think the world would be better off without him? Sure. The thought had crossed my mind, but I didn't kill him."

"They know that honey," Janelle said. "Simon did it."

"So, what did happen on the reception night?" I asked.

"I stayed at the reception for a while, but people kept asking me why I resigned as president of the board. So, I headed home. Mom told me she had a headache and was going to lie down. I sat on the couch and tried to watch a show, but all I could think about was Thornton's threat. What if he told Tiana before I had a chance to do it properly? Can you imagine the look in my little girl's eyes if she found out from someone else that I had been lying to her about her dad? I knew I had to do something to stop Thornton."

"I still wish you had told me before you left the house," Janelle said.

"I didn't realize you had taken a migraine pill," Ivy said as she picked jalapenos off her hot dog. "I would have never left if I knew that."

"You went to the ATM and withdrew money, right?" I asked.

My grandmother nudged me. "Leif told you that off the record."

"Well, it was off the record until you mentioned Leif's name," I pointed out.

"We probably need a Three Investigators' manual," Hudson joked.

Janelle chuckled. "Is that what the three of you are? The Three Investigators? Which one of you is Pete? He was my favorite character. I loved how he always said, 'Gleeps!'"

My grandmother smiled. "'Gleeps' would make a much better curse word than some of the other expressions folks use nowadays."

"Isn't that the truth," Janelle said. "Why do they always have to rely on the same four-letter words to express themselves?" Janelle asked.

Ivy smiled fondly at her mother. "You're right. 'Gleeps' is much better. It has six letters."

Janelle batted playfully at her daughter, then pointed at her plate. "You haven't had a single bite of your hot dog. You need to eat."

"I'm not really hungry." She looked at Hudson's empty plate. "You want it?"

"Sure," he said. "Don't mind if I do."

While Hudson ate the second hot dog, Ivy told us the rest of her story.

"I got as much money as I could out of the ATM. Then I sat there in my car looking at all that cash. That's when I realized it wouldn't stop Thornton. His twisted mind game wasn't about money. He had plenty of money. No, Thornton got pleasure by bending people to his will. He'd find out what their weakness was, the secrets they were hiding, or what insecurities plagued them—then he'd use that information to feed his incessant need to prove he was better than everyone else."

"He really was an awful man," I said.

Hudson looked at Ivy. "So, you didn't arrange to meet him that night?"

"No, I drove to that all-night diner in Williston instead. Sat there for hours staring into my coffee cup."

"Do you mean Frank's?" Hudson asked. "Isn't that the same place Erik originally said he was?"

Ivy looked at Hudson with surprise. "Really?"

"Leif knows all this," Janelle said to my grandmother and me. "Ivy's alibi checked out. They were pretty thorough this time."

"What do you mean?" I asked.

"During their initial investigation, Ivy told them she was at home with me that night streaming shows." Janelle took a sip of her iced tea, then said, "Which was true. When Ivy came home, we had a glass of wine and turned the TV on. When the police asked me about it, that's what I said. It never occurred to me that she might have left after I went to bed."

"It's okay, Mom," Ivy said. "You weren't trying to cover anything up. I'm the one who did that."

I looked down at my coffee cup, thinking about how both Erik and Ivy had originally lied about their alibis. Erik had said he was at Frank's and Ivy said she had been at home. How different things might have been if they had both told the truth from the beginning.

"What did your lawyer say?" my grandmother asked, interrupting my thoughts. "Are there going to be any repercussions?"

Ivy took a deep breath. "I hope not, but that's why we're meeting today."

The two women lingered at the table for a few more minutes, sipping on iced tea and chatting with Hudson about his plans for the library. Despite the attempt at casual conversation, the atmosphere was heavy. Two people had lost their lives, and Ivy's future was in jeopardy. Now according to my brother's latest text, there wasn't enough evidence to charge Simon. Knowing a murderer was still walking around town free as a bird made my stomach twist in knots. I was going to have to do whatever it took to help my brother put Simon behind bars.

* * *

"I still think I look like a clown in these," Hudson grumbled later that night as he laced up his bowling shoe rentals.

"Let me see," I said as Hudson stood. "I have bad news for you, Hudson. You couldn't pass as a clown. Everything about you screams librarian."

Hudson looked at his reflection in the plate glass window and sighed. "It's the cardigan, isn't it?"

"The cardigan is cute, in a Mr. Rogers sort of way," I said.

He arched an eyebrow. "Cute? Mr. Rogers? Not exactly the look I was going for."

"What were you going for?"

Hudson fiddled with the buttons on his sweater. "I'm not sure. Professionally competent in an understated way, I guess."

"No reason why you can't be professionally competent and cute at the same time." I tugged at Hudson's elbow. "Come on, enough fashion talk. We have stickers to hand out."

Hudson pulled a plastic bag out of the pocket of his cardigan. As he examined the stickers he had made to pass out at the bowling alley, he said, "I know these are a pretext for why we want to speak with Simon. But even if we don't get anywhere with him, at least we can remind folks that the library has a lot to offer."

"Speaking of Simon, do you see him anywhere?" I asked.

"Um . . . there he is." Hudson pointed to the other side of the building. "It looks like he's helping a couple with the ball return machine."

"Okay, let's go talk to him."

Hudson grabbed my arm and pulled me back. "Do you think this is a good idea? Simon doesn't look like someone you want to get on the wrong side of. Maybe we should leave the investigating to your brother."

I shook my head. "Leif's at a dead end with the investigation. He hasn't been able to find anything concrete that ties Simon to the murder."

Hudson wrinkled his brow. "And you think we'll be able to?"

"Can't hurt to try." I smiled at Hudson. "Take a deep breath. You can do this. Keep in mind you're a professionally competent librarian."

Hudson nudged me. "Cute, too. Remember?"

"Noted. Now quit stalling. Let's go have a little chat with Simon."

As we walked across the bowling alley, Hudson said, "I kind of wish your grandmother was with us."

"It's bingo night." I grinned. "Nothing gets in the way of bingo night. Trust me."

"When I was at his place for dinner, Pastor Rob mentioned bingo," Hudson said. "He said it would be a good way for me to get to know people in town."

"We should go sometime," I said. "It's fun."

Hudson looked down at his feet. "Do you have to wear silly shoes?"

I shrugged. "Depends on if it's costume night."

"I hate dressing up," Hudson wrinkled his nose.

"Better not let my grandmother hear that. She's famous in Why for her annual Halloween party," I said.

Hudson chuckled. "I can't imagine your grandfather wearing a costume."

"True. The two of you can be the spoilsports at this year's party."

"October feels like a long way off."

"It'll be here before you know it," I said as we neared Simon.

Simon was cursing under his breath as he tinkered with the machine. Clearly, he wasn't going to be receptive if we interrupted him now. While we waited to speak to him, I smiled at the couple standing nearby. The guy was busy instructing his date on how to avoid gutter balls. She looked skeptical, fussing with her hair while he talked.

"It's all in the wrist," he said, demonstrating how to hold the ball. "If your wrist isn't straight when you release the ball, it will end up in the gutter. Here, you try."

The woman groaned as she took the ball from him. "Geez, it's heavy."

"That's because it's mine," he said. "Yours is jammed in the machine."

As the woman tried to position the ball in her hands, she said, "My fingers keep slipping in the holes."

"Don't worry, your ball is a ladies' one. The holes will be smaller. Besides, it's pink, your favorite color." When she almost dropped the ball on his feet, he snatched it from her. "Maybe we should have gone to the movies instead?"

She bit her lower lip. "Could we?"

Simon looked up in frustration when the couple grabbed their coats and scurried off. "They break the darn thing, and then they take off. Nice," he said loudly. When he noticed me standing nearby, he frowned. "What are you doing here? I already told your brother everything I know."

Hudson took a step forward and held up the stickers. "We're here on behalf of the library. I wondered if we could hand these out."

"Hmm." Simon considered this as he put his wrench back in his toolbox. "Are you trying to poach my customers?"

"Poach? Certainly not," Hudson said quickly. "We're not in competition."

Simon shook his head. "Of course we are. We're both entertainment providers."

"Well, I like to think that the library provides information as well as entertainment," Hudson said.

"Information," Simon scoffed. "See, that's why you're not making a profit."

"Um, the library is non-profit," I pointed out. "It provides community service, free of charge."

"You know, as much as I hated the guy, I think Thornton was on the right track with his review of the library," Simon said. "You guys need to make money for the town, not be a drain on the coffers."

I was proud of how Hudson retained his aura of professional competence in the face of Simon's attack on the library. Personally, I wanted to take Simon to task, but I restrained myself. Instead, I said in my most ingratiating tone of voice, "I heard about how poorly Thornton treated you."

"Sweetheart, you have no idea." Simon plopped down on the plastic bench. "I paid him a ton of money to manufacture my clothing line, and all I got were boxes of jackets that no one in their right mind would buy. I can't even give the things away."

"That was the yellow jacket you were wearing the night of Hudson's reception, right?" I asked. "The stitching on it was pretty bad."

Simon thumped the bench with his fist. "Exactly."

"You know, when Thornton was killed, he was wearing one of those jackets," I said.

Simon nodded. "Yep. Thornton brought it to the library with him. When I was getting ready to leave that night, I saw him in the foyer grabbing it from the coat rack. He put it on, stared me right in the eye, and told me the rest of my shipment was coming next week."

Hudson leaned forward. "Really?"

"No. It was just another one of his lies," Simon said. "Thornton had been telling me that same story for weeks."

"What did you say?" I asked.

"I told him my lawyer would be contacting him. Thornton just laughed." Simon scowled. "I wanted to punch him."

"I can see how that would be tempting. A lot of people in town wanted to punch him." I tilted my head to one side. "What happened after that? Did Thornton leave the library?"

"No, he said he needed to go get something."

"So, he went back inside?" I asked.

Simon's shoulders stiffened, and he shot me a look. "I knew it. You're here on behalf of your brother. I already told him all this."

I held up my hands, then said in a slightly flirtatious tone, "I'm sorry. It's just that you're so easy to talk to."

Simon gave Hudson a triumphant look, as if to say,

'I've got it and you don't.' Then he turned back to me, giving me a smile that was a cross between a leer and a maniacal grin.

Hudson adjusted his cardigan, then cleared his throat. "I heard some rumors about your wife and Thornton."

Simon bared his teeth. "I'd watch yourself. Repeating rumors can get you in trouble."

I briefly placed my hand on Simon's arm. "He knows Michelle would never be unfaithful to you. Besides, from what you told me, Thornton was going out with Ashley."

"He was sleeping with her. They weren't dating. Big difference." Simon grinned. "In fact, did you know he had to pay Ashley to have sex with him?"

"Really? I hadn't heard that," I noted.

Simon nodded. "Oh, yeah. He gave her a big chunk of money before the holidays."

Hudson frowned. "Did she tell you that?"

"You betcha. Get a couple of drinks in that gal, and she'll spill her guts."

"So, let me get this straight. Ashley told you Thornton paid her to sleep with him?"

"Well, not in so many words. But I did see the two of them coming out of a motel at the beginning of December. Right after that, she started flashing a lot of cash around town." Simon leaned forward. "Here's something your brother doesn't know. This isn't the first time Ashley slept with Thornton. They hooked up years ago."

I furrowed my brow. "What do you mean?"

"Sorry, my lips are sealed." Simon patted my leg, then got up and grabbed his tool bag. He pointed at the ball return machine. "Don't touch that, okay? I don't need you breaking it any more than it already is."

Simon started to walk away, then he spun back around and jabbed a finger in Hudson's direction. "No handing out stickers. You got it?"

After he left, Hudson and I looked at each other, saying in unison, "Gleeps!"

CHAPTER 15
CHAMELEONS VERSUS GECKOS

The next day, Hudson called and asked if I could help at the library. "I know you aren't scheduled to volunteer today, but Carol is out sick. We were already short-handed with my reference librarian being on vacation and now with Erik . . . um, no longer with us, I don't have anyone to cover the front desk this afternoon."

I was caught up on my work for the day, so I agreed to come in. "Why don't I bring a pizza with me? I bet you haven't had much time to eat."

It took a few minutes to agree on what toppings we should have, finally settling for sausage, onion, and black olives. When I got to the library, Hudson eyed the pizza box with great interest. "I'll put it in your office, then grab some plates," I told him.

Before I could head to the kitchen, a teenage girl stopped and asked me if I knew where she could find books on genetics. As I showed her where they were located, she told me about the research project she was doing for her advanced-placement biology class.

"I'm researching genetic links to autism," she explained. "Did you know scientists can pinpoint not only what chromosome a disease or condition is linked to, but also the specific gene?"

"I know there's forty-six chromosomes, but I don't have a clue how many genes there are," I said.

"Somewhere between twenty and twenty-five thousand," she said.

"Wow, that's a lot. How do they keep track of them all?"

She laughed. "I'm not sure. Their names are made up of numbers and letters. It'd be a lot easier if they called them 'Fred' or something like that.'"

After I helped the teen locate a couple of books that might assist with her research, I headed to the kitchen. As I was getting plates out of the cupboard, I recalled asking Leif to run a license plate check on the string of letters and numbers the chameleon had given me earlier in the week. Leif had come back already, telling me he hadn't come up with a hit.

Assuming the chameleon had likely sent me on a wild goose chase for fun, I'd put it out of my mind. Now, after talking with the teenage girl about genetic research, I wasn't so sure. I pulled my phone out of my pocket, copied the string of letters and numbers from the text exchange with Leif, and then did a search.

My eyes widened when I read the top result—variants of the gene KIAA0319 were associated with dyslexia. "He was right," I muttered to myself.

"Duh. Of course, I was right, lady." The chameleon was perched on top of the fridge, smirking at me. "Sure took you a long time to figure it out. Sherlock Holmes would run circles around you. You're more like a Miss Marple . . . a doddering old fool."

"Hey, first of all, Miss Marple is a sharp cookie. She's a natural problem solver and a good judge of human character," I snapped. "Second of all, I wouldn't want to be like Sherlock Holmes. The man's arrogant and unfeeling."

The chameleon peered at me. "Oh, are we playing this game again? Well, first of all, Miss Marple spent more time knitting than she did solving crimes. And second of all, Sherlock Holmes was a misunderstood genius."

I narrowed my eyes. "You know, you could stand to be more like the chameleon in those insurance commercials. He's sweet and charming."

"What? Did you seriously just compare me to a gecko? Are you out of your mind, lady?"

I grinned, enjoying seeing the little guy so flustered. "Chameleons, geckos. What's the difference?"

The chameleon glared at me, and then I felt something land on my cheek. "Hey, did you spit at me again?"

"Sorry, I thought I saw a fly," he said.

I got a paper towel and wiped my cheek off. "Seriously, after I brought you that nacho dog yesterday, this is how you repay me?"

"What nacho dog?"

"I left it in the fridge," I said.

"Did you leave a note on it? The cleaners eat anything that doesn't have a name on it."

"I don't know your name." I threw up my hands. "What was I supposed to do, write, 'Don't touch. This belongs to the obnoxious chameleon who lives in the library who only I can see,' on a sticky note?"

"Well, you could have asked me," he grumbled.

I sighed. "Fine, what's your name?"

"Edgar."

"Nice to meet you, Edgar." I held out my hand. After a beat, he placed his scaly hand in mine and I squeezed it lightly. Then I rushed over to the sink and scrubbed my hands.

"I'm not contagious," he said loudly.

"Need I remind you that you do eat flies," I said.

"That's only because the cleaners ate my nacho dog. Next time, put my name on it."

"You need to earn your nacho dogs," I said.

"I already have," he insisted. "I gave you the gene number and now you want more?"

"I'm the one who figured out that it's related to dyslexia. But I'm not sure what it has to do with the murders . . ." my voice trailed off as I put two and two together. "Oh, I get it now. And when you were talking about Miss Marple, you mentioned—"

Edgar cut me off. "Maybe you should call your brother and have him check on a couple of things. Then, when you're done with that, go get me a nacho dog."

***

Later that evening, Hudson was pacing back and forth in his office while I spoke with the supervisor at Clean Me Up. When I hung up, he looked at me anxiously. "Is it all set?"

"Yes. Don't worry. She's going to make sure Ashley is assigned to clean the library tonight."

"I still don't like it." Hudson ran his fingers through his hair. "I can't believe your brother would agree to this plan."

"He knows it's the only chance we have to get Ashley to confess. Without it, they won't be able to convict her. Although all the evidence points to her having killed Thornton and Erik, it's still all circumstantial. We need Ashley to reveal something concrete which could be used to definitively pin the murders on her." I glanced at my phone. "Hang on, it's my grandmother. I need to let her know what's going on."

After telling my grandmother Ashley was the killer, she suggested I activate the speakerphone so that we could convene a special meeting of the Three Investigators. "Can you both hear me?" she asked. After assuring her we could, she said, "Okay, tell me what the heck is going on. How did you figure out it was Ashley?"

"I can't take any credit," Hudson said. "It was all Thea. She put the pieces together—the ladies' bowling ball, the yarn, and genetics. When she came into my office this afternoon and explained it all to me, I was blown away."

"Thea's a clever girl," Grandma said.

I chewed on my bottom lip, not sure how to respond. As much as I hated to admit it, Edgar deserved a lot of the credit. The chameleon had pointed me in the right direction, whether it was through books I should look at, a string of mysterious numbers and letters, or even his mention of Miss Marple. But I certainly couldn't tell Hudson that a talking chameleon was living in his library, and the lizard had helped crack the case.

"Talk me through it, you two," my grandmother said. "Start with the bowling ball."

"When we were at the bowling alley last night, there was this guy trying to teach his girlfriend how to bowl," I said. "She was complaining his bowling ball was heavy and that her fingers were slipping out of the holes. He told her not to worry. Her ball was lighter and had smaller finger holes."

"Don't forget, he said hers was pink, too," Hudson said. "Just like the bowling ball that you saw in Erik's apartment."

"That's right," I said. "When I saw the *Fundamentals of Bowling* book in the library this afternoon again, I made the connection. The ball used to kill Erik was a ladies' ball. If Simon had killed Erik, he probably would have used a ball that his fingers could fit into."

"How did she get a hold of the bowling ball?" Grandma asked. "Simon had fired her. She didn't work at the bowling alley anymore."

"Leif looked into it," I said. "Apparently, Ashley went to the bowling alley the night of Erik's murder to pick up her final paycheck. It was probably easy enough to 'borrow' a bowling ball while she was there."

"So, that means it was premeditated," my grandmother said matter-of-factly.

"When Ashley was cleaning the library, we think she overheard a conversation Thea and I had with Erik," Hudson said. "That led Ashley to believe that Erik had seen her go into the storage room the night of Thornton's murder. She panicked at the thought of there being an eyewitness, so she killed Erik later that night."

"I still think a lawyer would make mincemeat of that argument," I said. "We don't have any proof that she heard what Erik said. And remember, if she had listened to the entire conversation she would know that Erik said he saw an elderly gentleman go into the men's room."

Hudson shook his head. "But if she only heard a snippet, that would have been enough to scare her."

"What exactly do you think Ashley overheard?" my grandmother asked.

"The night Thornton was killed, Erik had been in the hallway near the storage room getting a book for a patron," Hudson said. "When Thea and I were asking Erik if he had seen anyone walk toward the storage room that night—"

"This is the conversation you had with Erik the night he was killed, right?" my grandmother clarified.

"Correct," Hudson said. "Anyway, I said something to Erik like, 'Did you see anyone walk past you?'"

Grandma asked, "And what did Erik say?"

"Erik said that he had seen someone in the hallway that night," Hudson said.

"So, he did see Ashley," my grandmother said.

I chimed in. "No, Erik saw an elderly gentleman go to the restroom, but if Ashley didn't hear that part, then she might have assumed Erik saw her."

My grandmother thought about this for a moment. "I can see why that wouldn't hold up in court. You know Ashley was cleaning the library that night, but you don't have any proof she heard your conversation, let alone what part of it she heard."

"That's right," I said. "Which is why I need to get Ashley to confess to killing Thornton and Erik."

There was a long pause on the other end of the line, then my grandmother cleared her throat. "I don't like the idea. I don't like it one bit. Surely, there's some other evidence . . . hard evidence that can link Ashley to the murders. What about this yarn you mentioned?"

Hudson smiled at me. "That was something else Thea figured out."

This was another awkward moment. Did I give credit to the talking chameleon for helping me make the connection? Or did I tell a tiny fib?

I went with the fib. "A patron was checking out some Agatha Christie books, and I remembered how Miss Marple was always knitting."

"Ashley is a big knitter, too," my grandmother said. "She was at the knitting circle at the library the night of Hudson's reception."

"That's right," I said. "When I saw Ashley at the library that night, she told me how she takes her knitting tote bag with her everywhere she goes, even to work."

"Ashley even takes it with her when she murders people," Hudson said dryly.

"Are you saying Ashley left some yarn at the scene of the crime?" my grandmother asked.

"I started wondering about that this afternoon," I said. "So, I called Leif and asked him about it. He said that there had been a ball of yarn at Erik's apartment. The police didn't think anything about it at the time."

"Turns out it was the same yarn that Ashley's using in her current project," Hudson pointed out. "Aqua-colored angora wool."

"Yes, but again there's no proof that it was hers," I said. "And even if there was, Ashley could probably come up with some story about why it was in Erik's apartment."

"Anyway, how did she get into Erik's apartment that night?" my grandmother asked.

"It's all connected to Clean Me Up," I said. "They provide cleaning services for Erik's apartment building. Ashley worked there before, so she knew Erik was a resident. That night, after she finished cleaning the library, she went back to Clean Me Up to drop off the key."

"Before she went back to Clean Me Up, she stopped at the bowling alley to pick up her final paycheck," Hudson reminded us. "That's when she grabbed the bowling ball. I'm sure she was planning on framing Simon, but she didn't think it through and chose a ladies' ball instead of a men's."

"It's important to keep the timetable straight," my grandmother said with approval in her voice.

"Okay, Ashley got the bowling ball," I said. "Next she went to Clean Me Up. She gave her supervisor the key to the library. Then, knowing she needed to get the key to Erik's building, she distracted her supervisor by telling her that her car had a flat tire. When the supervisor went out to check, Ashley slipped behind the desk, and grabbed the key to Erik's building."

"How do you know all this?" Grandma asked.

"Leif," I said. "He spoke with the supervisor at Clean Me Up this afternoon. She told him about the flat tire incident—turns out she didn't have one."

"That's interesting," my grandmother said. "But how did Ashley return the key without her supervisor knowing?"

"The following night, Ashley told her supervisor that some guys were knocking over the trash cans by the side of the building. When the supervisor went outside, Ashley put the key to Erik's building back in its slot."

"Didn't the supervisor get suspicious when she checked the trash cans?" my grandmother asked.

"No, Ashley was smart," Hudson said. "She knocked them over herself before going inside the office the first time."

"Sounds like your brother has been busy," Grandma said.

"He has been. Everything came to a head this afternoon, and he's had to check a lot of things out," I said. "Finding out about the key helped a lot. It explains how Ashley got into the building. Once she was there, she must have knocked on Erik's door and sweet-talked him into letting her inside. She probably hid the bowling ball in a cleaning bucket. Then, once she was inside, she set her knitting tote bag down . . ."

When I paused to take a sip of coffee, Hudson continued relaying to my grandmother what we thought had happened that night. "Ashley didn't notice when her ball of yarn fell out. Then she came up with some pretext to get Erik to bend down and pick something up off the floor."

"And that's when she hit him over the head with the bowling ball," my grandmother said.

"She was probably wearing gloves. That's why there weren't any fingerprints on the bowling ball," Hudson said. "It wouldn't have seemed odd to Erik since she was a cleaner."

"Hmm. Makes you wonder what she used to clean her fingerprints off the marble bust she used to kill Thornton," my grandmother mused.

"Ashley had some knitted gloves in her tote bag. She showed them to me at the library that night," I explained. "But I'm sure they're long gone by now. My guess is that she burned them in her fireplace along with her shoes that she tracked in the blood."

"Okay, so that explains why and how Ashley killed Erik," my grandmother said. "But now you need to tell me your theory about Thornton. Why did she murder him?" Before we could share our thoughts, Grandma said, excitement in her voice, "Oh, wait a minute. Ashley thought she had killed Simon, not Thornton. From behind, the two guys looked the same."

"Sorry to burst your bubble," I said. "But Ashley knew exactly who she was killing. She wanted Thornton dead, and she made it happen."

"I guess that makes sense when you think about motive," my grandmother said. "Ashley was the only person we had on our list who might have wanted to kill either man. Simon treated her terribly at work, but Thornton dumped her. I think if you're going to murder someone, it's more likely because you're a jilted lover rather than a disgruntled employee."

"There's more to it than being a jilted lover," I said.

"That's where the genetics come in." Hudson leaned closer to the phone, and then said dramatically, "Thornton was Logan's father."

When my grandmother didn't respond, I asked, "Are you still there?"

"Sorry, I'm just processing what you said. How did you figure that out?"

"It was something Simon told us at the bowling alley last night," I said. "He mentioned that Thornton and Ashley had been lovers previously. Years ago, in fact. Well, that got me thinking. What if Thornton got Ashley pregnant, but then refused to acknowledge the child or take responsibility for him?"

Hudson chimed in. "We think Simon figured it out

as well. He really had it out for Ashley. I'd bet anything that he was the person who called in the anonymous tip telling the police to look into who Logan's father was."

"Why would Simon do that?" my grandmother asked.

Shuddering as I remembered how Simon had leered at me the previous night, I said, "He probably made advances towards Ashley, and she turned him down. He wanted to cause trouble for her with the police."

My grandmother made a tsking sound, then refocused the conversation. "So, Thornton was Logan's dad, and he never acknowledged it," my grandmother said. "I can see how that would make Ashley angry, maybe even angry enough to kill. But why wait until now?"

"Because he stopped giving her money," I said. "Remember how you told me Ashley had been flashing large amounts of cash around town back in December?"

"Yes, that's what one of the gals in my book club told me. Ashley was placing large bets at the casino," my grandmother said.

"When Thornton and Ashley hooked back up, he was helping her out financially," I said. "But when he broke it off with her, the money stopped, too."

"We can't be sure exactly what happened that night," Hudson said. "But Ashley must have followed

Thornton into the storage room and argued with him about money. Then when he turned his back, she clobbered him over the head with the marble bust."

"Uff da," my grandmother muttered.

"Uff da, indeed," I said.

We all sat in silence for a few moments, then my grandmother said, "So, when you mentioned genetics earlier, you were talking about Thornton being Logan's father, is that right?"

"Yes, but it's more than that," I said. "It has to do with dyslexia and that's what cinched it for me."

"How so?" Grandma asked.

"Erik told us Logan has dyslexia. That's why he had been tutoring him," I said. "It turns out dyslexia runs in families."

"But Thornton didn't have dyslexia," my grandmother said. "At least, not that I could tell."

"You're correct." I started to take a sip of my coffee, but frowned when I realized there wasn't any left. Pushing my cup away, I said, "By all accounts, Thornton didn't have any issues with reading and writing. But that didn't mean he still didn't carry the genetic predisposition for dyslexia, which he passed down to Logan."

"Hmm. That's a stretch," my grandmother said.

Hudson smiled. "I said the same thing until Thea pointed out that there was someone else in the family who showed all the indications of dyslexia—Reginald."

"Grandma, remember how you told me that one of Reginald's old teachers had said he struggled in school and ended up dropping out? They didn't formally diagnose dyslexia back when he was in school, but it makes you wonder, doesn't it?"

"That's a pretty impressive deduction on your part, Thea," my grandmother said. "You must have done a lot of research."

Hudson nudged me. "Tell her the name of that gene."

"KIAA0319. But I didn't figure that out on my own. I had a little help." I shifted in my chair, thinking about the chameleon. Then I looked at the clock on the wall. "Ashley is going to be here soon. I need to get ready."

After reassuring my grandmother that everything would be okay, I ended the call.

Hudson frowned. "I agree with your grandmother. This is a bad idea."

"Well, we don't have a better one," I said.

Hudson came around the desk and pulled me into his arms. "Be careful, okay."

I laid my head against his chest for a moment, then pulled away from his embrace. "Promise me one thing?"

"What's that?" Hudson asked.

"Can I have a sticker when this is all over with?"

Hudson laughed. "Sure. What do you want it to say?"

"'The Three Investigators,' of course."

* * *

While I was waiting in the kitchen for Ashley to arrive, I checked the monitor Leif had hidden behind the coffeemaker for the millionth time. He had assured me that as long as Ashley and I stayed in the kitchen, the police would be able to hear every word we said.

"Just be yourself, sis," Leif had said to me. "You got her to open up at her house. You can do it again."

"It was the wine that got her talking," I pointed out.

"That's why we put a couple of bottles in the fridge," Leif said. "Keep the wine and questions flowing. Remember, a drunken confession alone might not hold up in court, so try to get her to say something that we can use to prove she murdered Thornton and Erik. There has to be some sort of hard evidence we've overlooked. You can do this. I know it."

"You have a lot more faith in me than I do."

"I wouldn't have asked you to do this if I didn't think you could. Heck, I wouldn't have asked you if there was any other way to nail this woman." Leif squeezed my shoulders. "Now, remember what you say if you feel like you're in danger?"

I gulped. "Gleeps!"

Leif kissed my forehead, then told me there was a squad car nearby. "I'll be hidden in Hudson's office.

The minute we hear Ashley confess, we'll be right here."

After Leif left, I paced back and forth in the kitchen, fretting about the task ahead of me. The sound of someone walking down the hallway startled me. Poking my head out of the kitchen, I smiled brightly when I saw that it was Ashley.

She looked at me quizzically. "Hey, what are you doing here? I thought everyone was gone for the night."

"They are. I had to stay late to work on shelving books." I rocked back and forth on my feet, trying to summon up my courage to lure Ashley into my trap. "Why don't you take a break and come chat with me?"

Ashley frowned. "But I just got here."

"No one will know. It'll just be between us girls." I motioned for her to join me in the kitchen, opened the fridge, and pulled out a bottle of wine. "I've had a hard day. I could really use a friend."

Ashley eyed the wine. "What's wrong?"

"What isn't wrong?" I pulled glasses out of the cupboard and poured a generous serving of wine into each one. After placing them on the table, I patted one of the chairs. "Come on, sit down."

Ashley shrugged, then sat down on one of the plastic chairs. She grabbed one of the glasses and took a tentative sip. "Hmm, that's good. What are we drinking to?"

"Certainly not men," I said.

"Oh, I knew it. You're having boy trouble." Ashley chuckled, then took a swig of her wine. "It's that library director, isn't it?"

I cringed. My plan had been to get Ashley talking about Thornton, not to have her think I was having problems with my love life. Not that I have a love life, mind you, and definitely not one with Hudson.

"Um, yeah. I don't know what to do," I said. "He doesn't want anyone to know we're seeing each other."

"By 'seeing each other,' he means sleeping with you, right?" Ashley gave me a sympathetic look before draining her glass. "Men are all pigs. They want all the benefits of a relationship, but no actual relationship. Hand me that bottle, will you?"

Ashley continued to drink while ranting about what jerks men are. Occasionally, I took a few sips from my glass so that she thought she wasn't drinking alone. Though by the time she had drained the first bottle, I don't think she noticed or cared she was the only drunk one in the room.

As I got the second bottle out of the fridge, I stated, "Thornton was one of those jerks, wasn't he? I can't believe he got you pregnant, and then didn't want anything to do with you or Logan."

Ashley leaned across the table and gripped my hand. "Thornton was a jerk," she said, slurring her words.

"That's why you killed him, wasn't it? He had all that money, but he never lifted a finger to help you or to help his own son. You were desperate, weren't you? So, when he wanted to sleep with you again, you made sure he paid for the privilege. He was generous before the holidays, but then he got tired of you, and dumped you . . . again."

Ashley sat back in her chair with her eyes wide. I waited, not sure what she was going to do next. Was she going to admit what she had done? Should I offer her more wine? Would that get her talking? Or was she going to pass out?

Just when I was about to offer to fill her glass, Ashley started laughing so hard her eyes watered. She regained control of herself, then looked me directly in the eye. "Me and Thornton?" Then she started giggling. "Sure, Thornton wanted to sleep with me, but I was in love with his brother."

It was my turn to be surprised. "You and Reginald?"

A smile played across Ashley's lips as she toyed with her bracelet. "I met Reginald a couple of years after I graduated high school. No one approved of our relationship. My friends thought he was too old for me. My mom wanted me to date a guy with a decent job, not go out with a starving artist. And of course, Thornton thought I wasn't good enough for his brother."

Ashley's eyes narrowed. "My friends and my mother would have come around eventually, but Thornton was relentless, constantly telling his brother to dump me."

"So, the two of you broke up?"

"No, we kept seeing each other secretly." Ashley looked off into the distance while she drank some more wine. "When I got pregnant, Thornton hit the roof. He told me I was going to ruin his brother's life. He wanted me to get rid of the baby, but I refused."

"What happened then?"

"The lawyers got involved. I signed some papers saying that I'd never reveal who Logan's father was and, in exchange, Thornton gave me a big check."

"But what about Reginald? Didn't he have a say in all this?"

"Thornton bullied him into submission." Ashley snorted. "That's when I knew I'd be better off on my own. I moved out-of-state to be with my parents and raised Logan on my own."

I furrowed my brow. "Why did you end up moving back to North Dakota?"

"When Logan got older, he started asking me about his father. I knew I couldn't tell Logan who his dad was—the lawyers had made sure of that. But I thought if we moved back to North Dakota, maybe I could figure out some sort of way to involve Reginald in Logan's life."

"Did that happen?" I asked.

"No, not until the very end," Ashley said. "By the time we moved back here, Reginald had moved on with his life. Thornton had brainwashed him so thoroughly that he didn't want anything to do with Logan. But when Reginald was diagnosed with terminal cancer, that changed everything."

"I can see that. Knowing you don't have long on this planet would make you reassess everything."

"Reginald reached out to Logan," Ashley said. "They spent a lot of time together, talking about their shared interests—art, hunting, and football."

"Logan inherited his artistic abilities from his father," I said. Then I did a double take. "Did you say hunting?"

"Yes, they both loved pheasant hunting."

"Did Reginald give Logan a hunting knife, by any chance?"

"Yes, it was the last thing he gave him. Logan carries it around with him everywhere as a reminder of his father." Ashley frowned. "How did you know about it? I told him not to show it to anyone. The last thing we needed was for people to ask questions about where he got it."

"He had it at the library." Remembering how flustered Logan had been when I caught him with the knife, I said, "Don't worry. I think he was pretty cautious about keeping it hidden from folks."

Ashley nodded. "Reginald also gave Logan a painting, but I told Logan that he had to get rid of it.

The painting was too big to hide."

"Oh, that explains it," I murmured to myself, remembering the painting I had seen in Erik's apartment. Logan had probably given it to Erik.

Ashley got up from the table. "I need to use the ladies' room."

"No, you can't. Not until you tell me . . ." my voice trailed off, unsure of how to get Ashley to confess. She had told me a lot so far, but she hadn't admitted to murder yet.

"Tell you what?" Ashley grabbed the back of the chair to steady herself. "I gotta get back to work."

I gulped, then blurted out. "Tell me how you killed Thornton."

Ashley cocked her head to one side, then slumped back down in her chair. After letting out a loud belch, she said, "Sure. Why not?"

Ashley's explanation matched what we thought had happened. She followed Thornton into the storage room, argued with him about money, and then hit him over the head with the marble bust.

I leaned forward. "What did you do about the blood? There must have been some on your hands, and your fingerprints must have been on the bust."

"I used my gloves to wipe off the bust and my hands." Ashley groaned. "My beautiful angora gloves . . . ruined, all because of that man. I had to burn them, you know. There was blood all over them. And on that stupid painting, too."

I furrowed my brow. "What painting?"

Ashley poured more wine in her glass and gulped it down. "Reginald's painting. It was hanging in the storage room. I stumbled and caught myself against it."

My thoughts flashed back to Logan's room. He had a stack of paintings leaning against the wall. I remembered noticing one with large yellow dots and dark splotches on one edge. It was modern in style, not like the florals that Logan painted. When I asked Ashley about it, she shook her head.

"I tried to burn it, but when Logan saw what I was doing, he snatched it away. He said he wanted it as a memento of his father." Ashley frowned. "He didn't realize that the reddish brown marks on the side were blood. I didn't have the heart to tell him."

I leaned back in my chair. This was the hard evidence that the police needed. The blood on the painting could be linked back to Thornton. Then I ran my fingers through my hair. How could I have been so stupid? Reginald gave that painting to my grandmother. She hung it up in the storage room temporarily while she figured out where to put it in the library. If I had realized that's what had been missing from the storage room earlier, could Erik's death have been prevented?

"Tell me about Erik," I said through gritted teeth.

"Why did you kill him?"

"Cause he was going to blab to the police." Ashley waved a hand in the air dismissively, as though murdering someone was a casual affair. "I heard what he said to you that night. He saw me go down the hallway to the storage room. Of course, I had to eliminate him. It was easy, really."

Easy? Killing someone was easy? I wanted to lunge across the table at the woman, but restrained myself. Ashley didn't notice how upset I was. She kept drinking more wine and talking me through the gory details of how she murdered Erik. It all lined up with what we had thought happened—getting the key from Clean Me Up, 'borrowing' the pink bowling ball, tricking Erik into letting her into his apartment . . . then killing him.

"You were supposed to think that Simon did it," Ashley said.

"Shouldn't have used a pink ladies' bowling ball," I said dryly. Then I furrowed my brow. "You wanted to pin Thornton's murder on Simon as well, didn't you? That's why you freaked out when Hudson and I talked to you at the bowling alley. I honestly believed you were worried that Simon was going to come after you and Logan."

Ashley belched, then gave me a huge grin. "Pretty good performance, wasn't it? I always wanted to be an actress."

I saw Leif out of the corner of my eye, standing in the entrance to the kitchen, his gun drawn. I held up my hand, hoping he'd hold off arresting Ashley. There was still more that I wanted to know.

"Simon saw you and Thornton coming out of a motel. If you weren't sleeping with him, what was that about?" I asked.

"After Reginald died, I told Thornton that unless he paid me more money, I was going to tell everyone that his brother was Logan's father. I didn't care what papers I had signed." Ashley slid further down in her chair. "Thornton agreed, but he didn't want me to come to his house to get it. So we arranged to meet at that motel."

Satisfied that I had the final puzzle piece, I nodded at my brother.

After Leif read Ashley her rights and handcuffed her, I remembered there was something else I needed to know.

"Before you take Ashley away, I have one final question," I said.

"Go on," my brother said.

Ashley looked at me, her eyes bleary. "What?"

"Do you put dill in your knoephla soup?"

CHAPTER 16
ONE-WORD ANSWERS

A couple of nights later, my family made plans to gather at the Prairie Dog Lodge for dinner. Naturally, we invited Hudson to join us. My grandmother pointed out when we were getting ready to leave that Hudson had become an important part of our lives in the short amount of time he had been in North Dakota.

"Yeah, it's been a pretty intense couple of weeks," I noted as I put my coat on. "You really get to know someone well when you're thrust into the middle of a murder investigation together. It's kind of like he's family now."

My grandmother gave me a sly grin. "Maybe he'll join the family officially one of these days."

"What's that supposed to mean?" I asked.

"Nothing," Grandma said innocently. "It's just that I've seen how you look at him."

"Let's get something straight." I put my hands on my hips. "I don't *look* at Hudson in any special sort of way. I look at him in the same way I'm looking at you now."

"You mean with daggers?" Grandma chuckled. "Grab your purse, dear. Your grandfather is waiting in the car."

I gave my grandmother the silent treatment during the short drive across the road to pick up Hudson. When Hudson slipped into the back seat next to me, I muttered hello, then went back to staring out the window.

"What's wrong?" Hudson asked.

"Nothing," Then, realizing it wasn't Hudson's fault that my grandmother was trying to play matchmaker, I said, "I was thinking about Logan and how tough it's going to be for him with his mom in jail."

"Well, he won't be completely alone," Hudson said.

"What do you mean? His father is dead and his grandparents don't live in the area." I spread out my hands. "He's got no one. Well, except for his cat, Henry."

Hudson grinned. "What if I told you he had a sister?"

My grandmother twisted her head to look back at us. "A sister?"

Hudson grinned. “Yep, and you’ll never guess who it is.”

“Seatrina,” Grandpa said quietly from the driver’s seat.

I burst out laughing. The whole idea of my grandfather knowing who *any* celebrity was, let alone Seatrina, was comical. “Have you been watching the entertainment news instead of the sports channel?”

“No.”

“It’s your grandfather’s idea of a joke,” Grandma said to me. “He must have heard someone talking about her.”

Grandpa switched lanes, then uttered another succinct response. “Nope.”

“Just ignore him,” my grandmother said. “Go ahead, Hudson, tell us what you know about Logan having a sister.”

Before Hudson could respond, my grandfather said, “Funny eyes.”

“Who has funny eyes?” I asked.

“Seatrina,” Grandpa said simply.

I thought back to when I first saw Seatrina at the airport. Her eyes had been the same unnatural fluorescent green color as her beehive hairdo, clearly the work of contacts. Grandpa was right. They were funny eyes, but then something occurred to me.

“What was funny about her eyes?” I asked my grandfather.

“One blue, and one another color.”

I slapped my leg. "Oh, my gosh. Seatrina and Ceely are the same person."

"I'm afraid you've lost me," Grandma said. "Who is Ceely?"

"A woman I met at the cemetery. She had unusual eyes, just like Logan," I said. "I can't believe I didn't put two and two together until now. That explains why she was visiting Reginald's grave. He was her father, too."

"Reginald had another child?" my grandmother asked.

"I think so. When I was talking to Ceely—or Seatrina, as her fans know her—she told me she had gotten to know Reginald a few months before he passed away. I'll bet you anything that Thornton paid off her mother, just like he did with Ashley. That's why she didn't have any contact with Reginald until he reached out to her when he was diagnosed with terminal cancer."

Everyone was silent for a few moments, absorbing the fact that Seatrina and Logan were both Reginald's children. Well, everyone except my grandfather. He was probably thinking about baseball.

"Thor, I'm still confused. When did you meet Seatrina?" my grandmother asked.

"At the house."

"Our house?"

"Uh-huh."

"He's not big on details, is he?" Hudson whispered to me.

My grandfather looked at Hudson in the rearview mirror. "I can hear you, son."

"Just tell us what happened," my grandmother said, clearly exasperated.

Grandpa turned into the parking lot at the lodge. "She came to the house looking for Thea."

When he didn't elaborate, my grandmother said, "I'm sure there's more to the story than that."

"She wanted to give back a scarf. Then she had some trouble with her contacts. She took them out, and I saw her eye colors. Same funny eyes as Logan."

"Why didn't you say anything?" I asked.

Grandpa placed the car in park and then shrugged. "No one asked."

"You've lost me," Hudson said. "What's this about a scarf?"

"Ceely . . . I mean, Seatrina was freezing when she was at the cemetery, so I loaned her my scarf. She drove away before I could get it back." I looked at my grandmother. "It was the one Freya made for me."

"That was nice of her to track you down," my grandmother said. "But where's the scarf now?"

"Hall closet," Grandpa said.

I sighed. "I wish you had told me it was there."

"Left a note."

"Huh? You did?" Then I grinned. "Oh, the piece of paper on my bed that said 'closet.' I wondered what that was about."

Grandpa opened the car door. "Throat's dry. Too much talking."

"We'll get you a beer in a minute, Thor. Close that door. It's cold outside." She turned to Hudson. "You started to say something about Logan's sister. What was it?"

"Pretty much that Seatrina is Logan's sister." Hudson shrugged. "Feels a bit anticlimactic now."

"How did you find out?" I asked.

"Seatrina and Logan came to see me this afternoon to discuss a special event they want to hold at the library. That's when they told me they're related."

Grandma furrowed her brow. "What kind of event?"

Hudson gave her a mysterious smile. "I think I'm going to let it be a surprise."

* * *

A few weeks later, I was circling a parking lot again. When this last happened to me, I was late picking up Hudson since I couldn't find a spot at the airport. At the time, I was utterly clueless that the reason the airport parking lot was jam-packed was because of Seatrina. This time, I knew exactly why there wasn't a spot to be had at the library. Turns out it was the same reason—Seatrina.

When word got out that Seatrina was going to

make a special appearance at the library, it quickly became clear that more people were going to want to attend than there was space for. A lottery system was set up for tickets. Since you had to be a current patron to enter the drawing, folks from far and wide, who hadn't stepped foot in the building in years, rushed in to register for library cards. After they signed up, some of them had even lingered, looking at books, asking questions about programs, signing up for online systems, and generally rediscovering a library was more than just a building—it was the heart of the community.

Prior to the event, Hudson had called me, letting me know that I didn't need to enter the lottery since he had a ticket for me. When I picked it up, I teased him about it. "Is this because I volunteer regularly at the library or because you like me?"

My face had grown warm the minute the words left my mouth. I sounded like a high school girl, wondering if a boy liked her and being awkwardly flirtatious about it. This was all my grandmother's fault, suggesting that Hudson and I might get together one day.

Fortunately, Hudson appeared oblivious to any possible romantic connotations to my question. "All the library volunteers got tickets," he said with a neutral expression on his face. "And of course I like you. Your family has been so good to me. I'm lucky to have you as my pal."

Relief washed over me. Hudson didn't think I was flirting with him. We were pals. Other feelings bubbled up inside of me. However, I pushed them down, firmly telling myself that being friends with Hudson was all I wanted. End of story.

Realizing that I needed to focus on finding a parking spot rather than mentally rehashing that incident with Hudson, I circled the lot one more time. When I didn't have any luck, I drove over to the bowling alley next door.

After locking my car, I turned to walk across the patch of frosty grass that separated the bowling alley and library.

"Hey, this lot is for bowling alley customers only," a man shouted behind me.

I turned and saw Simon wearing that same ugly jacket he had been wearing the night Thornton had been killed. When he got closer, I saw that it was actually a different jacket. It was still the same fluorescent shade of yellow, but it didn't have loose threads hanging from it, the zipper looked like it had been sewn on properly, and 'Bowling' wasn't misspelled.

"New jacket?" I asked.

"Uh-huh. It just came in from the manufacturer." Simon grinned as he modeled it for me. "Do you like it?"

"It's . . . um . . . eye-catching."

"I know, right?" Simon leaned forward and said in

a conspiratorial tone, "Turns out I didn't need Thornton after all. Someone contacted me on behalf of this investment company. They said that they were impressed with my designs and offered to bankroll the production of my new line of clothing. No strings attached. All I had to do was pay a small deposit as a show of good faith."

"Huh. Isn't that something?" I cocked my head to one side. "What's the name of the company?"

"I.M. Stultum." When I chuckled, Simon said, "I know. It's a funny name. They're a foreign outfit. I checked them out online. They're totally legit."

It took all my self-control to keep from breaking out in laughter. I was pretty sure that Simon didn't know the word 'stultum' meant 'foolish' in Latin. If he did, he might have figured out that the company name was a joke, meaning 'I am foolish.'

I started to tell Simon that he had fallen for a scam. Instead, he interrupted, telling me that since he was in such a good mood, I could go ahead and park at the bowling alley.

"Thanks. I'll catch up with you after the event," I told him. I just hoped that he didn't lose any more money between now and then.

When I finally walked into the library, my grandmother gave me a look that clearly said, 'Late again?'

Grandma motioned for me to join her, handing me a program when I sat down. I was grateful that she had saved me a seat. The place was standing room only despite the rows of folding chairs that had been set up. "They haven't started yet?" I asked my grandmother.

"Soon. You got here in the nick of time." My grandmother nodded at the stage. "Do you think Hudson looks nervous?"

"I would be. It's not every day you introduce a world-famous celebrity," I said. "She's really down-to-earth, though. I'm sure she'll put Hudson at ease."

"Have you met her?" a woman on my other side asked.

I turned, smiling when I saw it was Janelle. "Yes, a few weeks ago at the cemetery."

"What was she doing there?" Janelle asked.

"I think we're about to find out," I said. "I don't see Ivy or Tiana. Are they here?"

Janelle pointed up toward the front of the room where several kids were sitting on the floor. "Tiana is up there with her friends."

"And Ivy?"

"She's at home." Janelle frowned. "I keep telling her people will understand why she lied about being married, but she's too embarrassed to show her face outside of school."

"That's a shame." I squeezed Janelle's hand. "Please tell her we're on her side. The community needs people like Ivy."

"Thanks, sweetheart, I will."

"Shush, they're starting," my grandmother whispered to us.

Hudson tapped the microphone on the podium. "Can everyone hear me?"

"Yes," a few people called out. "We can hear you." One person shouted, "Bring out Seatrina!" Other folks chimed in, chanting Seatrina's name.

Hudson held up his hands for silence. A hush descended on the room, but before he could continue, Bobby Jorgenson pushed through the crowd and ran onto the small makeshift stage.

"Why isn't he wearing a shirt?" my grandmother asked me.

When Bobby spun around to face the crowd, I grinned. "That's why."

Emblazoned across Bobby's chest were the words, 'Marry Me, Seatrina!'

Janelle shook her head. "I hope that's not a tattoo."

"Even Bobby isn't that dumb, I think," Grandma said.

"At least he doesn't have that plastic wrap duct taped to his cheek anymore," I pointed out.

Bobby fell to his knees, yelling for Seatrina to come out and agree to be his wife. I had a feeling Seatrina had heard the commotion and hightailed it out of the place.

After a couple of guys in the audience escorted Bobby off the stage, Hudson began his speech. "I'm sure none of you came here to see me, so I'll make it brief." The audience chuckled appreciatively. After Hudson told the crowd about the new reading program the library was going to launch, he said, "And I'm delighted to announce that none other than Seatrina has made a considerable donation to fund this program on a permanent basis. Now, without further ado, let me present to you the one and only Seatrina."

The crowd got to their feet as the high school band launched into a rendition of 'Celebration,' this time slightly more in tune than it had been at the airport. Seatrina walked out onto the stage wearing her trademark beehive hairdo, iridescent make-up, and flamboyant clothes. But there was a marked difference in her appearance this time—her eyes. Instead of the colored contacts Seatrina normally wore in public, today she was wearing large wire-rimmed glasses which highlighted her unusual eyes—one blue and one hazel.

Seatrina basked in the welcome for a few moments and then held her hands up for silence. Once the crowd had settled down and sat back in their seats, she thanked everyone for coming out. "This program is really important to me personally. Learning disabilities are nothing to be ashamed of. I have dyslexia and if it hadn't been for the help and support from my mother, teachers, and reading specialists, I would have struggled in school and in life. Not everyone is so lucky in getting the help they need . . .

people like my brother included."

The audience looked at each other in bafflement when Logan walked out onto the stage and stood next to his sister. Seatrina whispered something in his ear, then handed him the microphone.

I felt my eyes tearing up as I listened to Logan tell everyone about the everyday struggles he faced because he was functionally illiterate. Then he talked about how the support of people like Erik had made a difference. At the end of his speech, the crowd jumped to their feet and gave Logan a standing ovation, cheering even more loudly for him than they did for his sister.

Seatrina embraced her brother, then asked the audience if they wanted to hear a few tunes. Everyone roared with excitement. As Seatrina belted out song after song, I made a mental note to add her music to my playlist. She truly had a stunning singing voice, and now she was using her celebrity status to raise awareness of dyslexia.

After the event wound down, my grandmother and I joined Hudson in his office for a cup of coffee.

"You know, I need to start looking for a new youth librarian." Hudson looked at my grandmother. "Would you help me interview candidates?"

My grandmother beamed at Hudson. "I'd be delighted. Also, I can help with the book fair."

"What book fair?"

"Oh, didn't I tell you about it?" Grandma gave

Hudson a quizzical look. “It happens every year in April.”

As my grandmother was explaining how the annual book fair helped raise funds for the library, Hudson jumped to his feet. “What was that noise?”

“Look behind you,” I said.

When Hudson turned around, he gasped, and understandably so. It’s not every day that a buffalo presses his face against your window, staring at you with soulful dark brown eyes.

“What does he want?” Hudson asked, taking a step back.

“He probably wants to say hi,” I said.

“Or he could be here because he heard us talking about the book fair,” my grandmother suggested.

“And why would he be interested in that?” Hudson asked slowly.

“Well, one of the ideas the library had to raise interest in the book fair was to tie it in with a buffalo naming contest.”

Hudson jerked a finger at the window. “This buffalo here?”

“Oh, that’s a great idea.” I smiled at my grandmother, then turned to Hudson. “No one in town can decide what to call him. Personally, I think his name should be Bufford.”

“Hagrid is much more distinguished,” my grandmother said.

Hudson took a deep breath. “Okay, fine. I guess I’m

going to be busy next month with hiring a youth librarian and getting a name for a buffalo. Oh yeah, I also have to organize a book fair. I think that might be the easiest task of them all. What could possibly go wrong? It's not like anyone died because of a book."

When Hudson and my grandmother started talking about how best to recruit a new youth librarian, I excused myself, saying I needed to stop by the bowling alley.

"Okay, dear, we'll see you back at the house. I'm making the chicken and wild rice hotdish your brother likes." Then she turned to Hudson. "You'll come for dinner, right?"

As I was heading out of the library, I heard a familiar voice call out. "Hey, lady, where are you going?"

Edgar looked up at me from a display of new books. Checking to make sure no one could overhear me, I said, "Home. Why are you bothering me, anyway? The investigation is over. Ashley is in jail. I don't need a guide anymore."

"Don't be so sure," the chameleon said.

Before I could ask Edgar to explain himself, I heard a whooshing noise, followed by a flash of light. "Stupid reptile, always disappearing," I muttered.

A snarky voice whispered in my ear. "Don't worry, princess. I'm not done with you yet."

THE CARD CATALOG

One of the things I love about writing a library cozy mystery series is sharing my love of all things bookish. Think of this as your personal "card catalog" of the books mentioned in ***Murder at the Library***.

It will probably come as no surprise to you, but I'm a huge mystery fan. It all started with Nancy Drew when I was a kid. When I wasn't reading about Nancy's adventures, I would occasionally borrow one of my sister's Three Investigators books. I recently reread ***The Mystery of the Whispering Mummy*** by Robert Arthur and it reminded me how cool Jupiter Jones and his buddies were. Gleeps!

While I enjoy serious mysteries, I often turn to more light-hearted series when I need an escape. A couple that are guaranteed to make me laugh out loud are ***Death by Pantyhose*** by Laura Levine and ***One for the Money*** by Janet Evanovich.

Of course, I always have a soft spot for the classic detectives like Miss Marple and Sherlock Holmes. Agatha Christie's ***A Caribbean Mystery*** and Arthur Conan Doyle's ***A Study in Scarlet*** are two of my favorites.

In addition to reading mysteries, I'm a big science fiction nerd. I've probably read ***Dune*** by Frank Herbert at least a dozen times. The movie and television adaptations I can live without, but the book is a classic that I'll probably re-read again and again.

The opposite is true when it comes to Star Trek. I'm a huge fan of the original television series and all the subsequent series and movies in the franchise, but I've only read a few of the books. One of those is ***Star Trek Discovery: Desperate Hours*** by David Mack. It was a lot of fun.

Although I love mysteries and science fiction, I try to read books in other genres. Some of those I've enjoyed include the western classic ***Lonesome Dove*** by Larry McMurtry and the children's book ***Magic Marks the Spot*** by Caroline Carlson.

The Odyssey is one of two ancient Greek epic poems attributed to Homer. I vaguely remember reading part of it in high school. To be honest, I found it quite dull at the time. But after recently reading ***The Song of Achilles*** and ***Circe***, two Greek mythology retellings by Madeline Miller, I'm tempted to give ***The Odyssey*** another go.

Did Edgar pique your interest? Do you want to know more about chameleons? If so, check out ***Chameleons*** by Chris Mattison and Nick Garbutt. And if you're curious about what it's like to harness the creative benefits of dyslexia, you might want to take a look at ***Dyslexia is my Superpower (Most of the Time)*** by Margaret Rooke.

I'd love to hear about what books you enjoy and if you've read any of the books I mentioned above. Email me at: ellenjacobsonauthor@gmail.com.

Sloppy Joe Hotdish

Hotdish is a type of casserole popular in the upper Midwest region. It typically consists of a starch, meat, and vegetables, along with canned soup, gravy, or sauce to bind it together. Grandma Olson makes a variety of hotdish recipes, but one of her family's favorites has a sloppy joe meat base and is topped with tater tots.

Ingredients:

1 pound ground beef
1/2 medium onion diced
1/2 green or red bell pepper diced
1 can condensed cheddar cheese soup (10.5 ounces)
1/2 can of tomato sauce (4 ounces)
1/2 cup ketchup
1 tablespoon dijon or yellow mustard
1 1/2 tablespoons brown sugar
1 tablespoon Worcestershire sauce
1/2 teaspoon garlic powder
1/4 teaspoon black pepper
1 bag frozen tater tots (32 ounces)
1 cup shredded cheddar cheese (4 ounces)

Directions:

1 – Preheat the oven to 350 degrees and grease a 9x13

casserole dish.
2 – Stir the cheddar cheese soup, tomato sauce, ketchup, mustard, brown sugar, Worcestershire sauce, garlic powder, and black pepper together in a bowl.
3 – In a non-stick skillet, cook the ground beef, onion, and bell pepper over medium-high heat until the beef is lightly browned. Drain and return to the skillet.
4 – Combine the cheddar cheese soup mixture and the beef mixture together in the skillet. Simmer on low for 5 minutes.
5 – Spread the cheesy beef mixture into the casserole dish. Top with the frozen tater tots, then sprinkle the shredded cheddar cheese on top.
6 – Bake for about 30 minutes or until the tater tots are golden brown.

Rhubarb Linzer Cookies

Grandma Olson loves to bake sweet treats to accompany the endless cups of coffee her family drinks. This cookie recipe uses rhubarb jam which Grandma Olson cans herself, but any store-bought jam will do just as well.

Ingredients:

1 cup unsalted butter, softened
1 cup powdered sugar, sifted
2 large egg yolks

2 teaspoons vanilla extract
2 cups all-purpose flour
1 cup almond flour
1/2 teaspoon salt
Rhubarb or other kind of jam for filling the cookies
Powdered sugar for dusting cookies

Directions:

1 – Preheat the oven to 350 degrees and line two cookie sheets with parchment paper.
2 – Whisk together the all-purpose flour, almond flour, and salt in a medium bowl.
3 – Cream the butter and powdered sugar together in a large bowl using a stand or hand mixer.
4 – Beat in the egg yolks and vanilla extract.
5 – Gradually mix in the flour mixture until combined.
6 – Turn out the dough onto a lightly floured surface.
7 – Roll out the dough until it is 1/8 to 1/4 inch thick. Note: You may need to put the dough in the fridge for a while to get it to firm up and be easier to roll out.
8 – Cut out 3-inch circles using a cookie cutter. Place half of these circles on baking sheet 1 inch apart. Using a smaller cookie cutter, cut out the centers from the other half of the circles to make 'windows.' Place the cookies with the holes cut out of them on the baking sheet 1 inch apart. Note: You made need to bake in batches.
9 – Bake the cookies until lightly golden on the edges, about 10-12 minutes. Remove the cookies from the oven and place on a rack to cool.

10 – Once the cookies are cool, place about 1 1/2 to 2 teaspoons of jam on each of the larger circles. Then place one of the 'window' circles on top. Dust each sandwich cookie with powdered sugar and enjoy.

AUTHOR'S NOTE

Thank you so much for reading my book! If you enjoyed it, I'd be grateful if you would consider leaving a short review on the site where you purchased it and/or on Goodreads. Reviews help other readers find my books while also encouraging me to keep writing.

I was one of those kids who always had their nose in a book and spent countless hours at the library. As an adult, I volunteer at my local library and am still a voracious reader. To my mind, libraries are an essential part of the communities they serve. In a way, this book is my 'love letter' to libraries and librarians everywhere. The world is a better place because of them.

My hubby is a proud born-and-bred North Dakotan who gets a kick out of the fact that I'm writing cozy mysteries set in his home state. I'm grateful to him for his character and story ideas and inspiration, as well as for his invaluable feedback as I wrote this book.

Many thanks to Susan for reviewing this manuscript from a librarian's point of view and to Jana for her insights into how library boards operate and suggestions for why and how someone might be murdered in a library. Finally, I'm so appreciative of my wonderful editor, Alecia, for her thoughtful edits and suggestions.

ABOUT THE AUTHOR

Ellen Jacobson is a chocolate obsessed cat lover who writes cozy mysteries and romantic comedies. After working in Scotland and New Zealand for several years, she returned to the States, lived aboard a sailboat, traveled around in a tiny camper, and is now settled in a small town in northern Oregon with her husband and an imaginary cat named Simon.

Find out more at ellenjacobsonauthor.com

ALSO BY ELLEN JACOBSON

North Dakota Library Mysteries

Planning for Murder
Murder at the Library

Mollie McGhie Mysteries

Robbery at the Roller Derby
Murder at the Marina
Bodies in the Boatyard
Poisoned by the Pier
Buried by the Beach
Dead in the Dinghy
Shooting by the Sea
Overboard on the Ocean
Murder Aboard the Mistletoe

The Mollie McGhie Cozy Mystery Collection: Books 1-3
The Mollie McGhie Cozy Mystery Collection: Books 4-6

Smitten with Travel Romantic Comedies

Smitten with Ravioli
Smitten with Croissants
Smitten with Strudel
Smitten with Candy Canes
Smitten with Baklava

The Smitten with Travel Collection: Books 1-3